The Hired Man

The Hired Man

MELVYN BRAGG

Hodder & Stoughton

LONDON SYDNEY AUCKLAND

British Library Cataloguing in Publication Data

Bragg, Melvyn
   Hired Man. – New ed
   I. Title
   823.914 [F]

  ISBN 0–340–58296–0

Published by Hodder and Stoughton,
a division of Hodder and Stoughton Ltd,
Mill Road, Dunton Green, Sevenoaks, Kent TN13 2YA
Editorial Office: 47 Bedford Square, London WC1B 3DP

Photoset by Rowland Phototypesetting Ltd, Bury St Edmunds, Suffolk
Printed and bound in Great Britain by
Biddles Ltd, Guildford and King's Lynn

To Marie-Elsa

PART ONE

ONE

As he woke, the word 'wife' raced up from the fathoms of his dream and broke the surface of his mind as gently as the moonlight met his eyes. And the word basked under the light, rubbed itself against his unnerved flesh, tumbled slowly about the lapping waves of sense before plunging once more down, taking its news back to the dying dream. In marriage he had found life, taken it and given it.

They slept naked, feeling bold. She had drawn the curtains so that they could see each other's bodies. In the deep flock bed, breath, warmth and memory intermingled – but he did not turn to her, had promised not to wake her. Just his hand settling on her belly: no sign when she lay like that: at what exact moment had she conceived their child?

When the church clock struck two, he got out of the bed, his feet cold on the bare boards before the heavy strokes had died away. Framed in the window he looked out and hesitated, turned to look at her partly uncovered by his exit. Her white face sank into a spread net of thick hair, drawn downwards, it seemed, innocent of the charge of life. In his desire was inexplicable pity. For the breasts, docile, lying softly together as she turned on her side: the fingers reaching out to where he had been with fragile disappointment. Why had he to leave her? Even for a few hours.

What more could there be than those thighs which parted sleepily, that waking glance which told him all there was to know, the end of desire in the beginning of their love?

Dawn had not yet come but his way was clear. A child's moon was settled largely and gracefully in the sky and thin bars of cloud trailed from it edged with yellow light, motionless streamers. The tracks he walked could have been currents in the sea, so plainly did they mark their darker way between the still fields. The low wind would intermittently flick the grass and moonlight broke whitely on it as on the tips of waves. The air was raw and he felt his skin beat into it as he went; it left a moisture on his face which he could lick for pleasure. The wind came across the mosses from the Solway Firth and he remembered how he and Emily had walked to its shore in the evenings at the end of the previous summer. The tang of sea air flicked his thoughts to pictures of her running at the edge of the waves, jumping high off the dunes, racing along the hard runnelled sand, her feet slapping.

Alone on the track, memories warming his mind, moving secretly among the sleepers; and on his own now, aged eighteen, married, the slight curve of his child smooth under Emily's white skin, away both from her parents and his. For hire.

In this spring of 1898, John Tallentire was one of thousands of agricultural labourers going to look for employment. In Cumberland there were seven of these Hirings, held twice a year at Whitsun and Martelmas. There the men who wanted to change their employer or the employer who wanted fresh men met and struck a bargain for a term – six months' work. John could have chosen to go nearby to Wigton on the Monday – but he was known in the district and wanted to be in new country where he could set up his family in his own way, be rid of all ties. So he had ignored the Whit Monday hiring and spent the day finishing off the two chairs he had made and stacking up their very few possessions as carefully as he could so that Mr Errington would, by example, be just as careful when he loaded them into the trap. For John was determined to do all at once. Usually, once hired, the labourer was free until Saturday, it was one of his two holiday weeks of the year. But he was going to ask if he could move in immediately. Emily was to come to Cockermouth later that morning – with Mr Errington and the furniture – and they would be away.

He had ignored the objections to this plan. Emily's father, himself a labourer, had been contemptuous at the way in which the young man was so lightly prepared to throw over a few days' rest. Her mother had worried about the practicability of finding a place which would have a 'tied' cottage free that very night. When he had told his own mother she had warned him – strictly – against the foolishness of setting up house where you knew no one, where no one could help you out in the hundred and one things you always needed when you started up. His father had only said 'Try it and see!' And he had made it even more difficult for himself by resolving that he would not be hired for less than fifteen shillings a week – twice as much as he had earned as an apprentice to the blacksmith.

It was eighteen miles to Cockermouth and the decision to walk it was proof of his confidence.

He skirted Wigton and pushed up towards the Roman Camp of Old Carlisle where, as a boy – and that seemed an age ago, isolated behind the reaches of his working life – he had played with his brothers. This play – most often in the scraps of time left over from gathering sticks or looking around his father's snares, collecting dockings or finding roots for his uncle to carve – now seemed like the most idyllic gambolling.

He paused to look down over the moon-shaped mounds and bowls of the camp beneath which were said to be amphitheatres, barracks, walls and defence-works to be had for the digging, and his legs itched to be running about there again with Seth and Isaac and the others. How steep that hill seemed when they had sledged down it – and at Easter the painted eggs trundling to the beck, the gaudy dyes running again, wetted by the grass. Seth had discovered the entrance to a tunnel and they had stored hazel nuts there – and he, being the smallest, had been pushed right down it by his brothers who used him as a ferret to find out if this tunnel led to others. A warren of tunnels, Seth had predicted or, better, a long-ranging system of tunnels, like badger sets, which would burrow down to Wigton and come up in the cemetery, into one of those stone tombs. But instead he had stuck in the rank foisty earth so that every cry seemed to fill his mouth with clamming dirt, though later, when his father had dragged him out, they had told him they had heard nothing. It was his silence which had frightened them so much that they even dared seek out their father for help. He remembered the beating he had received for the trouble he had caused and how he had loved his father who was hitting him. It seemed impossible that once he should have lost himself in there – a place he could walk past in a few minutes.

He went on along the track to Red Dial where he would pass the gates of the farm his father had been hired at for twenty-two years.

Often, on his way to school, he had stopped at these gates to watch the labourers taking to the land. To John, all these men were heroes. Heroes in their work. Labour was their fate and the earth the most demanding of gods. Every year they opened it and every year it would turn its back on them. Every year there would be some things perfect – a ploughed field, hedges, a crop – and every year it would return to what it had been. Only with luck and after the greatest care – 'husbandry' it was called, a word accurately descriptive of the necessary bond of intimacy – would a good harvest come, toss its head, and wait to be mown down, at once the booty and the defeat, leaving its stubbled stalks for pigs to root in. And he would want to jump down and be among them – to go and be part of what he saw, feeling arms soft that had not managed an angry team, legs feeble that had not walked a field a hundred times in an afternoon, his whole self unmade that had not been fired by such work.

At thirteen he had got his wish, gone down to a farm – he could see it from where he stood, a shroud on the pale fields. Winter then, and his wet trousers, hung on the bottom of the bed, often froze, slim splinters of ice crackling as he climbed into them at five o'clock in the morning. His legs chapped raw. The day's work would finish at six thirty and by seven he would be asleep. For that term two pounds were delivered to his mother a portion a week on Sunday afternoon, the only time he had off. A miserable collection of coins – less than two shillings a week – from which she would allow him threepence for himself, the rest to go towards her housekeeping. Nor would that threepence have been allowed – for what, she asked with no irony, had he to spend it on? Only sweets. But his father insisted that he must have something in his pocket to show he had a wage.

Yet his appetite did not sicken. Instead, now that he was among those men he had watched he found even more to admire in their strength, and especially in their tricks. Everything, it seemed, could be made a 'trick' of: there was a 'trick' about holding a scythe, a 'trick' about getting a straight furrow, a 'trick' about pressing the teats – and even in the tiniest things, about making your porridge last or washing your back, there was a 'trick'. These 'tricks' embellished the toil as appurtenances do war. And he became clever with fingers hardened and could plait with nine strings.

His father, after his third term, found a place for him in a blacksmith's at Wigton. He had no alternative but to leave the work he loved. There, starting in springtime he felt at first confined, blowing the roof-high bellows to a fire which scorched the down on his cheeks while the lengths of iron sizzled in the forge and the smith shaped, holed and hammered them. Soon he moved on to the making of screws and rivets (so difficult that it made his arms shake, his head drum with the impossibility of it), then to the hoops of iron for the cartwheels, the gates and fittings – he had spent his first year in as aching and dreary a time as he would ever have imagined. That he had now three and six a week to take home made no difference. He was shut out, unseen by the world he had been growing to. But as he began to conquer the work, the advantages his mother had spoken of claimed his attention, then his interest. The world came to him. There was never a time when farmers would not need something done to their horses, and soon he was outside on the square, in among the hooves of the beasts, nearly kicked to kingdom come by the first mare he was let shoe, doing all bar the bulls which the smith reserved for himself. It was work, this – no one could deny that – and his hours and labour matched those of any man his age; but also, there was the talk he would only rarely get on the farm. For those who brought their horses would always stay while they were being done and ask and chat without pause. He would have been there still but for his marriage. His father – after the rage which met that declared intention – had told him he would be a fool to leave when he was more than half-way through his apprenticeship. Yet he *had* left and 'filled in' for the fortnight before term. He wanted nothing with work that would not give him that independence he thought essential to a married man.

He put some dry bread in his mouth. Bread a few days old, you could not beat it in a morning, he thought, if he could choose anything in the world to eat, it would be that, with the crusty comb of white crumbling on his teeth, the yeast seeming to rise again as it met the heat of his palate. Then he looked last at what he would leave. By going to Cockermouth he would almost certainly be hired in the fells – and he intended to stay there for time enough at least to gather about him what Emily and himself might need. It was from the fells that the Tallentires had come – at least his grandfather had come from there. But such families as his were merely the numbers to the alphabet of history. 'Labourers – 10': 'Estatemen – 16': 'Foot-soldiers – 17': or more commonly, 'and a number of men'. His path to the fells was paved by no treasured remembrance of things past. Though he would call at his grandfather's for breakfast.

He would not stop to see his father. Their last encounter – after the wedding – would be sufficient for some time. Joseph himself had married at twenty. But it was not a question of age, suitability or anything else: it was a matter of obedience. He, Joseph Tallentire, did not want his son to marry and that should have been that. And he, Joseph Tallentire, a fiery particle, black-haired and cold-blue-eyed like John, a cocky fellow who had quickly become head labourer at the Roberts's and could have had many a better job had he not been so settled in his sports – his cock-fighting and terrier breeding – and the easy independence which his little authority gave him; a man who had made a reputation as a wrestler (Cumberland and Westmorland style), brought up nine decent children and taken them to church weekly, who had hunted on foot in John Peel Country just five miles off with men who had hunted with Peel himself, who knew a horse by teeth, hoof and hide and a man for hire by similar markings: he would not be defied by this boy who had had his behind slashed with birch, his head cuffed hard with a tough palm, his face almost knocked askew with the open hand, and the same who had been comforted when time was, and taught what was for his own good. He would not be defied. But John did defy him and, leaving his father the alternatives of defeat or disgrace, got on with his wedding preparations through the infinitely more pliable parents of Emily. Joseph had chosen that which could be called defeat, but he had not accepted it. He came to the wedding, as he said, 'for your mother's sake': he had spoken once since – on the subject of John's going for hire – and then, as most vehemently at the wedding, made it plain that no future dialogue would happily be sought by him. His mother, though not subdued by her husband, in this matter agreed with him because she, too, thought it stupid for him to marry so young and without means.

But as he walked past the track which led to his parent's cottage, he came to a shed, a black wall from the road, and smiled at his best memory of his father. Behind that shed on Sunday mornings after church was the cock-fighting. Joseph had never once taken his sons along with him. He'd let them feed the birds, shown them how to fix the spurs, but he alone went to the fights. They used to follow him and watch, hidden. Climb on to the shed roof, peep down at the ring of men, watching the high-prancing cocks, flamboyantly plumed, gold on their backs, stab at each other delicately.

It was a stranger that John then saw. Far from the man who had ordered them all earlier in the morning as they stood in a line to be examined for church. When he pulled open their mouths and lifted up their feet. And they, quivering before his regular fury – he hated church – would stay in that line, each holding an article. Then Joseph walked again; taking shoes from one, scrutinised, accepted; a collar from another; the studs and the cuff-links, the tie, the waistcoat and the jacket until he came to the smallest who held the hat. A parody of empire but no one dared think of smiling. Now, here, that same hat was tilted back on a face that ran sweat down to soil the starched collar and the shoes splashed through mud, the cuffs dirty from holding the birds, the murder in his throat dismissed by a loud laugh: waistcoat barrelled and bared, happy as larry. John would have liked him as a friend.

No time for that now. Emily had taken the place of them all.

TWO

As it was a holday, Harry Tallentire lay in bed an extra hour. He did not enjoy it. From half-past five until six was just bearable by making the most rigorous effort; but on the stroke of six his patience broke and every other minute he would be shouting downstairs to his wife for the time. Alice replied patiently, but the amused inflection of her words made it doubly impossible for him to quit. So he lay on the rack of his bed for that last half hour – scarcely making a lump under the puffy flock down, a spare, white-haired man, his voice agitated and querulous, wishing and willing the clock to move on but refusing to budge until the time was up; for though his patience might break, his will never would – and he always lay in bed for an extra hour on his holidays.

The small whitewashed room with the scrubbed floor was stippled by a wavering dawn light. Alice had drawn the curtains so that he could see – out across to the fells. He allowed himself to rest his head a little higher on the pillow so that he could look at this view. He was not quite sure about this; for was looking at a view lying in? On the other hand, sleep being impossible, he realised that a mere closing of the eyelids would be worthless. He could have buried his face in the pillow but he always slept on his back – straight out, arms by his side, toes to the ceiling, corpselike. He felt like a corpse, he said, lying there doing nothing. Doing nothing was the thing he hated above all. Yet if holidays were not different they were wasted. So he looked at the view, a landscape he had looked on every day of the fifty-seven years he had been hired at this farm.

Under the weak pulses of light the densities shifted rapidly and the leaves on the trees, the tips of grass, the innumerable pocks and rises, the streams, hedges, even the soft-outlined hills themselves seemed to shuffle in ceaseless interchange of tone and mood, as if the forces below such apparent solidity were ever throbbing, unwilling to be still.

Eventually he heard the clock strike half-past six and then, as always, Harry burrowed himself more deeply into the bed than he had done all night as if, for that second, to find and grasp unconsciousness as a talisman for the day.

Downstairs there was a piece of dry bread waiting for him – no more.

His breakfast was taken at half-past seven – usually after two hours' work – and even holidays could not interfere with the displacement of his meals. He put on his oldest trousers, clogs, collarless shirt, waistcoat and muffler, never 'dressing' until just before breakfast, and took the bread out into the garden to share it with the blackbird he was taming.

He had always kept part of the garden for Alice and this year had laid out even more of it for her. She liked rosemary, bergamot, thyme and lavender, roses for the summer and a few evergreens for the winter; he had brought in some wild flowers which she missed now that she got out less than she used to. But the vegetable plot was his chief concern and he looked at the stitches anxiously. He went to the wall and put a few crumbs on it, waiting for 'Dizzy', his blackbird. Saw him in the hawthorn as still as the bough he rested on; he fluttered and lifted – but only to the lowest branch of the apple tree. Harry waited.

The cottage stood on its own. He had got it when Latimer had made him 'estate-man'. This meant that he worked at the same work as the other labourers but was also responsible for hiring and seeing over jobs, for visiting Latimer's other two farms twice a term and checking things there. Even then, twenty years ago when he had got the job, he had been with Latimer longer than anyone else; slept in the byres there as a boy (his first job at ten had been crow-scaring) seen the farm grow, been married from the farm-house and, over these last years, helped Mr Latimer's sons to keep things going through the hard times by building up the flocks of breeding Clydesdales. Luckily this was not corn-land and so the competition from foreign grain and beef which was decimating large farms in the south was not as severely felt here. Before moving into this cottage he had lived in the row of nine agricultural cottages – two up, one down – which were hidden in a dip to the west of the farm. There his wife had given birth to fourteen children, twelve of whom survived, and now he counted his grandchildren in scores and even his great-grandchildren in half-dozens. Not that he had seen them all, but it pleased him to keep a record of them all – or rather it pleased him to do it for Alice who liked to go through that list, her lips forming the names, her head lifting after every one, eyes searching the ceiling, picturing what they looked like now. Two of his sons had gone to Australia and one daughter to Canada but even then Alice counted on a letter around Christmas to keep her informed. Joseph he knew of more than most of the others, for the two sometimes met at Cockermouth auction and Joseph had occasionally sent his children back to Embleton for a few days in the summer.

In the district he was known for his consistency in all things and his pride lay in keeping that record. Within that tiny locality he was erudite but this knowledge, though different not in kind but only in the material it drew on from that of educated men, he considered as 'knowing nothing' whenever faced by a fact or remark outside his experience. There were two books in the house he had read, *Pilgrim's Progress* and the Bible, and those were the only two books he had ever read. He played the fiddle in the church band and went there not as to peremptory parade once-weekly as did Joseph, but because he believed in it. He had drunk a lot in his young days but gradually eased off and finally become teetotal. In his dress he was as careful and conservative as those 'above' him and always wore a hard hat.

John's first sight of his grandfather that morning was of the old man bent double in the field outside the garden, his head jammed between straddled legs, jutting under his behind. Easily misconstrued. Thus bent, so that he saw the world upside down from as near ground level as made no difference, the old man moved down the field. To help him keep steady, his hands had fastened on his ankles, and to help him keep low, his feet were widespread and so his progress could be compared neither to a walk nor to a waddle but to a performance, one left in the fields by the departing circus. John laughed to have caught the old man like that, but though the laugh was clear enough, the performance was not interrupted until, having reached an intently desired spot in that field, Harry stopped and was suddenly unsprung.

He had been looking through his legs until he could see the top of the tree he intended to chop down. When he could see the top then, at that spot, he could mark to a foot the end of the tree's fall.

Without looking at his grandson who stood grinning at him over the hedge, he pushed a peg in the ground, turned, looked at the tree once more and then, having regarded John in silence for a properly admonitory period of time, said, slowly, as if talking to himself:

'Tell me – thou's been kept at school for a very long time – fourteen wasn't it?'

John was wary; shot was often primed with this powder.

'Tell me – there's a tree in my garden, that ash, theer, an' a fella' wants to lop it down because it's ower dangerous. Now then – use thee eyes a bit mair than for gawpin' at fwolks doin' a job and see that waa.' The wall he spoke of ran along the foot of the garden, stood about five feet high and was a well-kept length of dry-stone walling. 'Now Aa'm gonna cut that ash, and Aa'm not gonna have it fall into t' garden: it'll drop reet here where my feet is. How will that happen widout brekkin' that waa? Tell me that?'

John ran along to the gate, swung himself over it into the field and went to join his grandfather. The resemblance between them as they stood together was startling and both smiled in faint appreciation of this mutual flattery. The younger man looked at the tree, took a few paces forward and back and teased his grandfather with pretence of ignorance, for he knew quite well. It was one of the 'tricks'. After making your cuts in front and behind, you make another diagonal cut across the front, and as the tree started to fall it 'leapt' and, well judged, would clear even that wall.

So he fed the old man's complacency for a while and then said:

'I'd mek a bird-lowp cut, grandfather, and see if that did.'

The old man did not hesitate.

'Thou means *I'll* mek a bird-lowp cut – thou'd mek a hash of it.' Then 'Lookin' for work now, is'te?'

'I am. Is thou not gaan to Cockermouth thissel?'

'Aa've got the men I need.' He paused. 'Maybe Mr Latimer *could* manage another . . . know owt about a hoss?' he asked, well aware that John had worked daily with horses for the past three years.

'I can tell its arse from its tip,' replied John. 'On a bright day.'

'Language,' Harry admonished. Then, 'Mebbe we could . . .'

'No thanks, grandfather.'

'Aa wasn't through me sentence.'

'I'd raither set up on me own.'

'Mebbe we could do wid – some breakfast I was gonna say,' the old man completed, calmly.

He nodded and the two men walked up the field, over the stile and through the garden into the kitchen.

'Yen o' Joseph's,' Harry announced. 'Set a trough out for him. If he's owt like his fadder he'll eat us oot.'

His grandmother nodded to John happily and got down another basin into which she heaped a ladleful of porridge. There was flat bread, milk and a little sugar on the table as well as a plate of fancy cakes – another holiday concession.

John sat down.

'Stand up to give thanks,' Harry ordered.

John blushed and clattered to apologetic attention.

'Thank you Lord for thy bounty in givin' us this thy harvest. Amen.'

'Amen.'

'Sit down.'

They ate in silence or rather without talking, for the cooling slurp of his grandfather's mouth against the spoon sounded as regularly as the clock. John looked around the kitchen and everything from the black-leaded fireplace which almost covered a wall to the neatly marked jars in which is grandmother kept her stores encouraged him to dreams of his own domesticity which could not come fast enough. He admired the birds his grandfather had carved on the top of the chair-frames: the most he had been able to manage was a cross. And the shiny baking-tins his grandmother had – Emily's mother had given her three but that would not be enough, and they could not afford to buy more for six months at least and even then there would be more important things to buy.

After the porridge, Alice brought them the mugs of tea and then, nodding to John, took down a black pudding and set it in the oven. John blushed once more, for he knew that she had 'likened' it to Emily and himself – as was done with newly married couples – and that she would believe that their life would be happy if the skin held, disrupted if it burst. The idea of his prospects depending on a black pudding made him impatient – and then discomfited him – at the notice being taken of his new status.

And he knew, now that his grandfather was on the less demanding bread and so could be expected to allow speech, that he – the old man – would have words to say on it. He had seen neither of them for a long time. They had not come to the wedding, but he knew that old Harry disapproved, had seen it in the first glance, just as he knew his grandmother was having a hard time bridling her curiosity.

'Thee father's mekin a reet fool of hissel,' Harry began calmly. 'Folk tell me he's nivver off cock-fightin' nowadays.'

'It's only Saturdays,' John countered, half-heartedly.

'A fool can be seen any day of the week. Saturday included.' Harry paused. 'Next time thou sees him, tell him from me to quiet his daft sel. When a thing's been med illegal – thou stops. He could a' been a bailiff yer father, maybe an estate labourer, instead of gallivantin' around like a daft calf.'

'He works hard enough.'

'Anybody can work.'

'Well,' John disliked being his father's defence, but it was impossible to allow an attack to go unresisted. 'Well mebbe he thinks he'll enjoy hissel the bit of time he has over.'

'Enjoy what?' Harry inquired. 'A clown enjoys hissel my lad. That's no mark. And,' he paused and looked at John intently, 'it isn't Saturdays I've heard on. "Six days shalt thou labour" my boy – it's Sundays. Am I right?'

'I don't know.'

'Thou won't say.'

'No. I won't.'

'Well mebbe thou's right. I's'll see him and tell him in me own good time. Don't bother to pass that message on. A son should honour his father – and if you tell Joseph he's a fool, he'd strike you dead.'

'He would.'

John agreed out of respect for his father's reputation, but inside himself he felt better than ever at the remembrance of those two months before when he had done even worse to his father – totally contradicted his authority – and lived.

'Well,' said his grandmother, unable to hold herself longer and tactfully anticipating the severe quizzing which was concentrating in her husband's expression, 'tell us about her, John.'

And now there was no embarrassment because he was talking of her and not himself. But his talk could not describe her. He wanted to tell them that she had hazel eyes that could flare in temper and dare as much as he – but instead he told them what her father did. He wanted to say that the run of her calf, the whiteness of her skin – so white that he imagined he could feel the colour as his charged fingers trembled fearfully on her flesh – that such was his kingdom of heaven – and instead he engaged in the infinite crochet of relations until, by complicated cross-patterning, she was pulled closer to Alice through the husband of a friend who was her uncle. Could she bake? Yes. And turn a collar? Yes. Sew a straight hem? He was certain she could. Manage a house on very little?

'And that's t'first sensible question asked,' Harry said. 'See here. She'll have to mek do, my lad, on next to thin air with the money thou'll fetch. She'll hev that to do, no mistake.'

'I know.'

'He knows that, father.'

'As long as he does.' Then, in case the comment had appeared too surly, Harry smiled and his tone was cheerful. 'Well if she's half what thou says thou's done well. Aa was nobbut nineteen when we were wed.' He hesitated and then, with a shyness which made him look years younger he said, 'No – what worried me, lad, was givin' up a good trade. There'll always be a call for blacksmiths. Yer fedder was lucky to get you in there.' Harry wanted no explanations. 'Thou should hev stuck it, lad,' he said, 'whativver.'

The level tone in which he said that made John shiver – but only for a moment. However well-intentioned, they wanted to rule you. He did not dare tell his grandfather that Emily was to follow him that very day.

'I hev a smoke in t' garden after breakfast on a holiday,' Harry said. 'Thou'll hev time to join me?'

'I will.'

'Thou won't can afford to smoke?'

'No.'

Harry nodded, in approval.

Outside the cottage, they looked over the fields to the small church with the minute tower which just cleared the hedges. John encouraged his grandfather to talk of the old times. To touch on *his* grandfather who had boasted of fighting with Wellington and earning the title 'scum of the earth', of his father who had been a local prizefighter. He got the story of the two-day dance in Pratt's barn and the one about the wild dog of Ennerdale and then, turned eight thirty, it was time to leave.

'The skin never even blistered,' said his grandmother happily as he came in to kiss her good-bye. He was relieved. But refused the black pudding; did not want the bother of carrying it around all day.

Harry, having changed, walked some way down the road with him.

'Thou'll have to have this,' he said, handing him a piece of straw he had brought. 'In my time they twisted it under their hats so it popped out of their ears. They suck it now.'

John took the straw and popped it into his mouth. The end of it jabbed against his palate and he spat it out.

'I can be hired without that,' he replied, over-curtly.

They went up the hill which led on to the road to Cockermouth. They were silent. John's last remark had appeared to the old man to be groundlessly arrogant. It was up to John to atone for it, but he did not want to.

He was afraid of the temptation offered by the old man. Not so much in the hint of a job as in the attraction of his grandfather's look and temper, the contentment of it, the serenity.

About Harry's face and movements there was a veil of serenity – as distinctly to be seen as the spume of fever which hovers around many people today. It was this, perhaps, which sprang his back still spruce-like and gave grace to his work – and the work itself was not met head-on as it was with Joseph or attacked as with John, but done in ultimate service to a Creator who made less demands than men. Harry appeared as a man whose substance was unmuddied, whose life had been spent well, who walked in a serene self-containment out of which John's father had come stampeding like a wild thing and into which he himself could find no entry.

But he was not sure that he wished to find one – and it was this which caused the confusion. For in another glance he saw his grandfather submissive to the place given him by others, with notions which were the crumbs scattered by his masters and manners aped. And he could have knocked off that hard hat.

Yet he loved him more than any other man.

At the top of the hill, Harry stopped.

'So thou'll not work for thy grandfather.' He smiled. 'Mebbe so. Be on thy own if that's the way.' He held out his hand. 'I nivver fancied it meself.'

As John shook his hand, he felt a tide of home-sickness rush into his throat. He was gruff, to conceal it, and the men parted, John watching the small figure return down the hill to the grey stones of the cottage, slate grey like the outcrops on the hills and the steady figure in the watery morning light, as slate as they.

Harry did not go into the cottage, not wanting to meet his wife's question about what he *really* thought of John and his chances. He made for the shed, where he set to carving minia-ture wooden animals which he loved to carry about in his pockets and give away to any children he met on the road. Gradually forgetting his grandson.

THREE

Cockermouth was a small town, sandstone, granite and slate which lay as naturally at the confluence of the rivers Cocker and Derwent as a pebble in a palm. Roofs slanted in sharp diagonals of many-toned grey, shields which were never lowered; and nests, lichens, leaves and moss dappled them kindly as if in recognition that they would not be broken, had become, through time, affectionate to that which they obstructed.

He lengthened his stride past the castle, over the bridge and looked beyond the Ring, to the fair which sprang at his eyes, as if he had turned a page in a book from print to a gaudily tinted plate.

Yellow, scarlet and silver were the chief colours, on the roundabouts and swings, the clothes and jewellery of the gipsies, the plates of the potters. Tents had been erected the previous night and they stood before the caravans. The Fat Lady yawned as she sat on her stool pulling her boots on to unseen legs, the magic lantern show had already attracted a small crowd before it; behind the Boxing Booth the men swilled themselves, shivering and muscle-knotted in their straw-tagged long-johns; fairmen stacked the prizes carefully, arranging them on the racks within apparent easy reach. Canvas rippled in the cuff of wind and the fair-people – with their rich scarves and fancy waistcoats, dark skins and chuntering faces, darted incessantly from neighbour to neighbour, the rapidity of their speech making John's tongue feel wooden.

Around, between, among and beside them were the horses and ponies and dogs. Their noise, the skittering and fighting dogs scudding from booth to booth inflamed by the number of new scents, the horses jostling together or moving over a scattering of straw, ponies forlornly tied to the gipsy caravans, waiting to be sold, had the strange effect on John of making this uncommon dash of activity more human.

Nearer him – the fair was well up the street – was the market. The feature of this was the number of women with their butter, white at this time as the cows had not long been in the fields, each slab with its makers' imprint on it. Butter every few paces, white footstones.

John saw no one he knew. He noticed a few whippets and a man caging fighting cocks and thought that Isaac, one of his brothers, might be discovered around such sport, but was disappointed. For a second, his solitude clanged against him loudly and he saw the other side of his determination to be on his own, but only for that second. He went towards the Ring.

This was where those went – men and women – who were looking for hire. They did not stand there unmoving but drifted off and back to the market and fair, pulling out together across the street in ones and twos to buy teacakes or look in the windows – emphasising always, it seemed, that though they would be hired they could not be bought. Nevertheless, the Ring was well enough marked and the farmers left their traps and horses down the town to walk up to it, generally by degrees through the stalls and pubs before they came there to hover around the crowd and ask 'Is thou for hire, lad?'

John went up to it shyly, feeling very much a boy among men. There were all ages there, men of sixty chewing their straw, girls clinging to each other in dragging embrace, slouching in deliberate spite of their femininity clogs clattering on the cobbles. Unless they saw a good friend, in which case an overhearty greeting buffeted between them and the sudden stroke of companionship drew a space around itself, the men drifted blank-eyed, their gaze fixed on no one, like those abstracted by the sea.

There was little business in that first hour and John took his cue from a much older man who leaned against a wall, as if a mere spectator. But when he heard the words, 'Is thou for hire, lad?' he spun around. To face his brother Isaac grinning so widely that his cheeks were forced back to his ears.

'Aa'll giv thee a hundred pound a year to clean my boots,'

Isaac continued, his loud voice attracting some attention, the terms he was offering bringing more. 'Mind you,' he added, 'Aa nivver tek me boots off, so thou'll hev to catch us while Aa's movin'. And Aa can kick – by Christmas Aa can! – last feller had this job med an ivory necklace for his wife and took to wearin' a bucket on his head. Then he couldn't see – bucket blinded. So Aa stamped on it and now he's in a tent over yonder,' he nodded to the fair, 'The Man in the Iron Mask.'

John was so pleased to see his brother that he clapped his arms around him. The embrace was returned with a hug which nearly winded him.

'What the hell, boy,' said Isaac. 'Aa'm thee brother not thee mother.' John stood back from him, but could not take offence so cheerful was Isaac's expression. Seeing that he might have caused his younger brother embarrassment, Isaac immediately moved across to him and flung an arm around his shoulder.

'Seth's in The Bridge,' he said. 'He looks as miserable as ivver. Let's go and show him yer happy face.'

All protests about staying until he was hired were swept quite aside. A lad like him could be hired any time of day, Isaac declared, leading, almost humping him away – while drink would come only while money was in the pocket and there was money in the pocket now. And again Isaac protected John from embarrassment as by saying this he made it clear that the drinks would be on him, knowing that John would not be able to afford them.

'Is *thou* for hire, then?' John asked him as they strode through the parting crowd.

'I'm for owt!' said Isaac. 'Owt there is.'

Isaac was the oldest of the brothers, the second of Joseph's family, the one most resemblig the father in his build. He was married with three children and had been at every sort of work since his twelfth birthday. No job was held for long. For what in Joseph was occasional wildness tempered by the unquestioned though often bitter recognition that he could run only so far on a leash which fastened him to his place and type of work, had, in this son, gone on the rampage.

Isaac would go anywhere for sport. Sometimes he left his wife at home for weeks on end, without any warning – 'Aa tell her nivver to worry,' he said, 'there's no man comes home quicker than a dead man' – and the most she would hear about him might be from a tradesman who passed on gossip that there was a gang of men going round after a supposed pole-cat, or taking on all comers at coursing or such-like. For that reason he would always have a jar of money behind a brick near the fireplace, sufficient to last for two months – solid proof of conjugality, for he did not run after other women on these trips nor did he think for a moment that he treated his wife badly. That jar of money was his pledge, never long empty, for he was luckier than anyone John knew. He would win a pig in a bet, butcher and sell it on the spot and have enough for a month. Or turn from his summer sports to hay-making and bargain over every field – a bargain he could count on doing well from, for his rate of work was prodigious and the untrustworthy weather often made fast work a premium. Now he was going to have a go at the men in the Boxing Booth – you got a shilling for every round you lasted with them; and if that turned on him, he was off to the cock-fighting, while Seth had a whippet worth putting any man's shirt on and he thought he might do a deal with a gipsy he knew over some ponies – if the deal could be done fast for he had not cash enough to buy one. And if all that failed – he could always be hired.

Only the set of their eyes showed that they were related, but when John went through the small door of The Bridge there was no doubt about Seth. Though his hair was sandy and his skin almost tallow, the same blue eyes pierced the same slight face.

'Aa's in training for a fight this dinner-time,' Isaac announced, 'so Aa'll just hev a pint. An' another for me brother here afore a cat walks over his tongue.'

He pulled out the four pence and slapped them on the wooden counter, falling into immediate conversation with the man he first set his eyes on. John took his ale over to Seth who had smiled at him as he entered, but now looked miserable, as Isaac had described him, and was bent over his whippet, stroking its slim, bundle-muscled haunches.

In that low room, crowded with farmers and labourers, most

of them rawly complexioned, their jaws chunked blood-red, their throats burnt scarlet, hands thick-fingered and brown, smoke from their pipes as steam from jostling horses, Seth looked like someone from another country. He had gone down the pits at fourteen and worked there since, unmarried, energetic with a ceaseless ambition to change the miners' conditions. On this day, he had walked over from Whitehaven to see the fair and maybe give his dog a run. 'Bounty' he called it.

'How's married life treatin' you?' he asked, as John sat down.

'Not too bad.'

'You've put yer head into a hell of a noose there, lad. But here's to it – and your missis.'

He raised his mug and John clinked it with his own. Seth spoke more rapidly than Isaac or himself, as if the urgency of underground work allowed of none of the breadth of vowel, pause and gesture which characterised most country speech. And the dialect, too, was less apparent, though the twang of the words would still have baffled most visitors.

'Why'd you come here then?' Seth demanded. 'I thowt you'd go to Wigton.'

'Father,' said John: for shorthand.

'I see.' Seth paused and then added, gravely. 'He is a gay old bugger, isn't he? I mean, have you ever met such a bloody selfish man?'

'He's not that bad.'

'Only because he can't afford to be.' Seth bent down and tickled Bounty behind the ears. 'He's not as bad as some I suppose – but I'm thankful to be out of that house.'

'So am I.'

'Let's drink to that.' Seth grinned and raised his mug once more. The grin knocked all the severity off his face, and John relaxed. He always felt a little under examination for the first few minutes in Seth's company.

Then he was asked about their mother, about Jane and Sarah, about Emily's family, his own prospects – which Seth heard through very coolly – and finally he told Seth that he had visited their grandfather that morning.

'And he hadn't heard about Ephraim?'

'He said nothing. Why?'

'Ah.' Ephraim was another of Harry's sons and Seth had seen a lot of him. He worked in the iron-ore mines at Egremont, was on the committee of the Co-op and had been trying for years to get an effective union going. 'He's had an accident,' Seth continued. 'I went to see him in hospital yesterday. A crusher fell on him.'

There was only one question John could ask – and yet to phrase it was too bald.

'He'll live all right,' said Seth, savagely. 'But they'll get no more work out of him, so he'll be thrown on the rates – rot the bloody rotten lot of them. A man should have compensation for summat like that. It was their fault – they hadn't the decency to keep the bloody crusher in trim – he couldn't be blamed. And mebbe he'll get fobbed off with a few pounds – less than we'll collect in a hat. It's all wrong.'

'All wrong' was how Seth saw the world. The ideas of Ruskin, Morris, Owen, Engels and even Marx wraithed themselves around the columns of the British status quo as smoke from an ignored fire. But Seth had caught a whiff of them through their popularisers in the threepenny pamphlets his uncle Ephraim bought, and from some of the speakers who came to West Cumberland on their way to building up the Independent Labour Party – and this scent he had followed. For it seemed to him All Wrong that men should slave while others lorded it, All Wrong that the sick should suffer while the rich wore pearls, All Wrong that a man should be ripped from school to work at an age when many of those who would never work were just beginning their schooling, All Wrong that there should be hovels for some and palaces for others, All Wrong that a man should be shut out from learning at the very time he might see the sense in books. All: Wrong.

Ephraim's accident had shaken him; ever since he had begun at the pits, the uncle had been as a father to him.

'Tek this shillin',' said John. It was the only one he had. 'Put it in for Uncle Ephraim.'

'No, lad – you've a wife.'

'Tek it.'

The coin jutted out from the thick thumb and forefinger and would not be ignored. Seth nodded and took it.

'So you're stickin' to farm work,' he said, broadening his accent in appreciation of the younger man's benevolence. 'I thought you'd be cannier than that, our John.'

'It's what I can do.'

'You don't have to be specially bred to work down a pit. Come with me. Even apprentice's wages are better'n you'll pick up.' The idea of having his brother work with him – which had come to Seth just now – affected him strongly and he leaned out and put his hand on John's arm. 'Come with me, lad. Those farmers'll nivver improve things 'til they're starved out. You'll get nothing from them but "Do this! Do that! No, you can't hev Sunday afternoons!" We help each other int'pit. Things'll move there. Look what the dockers did. So can we.' Seth drew himself up, at that moment becoming grand so that his voice thickened and his face felt some colour. 'And when we stop,' he said, 'England stops.'

'Do you really think so?'

Seth reached in his breast pocket to pull out a worn and many-folded piece of paper.

'Read that,' he said. 'I cut it out of a pamphlet. It's word for word as it used to be.'

John read slowly. It was a reprint of some of the evidence given a Royal Commission on the Mines in 1842. Seth had drawn a square around a quotation described as 'The Evidence of a Lancashire woman'. The square was drawn in indelible ink. It read:

> 'I have a belt round my waist and a chain
> passing between my legs and I go on my
> hands and feet. The water comes up to my clog
> tops and I have seen it over my thighs. I have
> drawn till I have the skin off me. The belt
> and chain are worse when we are in the family way.'

The last sentence lurched into John's mind like the sick of fear. He thought instantly of Emily and tightened his eyes at the knowledge of her tender pregnancy. Seth took the paper from his hands.

'I thought it would sicken you,' he said, gently. 'But I keep it to remind me how much we've got done already in the pits. There's more, if you want to go on, about kids less than five year old working on their own in the black. Well,' he paused, 'that's been got rid of – and more will be got rid of. But you'll change little on the farms, my lad – especially here where it doesn't take a very bad man to think he can get away with murder. You get out of it – come somewhere where you've got Rights.'

'Emily wouldn't,' John hesitated, realised he had exposed a personal matter and in doing so risked exposing his wife to Seth's criticisms, yet the sentence was begun and could not be left unfinished. 'We're both country people,' he countered, lamely, 'I want nothing with towns.'

'Your work's more important to you than any of that,' Seth replied. 'You'd like it over there.'

John nodded but said nothing. He had been stirred by Seth's words and seen himself working with a gang of men, all friends, all fighting for their Rights.

'Think it over anyway,' Seth concluded.

'Think what!' Isaac demanded, descending on them like a rush of rocks. 'Don't be puttin' bad habits into t'lad, Seth. I knew a fella did nowt but think. Thowt as soon as he wok up. Fed on what other folk thowt. Ate paper like lettuce. Swelled his brains till't sweat of it steamed his hair off. Thowt hissel intil a frazzle so that he couldn't talk for thinkin' that much, wouldn't move for fear o' jostlin' a new thowt. Sat aa day on a wooden bench just thinkin' it aa in – til' his head got that heavy he had to wheel it aboot in a barrow.'

'Well,' said John, 'what happened to him?'

'O, he died,' Isaac replied. 'Just like ivverybody else.' He plonked his empty mug on their table and looked at Seth. 'Yen mair of those, and Aa's game for a shillin' a round wid any man.'

It was John who jumped up to do the honours, however, despite Isaac's frown. He had fivepence in his pocket and after buying his brothers a pint apiece had to be content with half for himself. Which was as much as he wanted, for he saw by the clock that he had been in the pub over half an hour; and Emily was coming nearer.

'This bitch of thine,' Isaac was saying of 'Bounty' as John returned, 'let's hev a good squint at her.'

Seth pushed the shuddering whippet from under his chair and Isaac took her up, opened her mouth, scrutinised her paws, ran his thumb along her muscles, felt deep into the scruff of her neck and then:

'She's a good-looker anyway,' he said, and dropped her back on the floor. 'Thou wants to git a bit of sherry intil her belly, and plenty of raw eggs. And see thou drags a scrap of rabbit's fur through her insides ivery so often. Cleans them out like a charm.' He picked up his mug, raised it to John and spoke solemnly, 'Here's cheers to you and yer bride who Aa hope to have the pleasure of meeting one day. And if she's half as good as thou deserves, old lad, she'll be a rare 'un.' Then the foam covered half his face and he sucked strongly at the lip of the mug. 'That was tip-top,' he said, sat down on a stool which was overlapped on all sides by his behind, his legs planted apart, hands pushed down on his knees – the greatest comfort and display thus being afforded to his belly – and beamed on the world.

'Aa hed a bitch once,' he began. 'And mind Aa thowt Aa was on 'til a good un. She would streak across a field that fast that they had a special patrol of rabbits out to warn ivvrything off 't track. She once stopped to offer a hare a lift. Aa called her Parton after me wife's maiden name. Well Aa fed this useless thing like a babby: black puddings and a cut of mutton – raw, thou knows, bloodied – eggs like Aa was tellin' you, sherry for breakfast – maybe a laal bit o' nutmeg in some broth, just to keep her titillated. Thou's got to spice up a lady dog John,' said Isaac, 'just like't real thing. Well, this bitch of mine was ready to run. Reet lads, Aa says to missel, El Dorado! So Aa took her up 'til a meet at Moresby. And Aa laid out on her. Ivvery farthin'. There's nowt like jumpin' in wid two feet. And dis thou know?' he paused, 'that daft laal tyke would do nowt but gallivant around wid to'other dogs! It would *not* run. As soon as it was slipped –

off it made for t'nearest dog to hev a roll about wid!' Isaac looked as flummoxed now as he must have done at the time – and it was at his expression more than at the story that John and Seth laughed. For the story had tailed away, as Isaac's memory had grown stronger, his bafflement more acute.

'Nowt but play aboot,' he muttered. 'But Aa got a good price for her,' he added, in vindication. 'If she went on rollin' aboot – then she would be a rare breeder – no mistake! Aa selt her for her prospects *that* day.'

They talked on for a few minutes more and then went outside. The sun was still shining, and business in The Ring was much more brisk.

'Look at them,' said Seth, 'like a lot of bloody sheep.'

'Leave them alone,' Isaac retorted, glancing at John. 'They can wag their tails when they come home – that right, John?'

'That's right.'

'Now then,' said Isaac, 'I'll just git missel a couple of pies and then Aa's fit.'

'O, give this bloody lark up,' said Seth, turning to John. 'You want nowt here.'

'Let him be.' Isaac spoke severely. 'He has a wife to look out for an' a life of his own to lead. Let him be.'

Seth nodded.

'But come up wid us and see't fight,' said Isaac. 'That thou *can* do.'

'Aa'd rather get fixed up first.'

'As you say.' Isaac stopped in his tracks, keenly feeling John's tentativeness about the hiring and yet unwilling to interfere in the other man's life. 'Well mebbe we'll meet up later on.'

'Mebbe so.'

'Grand.' He moved away. 'Come on, Seth!' he shouted, 'and bring that shiverin' bitch o' thine to see some real sport.'

They nodded to John and walked down through the market to the fair. As they went away, John felt as if two pairs of hands had torn bark off a tree and left him the white, trembling trunk. He would have loved to lead the life of Isaac but he did not have it in him. As for Seth, the temptation to accept his offer grew as the sound of the hiring grew in his ears; but Emily would never settle in a town – she was unprepared for it. And he would do nothing, not the slighest thing, which might upset her. To work in a place she would like was the least he could do for her.

She would be here in an hour or so. Mr Errington had explained to both of them where he would set her down, and John wanted to be there waiting, job fixed, luck-penny to hand. He had planned to get her a present – but his money was gone.

He walked over to the other labourers, feeling the heavy ale settling in his stomach. He took up a place beside a small stall where a woman was selling bread, and waited.

FOUR

Emily felt quite queenly sat in the trap. There was little furniture, for which, at this moment, she was glad as it gave her room to stretch her legs. She had never before been this far from home and she tried to store up every detail so as to be able to tell it over to John.

Her features were like those of many girls in that area. Rather broad-browed, strong-nosed, eyes firmly apart, a regular mouth neither thin- nor thick-lipped, and her complexion shaded from the cream of her forehead to that soft redness of cheek which would later harden. Her hair was brown, parted in the middle and laced into plaits under her hat. It was her eyes – hazel with a flick of green in them – which was her difference. They dared everything.

It was she who had urged John to leave the area when he had first, fumblingly, suggested it. She too wanted to be away. So many of the girls she knew were born and hired, married and settled within a mile or two of their own homes. She wanted to be somewhere new. It was she who had been the first to listen to and take seriously those simple daydreams of his – of everything being contented and undisrupted – and encouraged him in them. While, at sixteen, the force necessary to insist on and go through with the wedding amounted to a considerable authority over the circumstances of life as she had found them.

Straight-backed in the trap, only half attending to Mr Errington, she held her hands tightly clasped on her lap, squeezing every drop of adventure out of this journey.

Mr Errington was flattered to have such a pretty young woman for company. One who, but for the ring and the just noticeable child she was carrying, looked as fresh as a girl; as if marriage had whisked over her so lightly that it had not broken the skin of her youth. He put himself in the attitude of gallantry towards her – forgetting (which she did not) that his original offer had been phrased in terms of it 'making no difference to him whether the trap was full or empty as he was going anyway' – and it pleased him to let her stay in the trap as he walked the pony up the hill to Bothel, take her by the arm as he helped her down when they stopped for a drink, have approving looks thrown at him by those they passed.

Errington was a man of about fifty though he looked younger – 'he nivver works, that's why,' Emily's father had explained – who dressed well, kept his pony and trap in good condition and liked to hear himself called (even though the tone was always chafing) a 'gentleman of leisure'. He had inherited a row of cottages in Wigton at his mother's death and the rent from these, together with the rent from his fields – let to other farmers for grazing – gave him 'a modest sufficiency', he would say. He had never married and kept only a servant girl and one hired man for the limited amount of farming he now did. His leisure was spent driving about the place, to fairs and markets and auctions, to shows, meets and carnivals, and especially to concerts. For he had a good tenor voice and liked it to be heard. And in this busy life, he had acquired the habit of thinking of himself as a clever man, even a witty one, was careful to take many of the thorns off his dialect, read his *Daily Mail* for an hour after each day's dinner and offered an opinion of any subject at all, unprejudiced by the notion that ignorance might be a bar to argument.

After passing Bothel, they had the road to themselves and he began to sing. Emily would have liked to join in, but Mr Errington's tenor was a very self-sufficient organ. He gave her *Harvest-Home* and *The Useful Plow*, *The Farmer's Son* and *John Barleycorn*, *The Seeds of Love* and *New-Mown Hay*, holding the ends of each line that touch longer than required to let his tone be fully registered. Emily wanted him to sing *The Farmer's Boy* – John had told her that when Joseph was in a good mood, he would get them up a concert in the kitchen, and this song would bring him to tears. She liked him to tell her of his father being pleasant at times, for she needed it to mitigate the thunderous impression he had made on her and she could not bear to think that there was nothing but that sulphurous rumbling in one of John's parents. Eventually she asked Mr Errington to give it her and he, pleased, prepared its passage by a delicate hawk and a spit, discreetly shielded by his white hand. Then, with feeling, he began:

> The sun had set behind yon hills,
> Across yon dreary moor,
> Weary and lame, a boy there came
> Up to a farmer's door.
> 'Can you tell me if any there be
> That will give me employ,
> To plow and sow and reap and mow
> And be a farmer's boy?
>
> 'My father is dead, and mother is left
> With five children, great and small;
> And what is worse for mother still,
> I'm the oldest of them all.
> Though little, I'll work as hard as a Turk,
> If you'll give me employ,
> To plow and sow and reap and mow
> And be a farmer's boy.
>
> 'And if that you won't me employ,
> One favour I've to ask, –
> Will you shelter me, till break of day,
> From this cold winter's blast?
> At break of day, I'll trudge away
> Elsewhere to seek employ.
> To plow and sow and reap and mow
> And be a farmer's boy.'
>
> 'Come try the lad,' the mistress said,
> 'Let him no further seek.'
> 'O, do, dear father,' the daughter cried,
> While tears ran down her cheek.
> 'He'd work if he could, so 'tis hard to want food,
> And wander for employ;

Don't turn him away but let him stay,
And be a farmer's boy!'

And when the lad became a man,
The good old farmer died,
And left the lad the farm he had,
And his daughter for his bride,
The lad that was the farm now has,
Oft smiles and thinks with joy
Of the lucky day he came that way,
To be a farmer's boy.

The melody contributed much to its effect.

'Well now,' said Mr Errington after he had finished and allowed due silence, 'it's a grand name you've got for yourself.' He winked at her and ran his tongue around his lips, washing away the frivolous traces of song so that they were clean for conversation – or rather monologue and one which, judging by his delight in himself, he had been working on since the trip began. 'I've been breakin' your name up and brickin' it together again and it'll do a trick or two, O yes, it can jump!'

'Can it?' inquired Emily, politely.

'Indeed it can. Tallentire. Now take its beginnings – "Tall" – not much there you say, none of them's tall, more "short"; that's a mystery for a start. Then "*EN*tire" – entire what? I left off that road. But it's per*nounced*,' this was delivered with the greatest possible emphasis, 'pernounced "Tallent" – like the parable and you wouldn't grudge yer husband that, would you? And again – now this is very interesting! – that last bit "ire" runs back into "Tallent" for cover – so it's more like "Tire" – if you follow. Now hack at that a bit and you get "T'ire" – and your fella's off to be 'ired, that is *h*,' he blew on the H as if to cool it, '*hir*ed, has he?'

'He has.' Emily smiled. 'That's clever.'

'I'm not finished,' said Mr Errrington. 'The middle of it is "lent" – and I'm lending you this pony and trap – and the back end of it, that "ire", that's just another word for temper – like his father has. Now then, what d'you make of that?'

'I wish it would come out a bit better,' replied Emily frankly.

'So it might if I had a pencil and paper and could dig a bit harder,' he answered. 'There's no telling what you might get then.' He paused. 'Oh, I forgot – "Tire" – your man doesn't get tired, does he?'

'No.'

'I thought not,' said Mr Errington, complacently. 'Now you'd never believe what I hacked out of Errington . . .'

When John was not there to meet her, Emily was as startled as if she had found him there hurt. She had seen them meeting and spending the afternoon together at the fair before going on to the new cottage. As well as disappointment, then, she was a little put out. She had never been to Cockermouth Fair and might never again be given the chance. And then both these reactions dissolved under the hot fear that something might have happened to him; reassured on that by Mr Errington's proofless eloquence, she resigned herself to wait and at last felt pity that John should be finding it so difficult to get a situation.

Mr Errington's gallantry failed him. He muttered and looked around, but could not conceal his determination to go up to the fair. Its noise set his feet shuffling like a small boy's to a street band. The place he had chosen was safe, he pointed out; it was at the end of the town farthest from the Ring, just this side of the house in which William and Dorothy Wordsworth had been born (a structure second only to the castle in local importance), off the main street and yet overlooked by some cottages, so that she could always give a shout if she 'needed anything'; there was an angle in the wall, and the furniture could be stacked without harm, and finally, here was a likely-looking boy, now there's threepence for you, wrap it up in yer handkerchief – never mind, hold it in your hand and stand here and look after this woman, she's waiting for her husband, it won't be for long and threepence is a man's wage for the job. There; well, good-afternoon. If I see him, I'll tell him you're here: he won't be long: and good luck.

She hoisted herself on to the wall and looked around. There was not much to see and the noise from the fair, which she had caught sight of for a few moments as they had come up the end of Main Street, aggravated her. She kicked her heels against the wall, pulled off her hat and, to fill her attention, tried to shoo off the small boy. But he had squatted in the gutter, his gaze taking in both her and the bottom of the road (the direction from which danger could be expected to come) and would not move. Nor would he speak. She put her tongue out at him and threatened to jump down and smack his ears, but he stayed at his post unflinching.

Then she forgot about him and pulled out some cakes – only to drop them into her basket and snap to blameless posture as she felt herself being watched. She could see the man looking out of the window – just from the very corner of her eye – but she would not give him the satisfaction of a full glance: nor would she have him watch her eat. So she sat still.

Robert Stephens knew that he had been noticed and sensed that the statue-like attitude was a reaction to his observation, and this pleased him. Her coat had been opened and, as usual with Emily, it tumbled about her and so he could not see the obvious indication of a married woman; by her looks and attitude, he guessed her to be the daughter of a pleasant-faced man who had set her down, waiting while he went to find lodgings – which would account for the furniture. It was not often that he had such an untroubled opportunity to look at a girl like that, and he was going to take advantage of it.

In the downstairs room of his two-roomed cottage, he was preparing himself some tea. A schoolmaster in his early twenties, son of a ship's engineer in Barrow-in-Furness, he preferred to be on his own, even to make his own meals despite the alarm this caused among his neighbours. As he set on the kettle and laid out the table, he wondered if she would accept an invitation to join him. Probably not, he thought. Her father had looked rather a 'proper' man: still, he could take a cup out to her, or, better still, by the look of the weather it might soon rain, and then he could offer her shelter, which would be unobjectionable.

The cloth covered only half the table, on the rest, his notes were scrupulously arranged. He had seen as much of the fair and the market as he wanted during the morning and since dinner-time had been occupied in making a list of the birds he had seen at Monkerhill Lough while at his first school on the coast at Silloth. He taught the youngest class in the Church of England National Primary School in Cockermouth and the list was to be accompanied by his own drawings of the whooper-swans, Bewick swans and long-tailed ducks seen there. Together they would be pinned to the blackboard to be copied. He had also been making ready for his expedition on the following day when he was going with Mr W. G. Carrick, the well-known naturalist, to observe peregrines in their nesting ledges on the red sandstone cliffs at Whitehaven.

But this was forgotten as he bobbed up and down to look out of the window – until he could contain himself no longer and went out to her. Emily was relieved because her back was stiff. The weather, inevitably, provided him with an opening and the two of them were soon talking. He had noticed her ring almost immediately, and while this quenched his ambition (a tiny new flicker, easily damped down) – it did not mar his enjoyment at speaking to her – aided it rather by relieving it of a weight of responsibility he might soon have felt too pressing.

Emily told him everything in one dollop and soon he was as anxious as she about John's future which they were discussing when, unseen by Emily, John rounded the corner as it began to rain.

He had not felt jealousy before. Emily had been his first girl and there had been no question of either of them wasting their precious ends of free time on anyone else. Nor had there been other young men around to tease him by flirtation. He was unknown to it until that moment when it wrenched at him so viciously that he was brought to a standstill.

It was the fear that she could care for anyone else – in any way at all – which shook him; that and the overwhelming recognition of how much his love had led to dependence when such a casual sight could affect him so badly. He was at once outraged, though he realised how stupid it was – of *course* she could talk to other people, like them, be in their company (though he wished she was not smiling so happily) – and depressed, though again, there was some pride to be got from a dependence so entire that only a complete love could have made it so. These extremes stropped his nerves and all he saw salted them. He could have choked her, struck the man, snatched her away, left her for ever, given her up to him. Instead he brushed away the tears that had come and walked on, as steadily as he could, feeling that he was stepping out of a pillar of fire still burning behind him.

'John!' Emily exclaimed delightedly. 'Oh John!' She fell against him and thought his refusal to yield a mark of public manners – so she pulled herself away quickly – which he thought a sign of further rejection. The small boy ran away.

'I thought you would never come,' she said. 'I was just sayin' to this man here – he's a schoolmaster and, John, he knows where Wiggonby is! – that I would leave him to look after our things and come up that town and *make* them hire you. Oh, I *must* kiss you!'

And then, to John's complete bewilderment, the jealousy which had cindered his affection with tongues of scarcely tolerable flame slid away, and his aching lips filled with his former love as she kissed his mouth.

'Well,' she said, impatient the second the embrace was over, 'who is it? Where are we going? What did you get? What's he like? Come on, John, come on. I must know.'

'If you want to shelter from the rain,' said Mr Stephens tentatively, 'you can use my kitchen.'

'It's nobbut drizzle!' John replied, sharply, again tossed up by jealousy. Emily glared at him for his rudeness. 'Thank you very much all the same,' John added in mumbled monotone of courtesy.

'I should *think* so, John. This man's been very kind.'

Mr Stephens, though he had not sufficient perception to see right through the affair, had at least enough tact to know he ought to depart: which he did.

'Well!' said Emily, as the door closed behind him. 'And have we got so High and Mighty we can be rained on without worry?'

'I didn't like you talking to him.'

'And why not?'

'Never mind.'

'But I do. And I think you're shameful.' She turned away, biting her lip to keep back the tears and not until John had held and gently pressed her shoulders for almost a minute would she consent to turn around. 'Now *that's* out,' she said, 'what happened?'

John stuttered and then stopped.

'It can't be as bad as *all* that.'

'Mebbe not,' he murmured.

'Come on,' she coaxed him, quietly. 'Tell us.'

'I will,' he said, and the blush which had crept around his cheeks retreated as he tensed himself before her. 'There was only one fella Aa got an offer half-decent from at all!' he began, his eyes fierce with the memory of it all. 'The others hadn't this and didn't want that and some of them asked me age and offered *boy's* wages – to a married man! There's fellas down there now hasn't been hired yet and won't be this day. Then came this fella Pennington frae Crossbridge – and he would have me – but for twelve shillings, Emily, *twelve* not fifteen. He laughed at fifteen. And he had a cottage but it won't be free 'til tomorrow. So I took his luck-shillin' – but I didn't spend it. I went to look for our Seth to tell him that I would go down't pit wid him. And I would a' done, Emily, though I know you'd be worried at it. But Isaac had med a lot of money in a fight and taken Seth off to race his whippet and God knows where they've gone. I couldn't go look for them with thou waitin'. And now I can't find Pennington – and his shillin's binding. I must work for him!'

'I would have gone with you to the pits,' she said.

'But would thou like it?'

'No,' she said after a pause. 'No. I think I would have been miserable.'

'So it's just as well, then,' John answered, finding some consolation in that.

'Twelve shillings isn't bad if you've got a cottage,' she said, taking up and heightening his mood. 'There'll be many managed on less,' she added, so sagely that he laughed and swung her around in the narrow street.

'But we'll have to go back home tonight,' said John. 'I saw Errington and he promised us a lift – though he didn't seem ower keen on *my* comin'.'

'I'm *not* going back home,' Emily replied. 'Now say what you want, I'll not hear it. I'm *not* going back home and have ivverybody laugh. I'm not!'

'But what'll we do then?'

'We'll lodge in Cockermouth.'

'What on? I've nobbut this shillin'.'

'I've over a pound.'

'That's thine,' he replied. 'Thine only.'

'So I should sleep inside and you rest out in a ditch?' she asked.

That struck John as a good idea. Then she pouted and he tried to coax her and the rain came down; he spread his coat on the furniture which she took off and replaced by some brown paper which blew away as the wind gusted up behind the rain turning nasty and she chased down the street while he shouted at her to take care of herself; so she stopped to shout back at him and the papers blew into a garden.

Mr Stephens came out and made his offer. He had seen and heard all – though he revealed this most delicately – and would gladly put them up for the night in his cottage, if they thought they would be comfortable. It was this condition, this clause of truly hospitable consideration which finally allowed John to accept an invitation which Emily had lapped up on the instant of its being made. But there was still that scar of jealousy in John and also a sliver of uncertainty – for his experience over the last hours, being ignored and ignored and ignored in The Ring and then approached for such a low offer, being barged around in the fair-crowd and made to ask strangers about Isaac – many of them teasing him and giving him false answers, surrounded and drenched and maddened by the entertainments and goods, none of which he could afford for Emily, not one treat could he offer her – all this made his acceptance easier than it might otherwise have been.

As soon as he said yes, Emily darted into the cottage as if it were made for her, and John went across to take the furniture over into Mr Stephens' outhouse; the rain now slashing down, his luck-shillin' clammy in his trouser pocket, stuck against his thigh.

FIVE

When Mr Stephens went out to buy more provisions for tea –
though his excuse offered was that he needed some tobacco –
John sat in a chair on one side of the kitchen, Emily stood by
the window on the other side, both on their best behaviour. But
while he was most conscious of himself, clumsy in uneasy
gratitude, Emily was delighted with it all. After seeing Mr
Stephens disappear around the corner, she examined the small
room minutely, the books on the shelf – reading out all their
titles aloud – the three prints on the wall, 'The Education of the
Young Raleigh', 'Derwentwater at Dawn' and 'The Drunkard's
Children' – drew her boots appreciatively over the mat, picked
up the jug of pencils and finally came to the oven which was next
to the sink. Above the sink was a large cupboard which she
opened despite the disapproving suck of John's tongue.

'I could make some biscuits,' she said. 'Do you think I should?'

'Leave things be, Emily,' John replied, speaking softly in the
new place. 'Thou can't go using other people's stuff like that.'

'He would like some biscuits.'

'How dis' thou know?'

'He would.' She shut one of the cupboard doors only, not to
be defeated that easily, and then thought of a conclusive argument, 'I bet he can't make them himself!'

'Well, what's that got to do with it?'

'A lot.' But she swung the second door in her hand uncertainly.
'Don't you think he *would* like some?'

'How do I know?'

'There you are!' She smiled. 'You can't be certain. It'll be
done in a minute.'

'He won't want his kitchen mired up wid baking stuffs. That
I do know.'

'And who'll mire a kitchen up?'

'Thou's bound to.'

'I am not, John Tallentire! And anyway, it's clean dirt. It's easily mopped up.' She paused. 'He *would* like some,' she reiterated. 'I could make ginger snaps. He has some ginger.'

'Do as you please.'

'Wouldn't *you* like a ginger snap?'

'O, for pity's sake, Emily, stop keeping on!'

She slammed the door shut and went back to the window. She glanced at John quickly and then leaned forward, slipped the latch, and pushed it open. Through the rain came the sound of the fair, organ music squeezing enticingly away, unseen.

'So I won't get to the fair,' said Emily – and then, the second she had said it, she covered her mouth with her hand, afraid that her thoughtlessness might upset John. And so before he could say a word, she rushed on. 'Still! I've been to Cockermouth in a pony and trap!'

John got up and went across to her. She heard him but kept her back turned so that she would have his arms around her and then she could wriggle inside them to face him. As he held her she seemed to swell, as if another skin, another body, more calm and perfect than the one she had, grew out of her as token for that love of him which could in looks and words show itself so inadequately. He kissed her on the cheek and her eyes closed to feel his lips breathing so tenderly.

'I'm sorry about the fair,' he said.

'Don't be sorry.'

'We'll come next year.'

'Yes.'

He released her, held her on the shoulders for a moment and quickly turned away.

'There were some logs in his backyard,' he said. 'I'll chop them up for kindling.' Use the axe to cut out the feeling of obligation.

'O! That's good!'

'Emily,' he asked as he reached the door. 'Twelve shillin's *will* be enough, won't it?'

'Plenty!' she answered. 'And if you can chop wood, I can make biscuits!'

By the time Mr Stephens came back, the snaps were almost done, the table was laid, crockery out, a split log burned on the fire, there was a neat pile of sticks drying in the grate, and tea went well. They talked of the market and the fair, and then, Emily having noticed and praised his drawings of the swans, Mr Stephens held forth about his hobby.

'What d'you call a missel thrush down your way?' he asked John. 'Is it a shalary?'

'Yes. That's right. There is a shalary.'

'I thought so,' said Mr Stephens, happily. 'Even in our county it changes its name all over the place. There's storm-cock and chur-cock and shell-cock, shalary and mountain throssel – all the missel thrush!'

'There's something my grandfather calls a shrike,' said John, 'would that be another?'

'It might be. It might be! I'll ask Mr Carrick tomorrow. Shrike! I'll make a note of that.'

'There's something I call a blue-wing,' said Emily, boldly, pleased to be joining in a conversation in which she was proud to see John taking such an active part, 'and my uncle Tom calls it a blue-*back*.'

'That's the "field-fare",' said Mr Stephens. '*Turdus pilaris.*' And the Latin appellation – memorised so painstakingly – crunched between his teeth like barley sugar. 'Your grandfather might have heard it called the felty, or the pigeon felty or even the blue felty – and I think some call it fell fo!'

'Goodness!' said Emily, mouth half-open.

'Oh, that's just the beginning!' Mr Stephens responded. 'Now take the whitethroat – *syliva cinera* . . .'

But after the tea had been cleared, the cups put away, everything tidied, then the three of them sat round in broken sentences. Because of the regular placement of the chairs around the fire, they were quite close together – and yet the small spaces between them quickly became boundaries. John wanted to be in bed so that the night would be over quickly and he could move off the next morning; Mr Stephens had a neighbour who would lend them a handcart and John wanted to be able to push the furniture the eight miles uphill to Crossbridge, settle it, and return the handcart the same day. Already he was worried about their stores lasting until the Saturday when he might reasonably claim a few shillings to tide him over; Emily's mother had given them a box of stuff, sausages, bread, some tea, butter, bacon – but it would have to be spun out. He was burrowing into responsibilities, looking for them almost, for they gave substance to that which bound Emily to him – and still the shock of jealousy pulsed occasionally making him shudder so that he blushed to seem to be shivering.

The schoolteacher realised that his guests were tongue-tied in this strange place and, after a few openings had brought no more than murmurs of self-conscious or self-absorbed politeness, he did what he had found best to do on such occasions. For he was not a man who could slither into any shape required of him. His interests and habits had been too strictly and personally framed for him to be anything less than completely reliant on them. So he did what he was going to do anyway, what would most engage his own attention and invited others to share the preoccupation – which was as much as any man could do, he thought.

He took down a copy of Wordsworth's collected poems. John and Emily sat themselves up to listen, and felt most solemn: but the schoolmaster's plain reading gave them confidence and Emily's hand reached out to touch John's arm.

Mr Stephens was careful to read the short poems and finished up with one set not far from the place at which John was hired. Beginning:

> There is a yew-tree, pride of Lorton Vale,
> Which to this day stands single, in the midst
> Of its own darkness, as it stood of yore.

And John felt Emily's hand tighten on his own as the last lines rolled out:

. . . beneath whose sable roof
Of boughs, as if for festal purpose decked
With unrejoicing berries – ghostly shapes
May meet at noon-tide; Fear and trembling Hope,
Silence and Foresight; Death the skeleton
And Time the Shadow: – there to celebrate,
As in a natural temple scattered o'er
With altars undisturbed of mossy stone
United Worship; or in mute repose
To lie, and listen to the mountain flood
Murmuring from Glaramara's inmost caves.

That final line itself murmured through the kitchen and they sat silently, the organ music from the streets like the sound from the caves. John looked at Emily and saw a face on which such a keen reverence was trying to settle itself to gaze of understanding that yet again he stirred against the schoolmaster. He had no such means of casting spells over her. They came from a world out of reach. And he did not want to hear of what was impossible.

When the couple had gone upstairs to bed, Mr Stephens packed his bag for the next day's outing, bolted the doors firmly – for many of the men stayed in Cockermouth drinking for three or four days and would roam the streets at night looking for somewhere to sleep – and then, as if to atone for those first designs he had had on Emily, he picked out *Silas Marner* from his bookshelf and wrapped it up as a present for her. He pushed back the chairs and laid his blankets on the floor to fall asleep, as always, the moment he closed his eyes.

John could not sleep. He had stayed in bed until Emily was settled and then, very quietly, got up. The window in the bedroom was very small and all he could see through it were the roof-tops lit, as the previous night, by a full moon.

He could not recapture the certainty he had felt that morning. And it was not only that he had not got what he had hoped for, nor was it the jealousy which made him feel unsure. In The Ring his pride in being on his own had met with confusion and Isaac and Seth, too, seemed to challenge what he wanted, what he believed in, how he lived – though understandingly enough, he knew. It was as if he had caught an infection which was moving around all men but as yet lighting on few, something which would grow to cause fever where there had been force. He shook his head, abruptly. No wonder you get like that, standing in your bare feet in the middle of the night, his mother would have said. And he remembered Isaac's story about the man who thought too much and smiled once more.

Not until dawn, however, could he fall asleep. He lay in the bed, touching Emily with fingers too rough for her skin, wondering what he could give her that would even approach what he thought of her; waiting to be gone to his own place.

SIX

John's restlessness continued over the next few days – forcing him to a temper which shocked Emily that all that she had seen in him could be banished by such an unknown mood, or into a brooding alike as alien to her knowledge of him. His work around the cottage soon done, he scattered these unsettled moods around him, seeds which were always covered over by a mutual coveting for warmth, yet waiting only for time to send tremors through the even surface of the life their love played on.

The restlessness retreated when he began his longed-for work; hated work in those few odd moments when inactivity had percolated through the habitual demands of his skin and nerves to give him a rare perspective on his existence; despised work when after telling Emily all that Seth had said to him, the words of his brother spun on his mind – so that he saw himself as a drudge, bound to tread on a ceaseless wheel, eyes to the ruts he trod, unable, unfitted to look about himself as Seth did and see a purpose; feared work as he stood before Mr Pennington that first Saturday dinner-time, hearing his first orders; once begun, longed-for work which served his demands and gave his life a shape, continued that sculpture between himself and toil, filled his day and stilled his questions. If it did not draw from him the quality of response it drew from his grandfather, then it was not for want of trying, for 'work,' he said to Emily, 'is all I'm good for.'

Pennington was not a difficult man to work for, once it was accepted, as John had been trained to accept, that every daylight hour would be squeezed dry of its labour. He had taken over the farm from his father and nuzzled into it as greedily as a calf into its mother's udders; only he was never full. Other life in Crossbridge infiltrated his thoughts and actions, market prices jarred them, his family were invested in them, the seasons were impressed on them, but it was his farm, its every present occupation which had fed and formed them. The world outside the farm was in every way beyond him and by the time the pulses of change and alarm reached him from the cities, they were no more than remarks along a lane, scarcely worth breaking his stride for. He had been left 270 acres of farm and 240 acres of fell for his sheep and not a yard had been added or substracted, the milkers stood at the same number and there were still about a score of Cumberland pigs which were so fat they could hardly trot but which, once butchered, gave bacon whose slim streak of lean tasted, it was boasted, like no other. He kept three working horses, about two dozen hens, fewer ducks and geese and only one of his sons at home.

His tenancy of the farm was far from lifting his circumstances into comparison with those of the few gentry around the village. In outlook and habit he was, to them, not indistinguishable from the labourers but certainly much nearer to them than to any other class. He dressed about the farm exactly as John did, he worked the same hours, did the same work as John did, and he spoke the dialect with no hint of landed advantage in his tone. With education he was less well equipped than some of those hired by him and that great tangible distinction – the money – was taken away to be stacked out of sight and kept for keeping's sake as soon as it had accumulated to a pile of ten pounds. His answer to the bad times was to dig himself in harder; his father had had four hired men and kept two sons at home; he had a single man living in, one married man and three of his sons out earning elsewhere money which would come back to their home farm. That his father had gained leisure-time by a superior labour force did not trouble him; his sights were on survival, his ignorance forestalled experiments or even such changes as might reasonably have been expected to bring about improvements: he made do with less and hung about Cockermouth until someone was forced to take his mean offer of twelve shillings.

One of his economies had been to cut out drink and he was pleased to see that John so rarely bothered with it – though this approval ignored the exigence of his hired man's economy with such lack of understanding as made it formidable. No less. To be able to ignore what he was part cause of and walk around grunting approbation of an abstinence all but enforced by his own miserliness needed extraordinary powers of insensitivity and blindness.

Pennington did not, by this self-denial, miss a great deal – or so he reassured himself, the memory of those evenings in the pub, The Cross, fading as far away as those of his father merely supervising some of the work. Gossip could be gathered over a dyke while on a job.

Crossbridge was a fairly typical fell-village, placed at the first abrupt elevation of fells which, a few miles from the Solway, shuts out the easy passages of the plain and cordons the lakes and peaks in wholly distinctive life and beauty. A church was there, two pubs and a Hall, whose last resident's uneventful branch grew directly from the transplanted roots of Normandy. There were two or three gentleman farmers, and land agents for the aristocracy who owned far the greatest portion of territory, coming themselves only to flatten it with the hooves of hunters or pepper it with shot. Pennington's farm was leased from Lord Leconfield. There was a school, a carpenter, a tailor, three shops, a blacksmith, a shoemaker – who specialised in the locally notorious 'Crossbridge Boots' which at first wearing seemed to drag alongside the foot like a ball and chain – a band, an occasional cricket team, and the oldest Friendly Society in England. Sufficient people for there to be plenty of room for finely-distinguished classes. Among the local labourers, the names Edmonson, Sharpe, Spedding, Branthwaite, Wrangham, Dacre, Bragg, Tyson, Edgar and Dalzell met, married, and you could warn a stranger – as you could in many villages and at that time in streets and districts throughout England – that care should be taken in talking of someone because you would be certain to be addressing his relation: if you offended one you offended all.

What gave Crossbridge a grip on the times, however, was not this rural net, which had always been and still is, now fatter, now lean, but the opening of iron-ore pits in the village. Haematite had been mined at Egremont for centuries but now the demand for ore drove shafts down all over the area. Knockmirton, one of the fells which looked down on Crossbridge, was opened and haematite extracted from the slate; two more shafts were sunk in the village itself and men who could not find or rejected farm-work were stopped from joining the long drift from the countryside by the prospects in the red, lung-caking ore. Emily heard the buckets whistling down the fields to the railway on the loop, the iron-ore miners passed by the labourers in the fields, and a red stain spread in the streams.

Their cottage stood about a hundred yards from the farm in that area of the loping village which clustered around The Cross. It was one of three, but they were alone, for Pennington used one of the empty cottages as a store-house. The other he left empty in case catastrophe compelled the hiring of another man. As both of them had expected, there was one room up, one down, a very small garden and some outhouses. The space was more than enough for their furniture.

Emily had not reckoned on being so isolated, but after worrying over it for a while, she found reasons to like it and would then have it no other way.

Though tiny, the cottage was not easy to manage. The rent paid by John was so small that it was not worth Pennington's while to make improvements and so if slates came loose or the back wall was persistently damp, if the flags on the floor cracked and the window-frames rotted – it was of no interest to him. Emily either had to do something about it herself or persuade John to disturb himself into further action after his return from the day's work. And the washhouse was in such a state that it took her a week to clean the dolly-tub alone; the mangle was broken and John's attempt to mend it revealed that it was riddled with wood-worm: until a new mangle could be afforded, she had to rely on beating and wringing the clothes.

At the least flush of rain, there would be a trickle as the water from the gutter splashed down into the doorway made sloping by the trampling of feet. The first time this happened she was out, and returned to find mud rising between the flagstones in her kitchen, a puddle collected around the fender, seeping in to wet the only sticks she had chopped, and the second-hand mat she had bought sodden with dirt. The rain had not stopped and a bucket was all she could find to catch the overflow from the gutter; she could not get the fire to start and eventually ran out of matches; cleaned, the precious mat hung miserably from a knob on the oven, refusing to dry and losing all its attraction, smelling like a damp hide; however quickly she scrubbed the floor she could never beat the water coming in and the mud plastered her apron until that too had to be washed. When John came in, he found her crying in a chair, the kitchen reeking of wet and smelling of the mat, wood unlighted in the fire and no supper on the table. He had bricked up the entrance, making a three-inch barricade against the water, and promised to mend the gutter when he got the time. He had not lost his temper – for which she was grateful, but there was an unspoken impatience so obviously charging him that she wished that words *had* flown.

Despite this, once she got the fireplace black-leaded and distempered the walls, picked wild flowers to put in jars on the table and cut her curtains from the old set her mother had given her, ruddied the doorstep and organised her food – the cottage shone for her and she was pleased with herself. Given the money she had, it was not easy to solve the problem of food; tea was an expense, as was sugar, flour and salt. Pennington only truculently kept up the tradition of part-payment in kind and the potatoes he handed over were never enough and often half-rotten; a few turnips could be relied on, but he had let his domestic vegetable patch go and any carrots, cauliflower or lettuce had to be bought or found in John's own garden. He had felt compelled to follow his grandfather's example and give a part of the tiny plot over 'to Emily' (though he dug it) for flowers, which left him only a few yards for himself. Considering that the bottom of the garden bounded a field of grass, it would not have been over-indulgent for Pennington to suggest that John take enough ground there for half a dozen stitches of potatoes, but the thought did not occur to him. Eggs had to be bought, as did fruit – there was no orchard and even cooking-apples had to be purchased – but there she was lucky as John did not care much for fresh fruit. They ate fish only rarely and meat no more than once a week. Pennington was apparently more generous with flesh, once offering her a hen, another time offering John part of a sheep, but on neither occasion had these been killed for eating; they had died almost likely of a scabrous disease and both John and his wife had no reluctance in refusing the offers. John planned to buy a piglet sometime and feed it up, but until then he would make do with porridge, broths, bread, jam and meatless hot-pots.

One reason why she soon accommodated herself to being so isolated was that the position made her a friend. Sally Edmonson was a year younger than Emily: she worked at her father's farm – The Beck – three fields away. The youngest of six children, there was no binding necessity for her to stay at home, but the family was too easy-going to demand that she go out as a servant girl and they liked to spoil her around the place. 'Pet lamb', her father called her and like a pet lamb she had been given so many privileges at the beginning that only the most brutal action – which the Edmonsons would never have considered – could have re-set her in the type of her sisters. To her, Emily was a new face, which was welcome; a married woman, which was intriguing; poor, which kept the balance right; almost her own age, which meant they could talk; and above all cut off from everyone else so that trips there did not bring her into contact with the rest of the village who knew all there was to know about her and were perpetually patronising with their 'What time did *you* get up this morning?' and 'What's it like to do no work?' She could slip out of the Beck by the back garden and be over the fields without anyone noticing. And, finally, though cut off, Emily's cottage was near to the Penningtons' – and there lived Jackson.

Both girls accepted and swore friendship after the first meeting and neither was the sort to apply any stingy rules of careful visiting to pickle their affection in a considered regularity. Sally ran up to the cottage whenever she could and Emily would rush through her work to be the better able to listen to her.

Sally brought the village in. All her life she had listened to gossip about those she had grown up with and such interpolation as she had been allowed had been treated as the cue for a joke, rejected as trivial or merely listened to, having no more effect on the general conversation than the wind outside the door.

Now she had a clear field and she raced through the uncut grass
– did Emily know about Alfred Dalzell's gin? Did she know that
Joseph Wrangham had a donkey that could count? And Mrs
Dacre wasn't really Mrs – honestly; Jackie Branthwaite had won
the ten-stone wrestling championship and the vicar stuttered in
his sermons (Emily had not been to church; John worked on
Sunday mornings and evenings; she would get there after the
baby was born); 'Major' Spedding had stolen a corpse from the
pub that belonged to a young medical student and 'Lollop' Tyson
kept a pet fox he had found in the woods as a cub. Jo Edgar had
not spoken to his wife for fourteen years and Annie Dacre was
daft. Joby Stoker had put his mother in the workhouse and
Mrs Allan had triplets. Lord Leconfield's son had hunted in
Crossbridge that winter and a three-headed calf had been born
at Winnah.

The news plumped Emily as surely as the child inside her,
and on hot days, they would take the chairs outside the cottage
where, while Emily sat knitting clothes for her expected child,
Sally would prattle away, dart off to snatch at some flowers,
shoo away birds from the stitches, tramp into the kitchen to
make tea and come out with some cakes or biscuits she had
brought up with her, hidden in her pocket as a surprise. They
were very alike in looks, though Sally's hair was darker, her
eyes grey; the chief superficial difference lay in their relationship
to the clothes they wore. Emily had on her second dress, a dark
brown one which she wore on every day but Sunday and whose
washing on Saturday night was always done with the worry that
it might not be dry by Monday. On top of that, she had a large
coarse apron which went from her shoulders to below her knees,
with two deep pockets for pegs and her handkerchief. The dress
had many underskirts to it and she had yet again let out the
waist to accommodate her growing belly. She wore no jewellery
and her hair was always parted in the middle and coiled up at
the back. Only once, tired out by Sally's pestering, had she let
it down for her friend and then it had fallen on her shoulders,
over her breasts and down her back like a sudden glorious rush
of leaves. Sally had wanted to brush it for her, but Emily had
gone far enough and began to plait it up again almost immediately.

Sometimes she wore a white blouse with an old skirt a sister had given her, and then Sally would make a necklace of flowers, buttercups, primroses or daisies and set it around her throat.

What caused Emily most shame was her clogs. She had a pair of shoes for such an occasion as never seemed to arise, the boots she wore when she went into the village, and then the clogs for about the house. They had rubber soles with rubber instead of iron corkers, a little brass guard around the toe and the holes for the laces were rimmed in brass; the leather was brown and the entire effect one which in a later age less conscious of the rigid liaison between money of a certain quantity and goods of a specific type, would have been considered chic. Never by Emily. Though she never dared abandon them, she hated them and would take any opportunity to tuck her feet away under her dresses or lean on one foot only so that she could draw the other back. Clogs they were – even though a far throw from those boats of naked wood and iron in which her mother so compliantly sailed – and clogs they remained. The clatter they made sometimes maddened her as much as a can tied on a dog's tail. These clothes then plainly suited her as much as they did a hundred other women; but perhaps because of the clogs, or that heavy line of pegs in the bottom pocket of the apron which swung sullenly before her, she appeared to shake herself free from them as she walked as if making it clear to all that she was but temporary captive to them.

While Sally was a most willing prisoner. No clogs there – except around the farm, to be kicked off as soon as she reached the edge of the yard and the shapely buttoned boots pulled on in their place. Her skirts were mauve and wine and violet blue, the blouses frilled, worked with designs, neat on the wrist. She wore a bracelet every day and the apron was tugged over her head and off as she ran away from the farm. As *she* walked, the clothes made a swirling fanfare for her, and she felt the colour and flourish of them lift her ankles, swing her arms and encourage her hair to tumble down.

The innocence which encapsulated Emily and her new friend was not unlike that simple layer of pure light which in paintings lies across so many medieval ladies like the flattening blade of a chastening sword.

They talked of men as they talked of children – Sally bemused and all-open to her love for Jackson Pennington – and Emily still bound in her first passion for John: the one as ready to be picked as the ripest plum, the other sounding of the complete interlocking of the night. Sally dusted over her demands and desires with a dumb-show of metaphor – now asking Emily who, besides her John, was the handsomest man she had seen in Crossbridge, whether she liked blond or black hair in a man, what she thought of the Pennington farm 'as a house to look at', skirting her object as deftly as she pirouetted around puddles in the lane. And Emily, remembering the first ecstatic clash of their two virginities, could weave nothing around John but public platitudes: even to herself the details of that intimacy were never admitted and the words which at that time were starting to be used to describe the finest sensations of love would have bruised her like stoning pebbles.

The two girls talked chiefly about Sally's prospects. Being married, Emily's prospects were considered to be closed. But for Sally – the world waited. She could leave home and work in a department store in Carlisle – her mother had said so. Or she could go and live with her sister, for a time, in Barrow and there learn to be a lady's maid. More realistically, she could be employed as a companion by Mrs Arnold, 'but she's such an old mope, Emily! And I would have to read to her every day. And the *smell* in that house – dad says she must have mixed moth-balls in the paste before she had her papering done. She's *shivery*!' or she could stay at home, 'but who wants to stay at *home*' she exclaimed with an admiring glance at Emily. 'I've seen all there is to see there.' Or, finally, and she proposed this skittishly – pawning it on to her father as a suggestion entirely of his invention and one so far-fetched as could only settle in such a ridiculous place as his head – she could get herself married. 'But who would have me?' she complained – and hurried to add 'And who is there that I could put up with?'

As Sally began to recite the rosary of her 'possibles', ticking each one along the string of her self-assurance with a cancelling click of her tongue, Emily tensed herself, for she knew exactly where this would lead and dreaded the subject. Jackson Pennington, son of John's employer, was the village beau: he had run off from home twice and been told, it was known, that the next time would be the last time. Taller than most of the men around him, he would still lean forward into his toes when standing talking, as if every extra inch were a point in his favour. He was blond-haired, good-looking, had totally escaped from the pinching myopia of his father and, within limits, he was dashingly dressed, never afraid to put on his best suit just to go out for a stroll, a scarf fluttering around his neck not, as with John, tucked well into the high-buttoned waistcoat. There was talk that his first disappearance from home had been to go and live with a married woman; that it was he who had set the ferret among Braithwaite's brood-hens and killed them all to get his own back for a lost fight and he *had* been found drunk on a tombstone one winter morning and terrified the vicar coming in to celebrate early communion – but Sally could shut all these stories out of her mind with little effort.

Emily endured the talk because Sally was so eager to have a confidante. And she wanted to keep Sally's friendship; without her the days would be lonely. Moreover she liked her, loved her – and one day she would tell her . . .

She had met Jackson on her very first day. John had unloaded the furniture, and immediately set off to return the handcart – taking a few sandwiches with him to eat on the way, so impatient to be quit of this last link with past obligations that he could not bear to stop and share a meal with her.

Alone, and, she found, glad to be alone in her new house, Emily had spent the first hour sweeping and cleaning. John had brought two buckets of water from the Pennington farmyard where the tap was, but these were soon used. She set off on the first expedition from her cottage – feeling it to be no less than that, the unfamiliar hills bounding the landscape, the short track to the farm unexperienced, and the compound of panic and excitement stirring nervously inside her as she realised that she knew not a soul in the village.

She saw Jackson under the pump, stripped to the waist, dousing himself. When he adopted a flamboyant expression of surprise at seeing her, she had smiled, recognising the beer which leavened reactions to caricature: harmless, she thought, remembering the clumsy clutches at dignity of those she had seen drunk in her home village. When he parodied gallantry and filled the buckets for her then his attentions were excused, she thought, by her telling him who she was. And when he insisted on carrying the buckets down to the cottage, she had taken his flattery and mock-advances as no more than mildly drunken high spirits. Besides she was glad to find someone so lively and friendly in this new place, while she could reassure herself that her married state made her invulnerable, so she chatted excitably, pouring out her life-story and her plans, constantly mentioning John – the name like a charm to keep her safe – unaware that this openness could be construed as evidence of compliance, her naming of John as deliberate incitement, her excitement as anticipation.

He got himself invited in for a cup of tea and she sliced the loaf given them by Mr Stephens: as she cut it, she remembered doing the same thing for John an hour or so before – and looked at Jackson anxiously. Fingers locked together, arms behind his head, he tilted back the chair and gazed: convinced that he was overwhelmed by this unknown woman, and feeling great freedom in the fact that he was unknown to her, that their being together in this cottage would be unknown, that he would be able to see her whenever he wanted to. She put down the knife and rubbed the palms of her hands down the thighs of her dress – afraid, unable to speak, in case she should be the cause.

Jackson stood up, the effect of the beer returning in that warm enclosed space. And stepped towards her. Her head still flinched as she remembered that first step – but at the time she had stood, rooted, arms suddenly quite forceless. This first rise of terror made her face appear only more enticing, inflamed, it seemed to Jackson, with the same thoughts as his own. He had grabbed her: even in thinking of it long afterwards, her hands crept up to those parts of her arms whose bruises she had at such cost hidden from John. The shock had torn all restraint from her and she had kicked and screamed until he had been forced to use his strength not to subdue her but merely to keep her quiet. A hand clasped over her mouth had been bitten deeply and she still remembered the blood on her tongue and Jackson's yell. He let her go and she took the knife from the table, and stood, panting, outraged – the blade most steadily held, its point firm for action should he dare come near her – which he dared not.

After he had gone, Emily had wept as she had never done before. For at once not only herself, but it seemed her unborn child, John, their love, all that she had grown for, had been violated. It seemed to her that she would never recover from it, that she might as well give up everything at that moment, that she must rush home, kill herself (for she felt that somehow she was to blame and this swelled immediately and spat its poison back into herself) that everything was 'finished, finished, finished', she had muttered to herself, letting the water from the bucket, which had been knocked over in the fight, soak into the hem of her dress without budging. And then she had heard footsteps, rushed to the door and shrank back to its frame as she saw Jackson yet again – this time meek, apologetic, holding out a chicken in his bandaged hand, as atonement; almost comical, he looked, but there could be no laughter. Seeing him (whom she thought she ought to loathe) now so docile before her, she felt without either will or sense – and took what he gave her, turning silently away from his 'Sorry'.

This strange full-circle had exhausted her. Where his attempt in itself might have shot through her and away this sudden turn on his part sealed his action up and kept it thrashing within her, impossible to respond to, impossible to reject. That she had determined John should know nothing of it made this enclosed knowledge lodge sickeningly in her. When Jackson came around to see them both – she had to be polite and pleasant. When over the next few weeks he brought her flowers – having easily slipped away from his father and John in some distant field – she had to accept them for fear he would ask about them in front of John the next time he came. This torture lasted for almost a month until she could no longer bear it and was prepared to tell

John and leave the place whatever the consequences. Jackson heard this threat solemnly, repeated, again, as he always did, that he was sorry and said he would keep away. A few days, a week, a fortnight passed, then Sally arrived and Emily felt almost free.

One thing nearly gave it away. Word came from the Pennington household that Mrs Tallentire might see her way to spending her hours between breakfast and supper within the walls of the farm – to do work as a servant-girl which Mrs Pennington had long required, no one until now being found suitable. Wages, the word continued in a more muted tone, could be arranged.

John thought this a marvellous opportunity – just for a few months until the baby got too 'bad'. He was carried away by the benefits it would bestow; there would be more money – and she could have *all* her wages to do with as she pleased, 'a dress and things'; she would have company and get to know about the village; he would see her more often through the day as he was frequently in the farm and the yard; they could walk back together at night . . . Emily was adamant. She would not go. At first out of curiosity, then out of anxiety, then in anger, John asked her why not. At last, when she sensed his suspicions grow warm to her secret, she said: 'Anything that can be done in my own cottage – washing or baking or anything, I'll do for them. But the *two* of us need not be bound to them. Besides, you've given me my own house and I want it kept right for you. I want us to enjoy it – when the children come it'll change soon enough. I'd do without any amount of dresses to have it right for us these few months.'

Spoken so calmly, that, coming after one of John's more heated outbursts, it not only reassured him but reminded him of his love so that he put his arm around her to beg forgiveness for his temper.

Her answer he carried to Pennington with no little pride.

By that, it seemed that she had cut herself off from Jackson, would be no more forced to see him than his father, and somehow, by wishing, even the memory would be shaven down. The more she grew to command the lonely cottage the more confident, she became and, to her surprise, she saw herself behaving as before, laughing, kissing John, thinking the same thoughts. By ignoring it completely it would be erased.

Yet there was one further incident which checked that hope – though it did not break it.

An early summer Saturday, John had been out turning the hay since early morning. His supper was warm on the hob, the table laid with a white cloth, water hot for him to bath in, the lamp on, herself tidied up, everything ready. One thing more, she thought, would make it perfect and she took down her shawl, looked out a big jug and went up to The Cross to buy him a pint of ale.

She knew from Sally that many women went there on a Saturday night – to the 'Jug and Bottle' entrance – and that some of them stayed there to 'push a few into theirsels', as Sally had impressively expressed it. Further, by her friend she had been warned that though most of the families at Crossgates were 'as decent as you've a mind', there were, in that row of cottages built to serve the iron-ore mines, 'one or two families,' said Sally, 'only one or two mind you, where the women are,' she had paused to whisper, 'awful.' And that these women were regular visitors to the 'Jug and Bottle'. This Emily remembered, and also she realised that Jackson would most likely have slid early out of the work and be drinking there – but she was not going to let anything stop her – it would take no more than a minute – and she pressed on.

The small corridor which led to this off-licence bar was crowded with women and children, many of whom had been helping in the fields now that some of the farmers (Pennington was behind-hand) were beginning to bring in the hay. The women's faces were red from the sun and redder from the ale; voices loud and assured, knowledge of each other complete, they fell silent as she joined them and despite her resolution not to be afraid she had shivered and her fright had gone right to the nostrils of the fiercest. Emily's smooth and pretty pregnancy and the boldness which fronted the timidity provoked them. At first she was merely bumped, then barged, then accused of barging, then accused of lying when she denied it. When she raised her voice accused of arguing, when she fell silent accused of sulking. When she turned to go accused of putting on airs, when she turned to reply, cuffed. And she threw her jug into the face of the woman who did it. Wiping her brow she discovered blood from a tiny cut made by the jug and the sight of this launched her against the stranger, both hands clawing.

What Emily remembered was that Jackson had come in with some other men and separated them, had held off the other woman with one hand and made her friends laugh at her. Had walked her home quickly and, at the door, explained all to John. And she remembered having been held most tenderly as they had walked back towards her cottage.

Jackson had not exploited this circumstance, and she was grateful. Wove reasons for this into her thoughts of him. For she could not prevent herself from thinking of him – so distant now, she thought, nodding cheerfully as they passed one another; no more.

When Sally spoke about him she felt such a cheat that she could not bear herself. Sometimes she could scarcely contain it, felt as a jealous woman – but always kept the secret; and to Sally's final appeal 'So that only leaves Jackson Pennington. Doesn't it, Emily? Doesn't it?' her reply was given with an emphasis of agreement far stronger than necessary.

'Yes, it does, Sally. Only him!'

SEVEN

Emily kept all this from John. She did not want to imagine what would happen. There was some consolation in her conviction that he suspected nothing and this had to be sufficient balm for her guilt.

But without seeing or hearing anything directly, John experienced the effects. The thousand flexible strands which held them together tightened: words meant kindly sounded indifferent, a casual glance would be coloured to cruelty or reproach by the interference of secrecy. Less and less was he able to feel her moods. Once he had known what she would think about everything: rested on it as on part of himself: they had been one.

The flaws appeared immediately.

When, after Jackson's assault on her, she evaded his eyes while undressing for fear he might see the bruises on her arms – making an excuse to go upstairs well before him and have the sheets up to her chin until he blew out the candle, or, pleading cold, retiring down the stairs to dress for bed before the low fire – he felt repulsed. Yet he did not ask 'What's wrong?' in such a way as would once have pulled inevitably on the loose thread and unravelled all the length; if he spoke the words now, they were toned in resentment and delivered with clumsy vehemence. She was also at this time nervous – and for this he was more inclined to blame her at being so weak that a little solitude could make her jump; pale, which he put down to the child, overlooking the evidence he had so far had – that the child had increased her buoyancy, heightened her colours; she looked at him sadly, and in that he saw neither a plea nor a pain – but reproach for the circumstances into which he had brought her. When she was tense he could not leave her alone, as formerly, and allow that splinter to work itself free in the cossetting of his companionship, but he must pester her and drive it in further until the hurt was numb.

As yet, such reactions were not set hard in him. He still felt all his former love on days when he would see her outside the cottage as he waved to her from the fields, or look down on their home from the hillside as he went among the sheep. And perhaps, he sometimes thought, his irritation was simply to do with the fact that they could not make love together so often. He had once heard that the moment a woman became pregnant then everything should stop. Both he and Emily had been unable to stop themselves. But now, the warning pressed into John's mind and he was influenced by it. That he allowed himself to be influenced was an act of spite against himself for treating Emily in a way which made him feel ashamed. So he desisted from that in which much of their communion lay in order to punish himself; which increased his exasperation and led to his treating her worse. Constantly his mind referred to the jealousy he had felt when seeing her with Mr Stephens.

Sometimes he thought he saw the tips of a root of external malevolence reaching into him, possessing him. For after days of peace and quiet, when he would see her smile as it had been and watch her as she stood at the window, waiting to be held by him, when Sally would flutter in with a mouthful of gossip, or he would again polish the ram's horns he had found on Knockmirton fell then, quite suddenly, as if a poisonous root had squirted out venom, he would be unable to stop this feeling of strain and temper and sometimes savagery. He wanted to hit her, hurt, destroy her.

So that, at such times, he looked at Emily as if she were merely the woman who happened to be sat near him in a chair, with no more right to be there than anyone else, tied to him by nothing more than an instinct which would pass – was the first awakening to this knowledge the root which spread the poison? – and there, always there, not to be moved, her enlarged belly fixing her to the spot. Though he caught sight of himself spinning in this vortex he was helpless to aid himself: and even if he remembered the pulse of what had been he was incapable of recapturing it.

The mood would pass, he would feel it go out of him, slip away, discard him, and he would walk like someone taking first steps, amazed at the trivial cause of such a thing, look at what was before him with clarity, the mists of his locked-in fury evaporated.

Emily gave herself the simplest of all explanations for that which shook him so totally. Which was that he worked too hard. Having grown up where men could be made senseless through work, she could reconcile herself to that and would go no further.

His work indeed filled his day, or rather it made of it a structure into which he climbed to ride through the minutes and hours and weeks of toil, full pelt. Never had he felt so capable of work for though his body could be sated, it could not be satisfied. The marriage, the approaching child, the new place, the freedom from those who watched and knew him, the determination to make Pennington recognise his value and so be forced to offer a less insulting price at the next term – all this goaded him into the work. It was not so much that he put everything into his work as that he looked to the work to put everything into him. Labour was his school, his opportunity, the stuff of his imagination and increasingly the object to which his senses reached. He attacked it and wanted his blows returned, to go harder, daring it to give him limits.

It could be seen in the way he did everything. At his arrival at the farm, Pennington's miserly ways had left the biggest field unploughed. A good test for his new man. And John took it up willingly on his first day. He had been round with the horses the night before to brush them (they were so startled at being groomed – cleanliness and smartness had to pay their way on the open market with Pennington – that they almost kicked the stall down), had them harnessed in the morning and out into the lane as Pennington's slow feet shuffled to a stop at the unaccustomed sight of groomed horses, dressed and ready without any of the usual hindrances which necessarily beset such pinched methods as he generally employed. Once out of the lane and on the road to the far field, John swung out his boots, clacked his tongue at the two massive Clydesdales before him and had to prevent himself from flicking them into a trot or pulling them back into a rear of delight. The dawn air chapped his cheeks and clipped his ears – encouragement to go faster: the horses were restless and one was much stronger than the other – but he felt his muscles flex at this extra trial.

The land was stony, there would be many pauses for clearance, he would have to hold the plough deep, the ground would be tough under those stones – but this was nothing as he tied up his team and walked down the curved field. It sat like a shallow bowl upturned so that when he broke off he could see only the heads of the horses. He strode back to them straight up the line he would plough, his mind locked on keeping that line straight as a rod on his return.

As the day went, his back tightened until just to move was to cause pain. Gulls came in from the sea to swoop and turn around his head. A large stone almost buckled the iron tip of the plough. The weaker horse listed over to the stronger at the slightest relaxation of the biased hold. Heavy wet earth fastened itself on to his boots until at times it made a second pair so that he walked in earth on the earth; and a fine drizzle moistened his drawn face until it glistened whitely. But behind and before him lay the straight furrows. As he paused after turning the horses he would look up the hill to them, get down on one knee to confirm their straightness and stiffly rise to stand on tip-toe trying to peer over the brow and be clearly certain that they continued as immaculately on the other side. Then came his pleasure: for the field looked as if it had been waiting to be opened up, the fresh runnels and steep little banks of earth revealed by the plough attending him to put their regularity across the featureless ground. When he closed the gate in the evening, saw the greening hedges holding fast the long lines of dense brown earth, the gulls still turning in the dusk, darkness coming down the fellside to cover what he had done, the curtain to his performance, the field in which he had lived for that day was proof in use and beauty of his work: undeniable.

Unlike love. Feeling uncertain, he turned to what was sure;

and it was through work that he reached out to fasten his transient grip on the planet.

There was nothing to stop him – certainly not Pennington who presumed on total service and was only moved to comment when that was not forthcoming. He could work fourteen, fifteen – all the hours God sent. There was nothing to hinder exploitation. Joseph Arch had formed an agricultural union in 1872 and himself gone into Parliament in the election following the labourers' first use of their vote; but the union fizzled out in the damp of the long agricultural depression and Arch saw his work undone. Pennington was in no danger from that quarter. Throughout England at that time, work was pitching so many men into a condition outwardly like slavery that the ugliness of outward forms, such as the new towns, was no wonder; they were sores, wounds, infections on the body of a land groaning with strain. Yet in so far as the condition was *not* slavish, freedom presumed if not enjoyed, work was a source, for some the only one, which could nourish those who fed it.

And there were many ways John could take on the Pennington farm; he could find an endless quantity of work and so strength need never be exhausted for want of application; difficulties he could discover in how to make do with rusting implements and fallow ideas – and this tested him, for the presence of difficulty was, to him, essential. He could achieve perfection in hoeing and win victories even over the weather. While, in his relation-ship with Pennington, there was the pleasure of a fight.

Pennington never thought of regarding John as an equal, and neither did John. He took a great delight in doing things before the farmer asked for them so that the man was stumped for a suggestion and would glare out of his small eyes vindictively until, after a certain play, John would propose his own next job. Or, seeing the chance, he would not do as ordered, wait until the storm burst then either prove the greater urgency of what he had done or argue once again, often with Jackson's support, about the worth of what had been originally pronounced. He eluded Pennington's table by taking all his meals with Emily just as he sometimes met his criticisms by direct action – as when Pennington had forced him to go out with a ramshackle cart –

clearly in need of repair – which John had driven so hard and badly that a wheel had come off half-way to the field. This confrontation with Pennington led to no boasting on John's part and, though it was spurred on by the resentment he felt at being so cheaply hired, it did not express itself in personal dislike for Pennington with whom he would have said he got on 'well enough'. It was essential to him that he laid down his rules: were he not to do so he would, he knew, have been walked all over. For though Pennington was dulled, he would have trodden as hard on John as he possibly could, given a chance: his nature was to wear down things and people until they fitted smoothly into his own proportion. The hired lad who lived in the house would have run up a tree if asked. The only way to prevent that was to obstruct it – and that could be a pleasure.

The cottage and the farm; Emily and the work; what could be and what was; these facing sides made the cliffs for his valley. There was little time and less inclination to join that young gang of men – led by Jackson – who followed the dogs, played football, pitch-and-toss, went to dances and flung themselves into as much as possible before they met their match. And despite his talk to Emily about being 'on his own' and 'starting out again', he was rather shy in the village. As keenly as her he missed the thatch of long-known friendships: those daily minute acts of recognition which seem so transparent as to let in the whole world but which, once abandoned, are seen as walls which kept the elements out. Many a time he sickened to be back at home and had to force this denial of his hope back down his gullet. He was out of touch with himself as he appeared. For he thought that he had become surly, almost a recluse, part of nothing but the farm and the cottage – unaware that people were beginning to know him, note his habits, fit him in: he would have been astonished to know that he was generally regarded as cheerful and contented, that people liked to see him about his work, hear him whistling and singing to himself: he would have denied that he did so, unable to make a real connection with the village, bound by the spell which he had cast over himself.

Emily had encouraged him to go to The Cross about once a week but after her fight there he rarely stepped in the place.

One disappointment which followed this decision was that he missed the company of the iron-ore miners who used it. He admired the way they made as if to despise the work they did – and on such occasion he would sincerely join in with their contempt; that he himself had to be up in the small hours of morning, willing to go out and get ready for a day's scything the hay was quite another matter. He liked also their collective intrigues about wages – what they would do, what benefits they wanted – his own contribution to the Crossbridge Friendly Society appearing in comparison the most fragile camouflage against fortune. And one night, after he had seen them entering the pub as he drove past with a load of hay and rather sadly endured their chafing he determined to ask Emily if she would mind if he left farm work at Michaelmas and joined those better paid, fresher, altogether freer men in the iron-ore mines. She would not answer him at first. He knew that she objected but he thought the objection based on her unwillingness to leave the cottage, to go and live where she might be in daily contact with the women who had fought her, to uproot from the place she daily made more in her own image. None of these objections, when he proposed them to her were confirmed by that particular tone of conviction which he would have recognised as conclusive.

Patiently he waited on her reply. Her silence was objection enough and already, as when Seth had urged him to come to the pits, he was easily ready to pass the chance over it if would hurt her. The moods which had built up in him and despite himself broken on her and the work which had sated him but in his exhaustion made him no more than an object of fatigue some nights – these were now regretted and wished all away. They seemed the twistedness of uncertainty and selfishness beside the love which at this moment flowed between himself and his wife. He felt her resistance and, through that, was allied to her again. He would not go, she need not reply. He knelt down and rested his head against her and his face was broken into patterns by the fire.

It was not until some days later that she told him her reason. She could not think of his working under the ground, she said. She had laughed in admitting it, but the force of her fear was

plain. No, as he took her hand and teased her that he would dig
a hole in the garden for practice, to let her get used to it, no
she could not bear it. This answer aroused such a feeling of
gratitude in him – that he could be considered with such tender-
ness – that far from blaming her or telling her she was silly, as
she had expected, he had kissed her and caressed her there in
the kitchen.

Later, when he was at the work he most liked – on the hills
going round the sheep, checking each one, he thought that
perhaps it was because of the child; with one part of her in
darkness she wanted the other in the light.

The impulse to change his work left him. Emily's concern
again unlocked his feeling for her and he was glad that his work
took him on to the hills where he could always see the cottage
and watch over her, waiting for the birth. At that time they
were beginning to cut down the plantations of spruce and larch
and the woods sounded and re-sounded with the ringing of axes
on the trees, bells for the birth of his child. Large carts took the
wood down to the yards, the horses drawing the huge stacks
higher than the cottages they passed, from a distance resembling
antique engines of war.

John loved their new place then, the peace at the little
tarn of Cogra Moss to which he would take Emily on Sunday
evenings, and the strange feelings, at once wild and heavily
peaceful, which swept him as he stood on top of Blake or
Knockmirton and saw before him range on range of interlocking
fells which seemed to shift as purposefully as clouds whenever
he moved; and behind him was the plain, the sea. Tranquillity
settled on him so drenchingly that it seemed his feet could never
move from the spot; every sort of man had passed from the sea
to these hills, all as transient as he would be – there was no fear
in it; and the landscape seemed to change and swirl in front of
him, as the light on the hills; the only thing which rested still
was that cottage down there, with Emily.

In October she gave birth to a daughter – May. Soon after
that came the term and John forced his original asking price out
of Pennington who, urged on by Jackson, eventually allowed the
benefits of the bargain to his side impress themselves on him.

Emily's mother came up for a week just before Christmas and the child was baptised.

On one of his holidays, John went to Cockermouth and bought Emily a new shawl and May a christening cup and these purchases took all that he had saved from his first term's wages.

EIGHT

Just after the New Year, Isaac landed. The money he had won in the fight at Cockermouth had been lost on Seth's whippet, 'beaten by a *real* speed-merchant,' he said, 'Aa'd back her agin any other – but not agin that thing. And there was nobbut a snout in it for a' that. Anyway, she skint Seth and me – so Aa had mesel hired by Parkinson o' Bothel. A right statesman he is: he's got that many hats it's a wonder his head doesn't get lost and he has hisself bath'd ivery other day! There's no dealin' with him! So Aa moped around theer for a bit – 'til Aa bowt this cock from a feller at Mealsgate – Silas Hocking his name; you won't know him – an' by the Lord he was a good 'un. Old wash 'is fancy breeches – Parkinson – he has spurs all polished up, hanging in his stable like some bluddy ornament. So Aa clicked them a few times – he wouldn't miss them, ower busy keepin' 'is hats on – and away we went boys! Aa've nivver seed a strike like that cock hed. It could a' ripped the liver out of a sheep – pardon me missis. So Aa collected a packet on that, fettled up our old lass, filled the jar, John, filled the jar! That's a man's life-work, filling the jar! – and Aa'm gonna hev mesel a few months' huntin'. Now then,' he turned portentously and politely towards Emily, 'Aa don't want to butt in on folks, if they're busy. Say the word an' Aa'll be off.' He was shy before Emily and attempted none of his jokes, altogether uneasy in any female company but that of his wife, 'An' you've got yersel a babby – they tek some cleanin'. But,' back, with relief, to John, his body shifting direction with the words, 'this Mellbreak pack's havin' a hell of a season, Aa've heard. Hardisty – he's huntsman now. Aa knew him when he was whipper-in wid the Blencathra – he tacks like a bloodhound, yon fella. They tell me he could sniff them out of a rock face. An' your house is handy for it see? If

Aa could leave me bag here, missis,' again to Emily. 'Aa'd pay for me feed. Thou wouldn't see a great deal of me anyway – but this could be a basis, kinda thing, for me sport.' Putting the sport before himself lessened his fear of imposing on them.

There was no question, he must stay, and Emily was moved to see how grateful Isaac was for this simple offer of accommodation. Moreover, there would be no word more of his paying anything. This he would have protested at had he not realised the mutual embarrassment which would result, so he made a note in his mind to buy some pans for Emily with the money he had set aside for his keep.

The Mellbreak he spoke of was a pack of foxhounds which was followed on foot. No horses could hunt where these dogs travelled – on the fells. And possibly because of the pedestrian effort involved, there was no aristocracy to make the occasion courtly, nor that gentlemanly professionalism of men in love with horses and sport but also conscious of a fine nerve of correctness which gave to hunts such as those described by Siegfried Sassoon the knightly aspect of a personal quest. The Mellbreak hounds were owned by the tenant-farmers and their labourers and kept at home by them through the summer. In the autumn they would go to the kennels for the huntsman and his whipper-in to work into a pack. The huntsman himself did casual work in the summer and claimed huntsman's pay from September: his wage was met from donations by the various hunt committees in the villages from which he would set out, and the food for the dogs was as often as not provided, in dead carcasses and left-overs, by the men – themselves living on very strict budgets – who owned them.

When the season opened, the huntsman, in red coat, red waistcoat, red tie, hard black bowler, brown jodhpurs and thick nailed boots with black leggings going from ankle half-way up his calf would blow the small horn he kept in one of his pockets – and they were away. He would settle in a village, staying free of charge in the pub, and – as still today – hunt around that locality for about a week before moving on to the next spot. At that time his range was not as wide as it became, and most days he would be out around Loweswater Lake, hunting under the dominating cone of the Mellbreak fell from which the pack took its name.

All the men involved were mad on the sport. They would set aside good cuts for their dogs, go without a drink themselves if the hounds needed some sherry, look out for the foxes in the summer, note down bolt holes and badger sets, bet on the staying power or speed of their hounds, and talk, talk and talk of nothing but the hunt throughout the winter. Unlike Pennington such men did not bore on as if all seasons were one but saw where work could be quickly got away for that day, set aside, even neglected if the pack was running well.

The hunt was centred around Loweswater, and as the lake was no more than two or three miles across the fells from Crossbridge, Isaac was wise in his choice of a base. In fact his qualification to Emily, that she would not see a great deal of him, was well advised. As often as not he would be invited to stay with someone he had got talking to after the night's drinking which followed the sport, or the hounds would have taken him so far from Crossbridge that he would find a barn or knock on a cottage door for the night.

In a previous season Isaac had got in with two much older men who clearly remembered Peel's day: they had half a dozen dogs of their own. For a whole winter the three of them had chased everything over the countryside, often dropping with fatigue where they stopped at the end of a long chase, sleeping in their soaked clothes behind a hedge. That time nothing in the world mattered to him but the sport; the three men walked and clambered over the fells until all soreness of muscle gradually turned into a tirelessness of limb which made them capable of what appeared to others incredible endurance. As when they had chased one vixen four days and ended up in Lancashire for the kill; and been laid up in an abandoned cottage near Shap, they had seen the rare sight of weasels packing – racing down the hill wailing with hunger, more terrifying than anything Isaac had seen or heard in his life: that time had been the happiest in his life. He had learnt from the older men and grown to be as knowledgeable as they, he had listened to stories and details every night, he had been freely bound to the sport he loved more than anything, and in the empty hills felt himself as contented and as strong as he could be.

Strength was something taken for granted in the farming areas; from childhood most of the men had lifted and hauled weighty objects, walked miles to bring sheep down from the fells or sow a field, pulled and heaved against horses and stones – their bodies were not puffed with that lovingly delineated muscle which in the sculpture of Greece imbues the forms of apparent gods with the shades of narcissism – they were often fat and bulky, as Isaac was, or tending to be scraggy like John – but their capacity for endurance above all set their bodies in an unvaunted power which was adamant.

On the occasions when Isaac *was* at the cottage, Emily enjoyed it greatly. He would talk for hours on end and, as he grew to know her better (though he always called her 'missis'), would make her laugh, her laughter warmed by the thought of these, her two men, as brothers. He set snares on Blake and sometimes brought her a rabbit or, once, a hare. Above all, his presence protected her, and she realised how much even now with the baby a few months old, she feared that Jackson might return to confuse her. He had come down once or twice since the birth, but the demands of the baby, or the entrance of Sally, had caused him to sheer off in disconsolate haste.

John, too, was glad to have his brother about the place and he grew to envy those early departures when Isaac would steer off across the field, his arms swinging beside his thick body like short oars on a boat, impatient to be with the hounds. John curbed his envy as best he could and even felt ashamed of it – and he realised that he could never be as adventurous as Isaac – but he could not eradicate it, and as his cold-swollen fingers cut up turnips for feed, or as he trudged up Knockmirton to look over the sheepfolds after a snowfall, he wished that he, too, could sail away on a free morning.

'Well why don't you come?' Isaac asked one night. May was upstairs in bed and the three of them were sitting around the fire, curtains drawn, light from the lamp toning everything in deep browns and blacks like Flemish kitchens, the wind rampaging around the isolated cottages, 'catching its tail,' said Isaac, 'chasin' itsel intil a bluddy fit – stupid ornament' – and John's eyes immediately went to question Emily's reaction and then moved away again, irritated at this dependence.

'Yes, why don't you, John?' Emily said. 'It would suit you.'

'It would suit him as snappy as a garter, missis. Aa can see thy John puffin' along there lad, tryin' to jump on to t' fox's back – it would buck him up, no trouble.'

'Ay, but I just have Sunday afternoons. What use is that?'

'Thous can claim a long weekend – Saturday dinner-time 'til Sunday tea-time – one week in three my lad – and mek no hesitation. How many time's thou taken it?'

'Hardly more than three or four,' said Emily.

'Well git stuck int' that Penitent o' thine. Tell him thou has a brother needs entertaining and tek a *full* Saturday – and t'Sunday to mek up for what thou's owed. He has thou workin' like stink. Thou mun throw some of his own muck back at him.'

'He doesn't drive me to the work,' John interpolated quickly.

'No – thou needs no whippin'. Thou's like our mother – she'll tidy up her grave and pop up in heaven with her pinny on. But that's all reet,' he conceded broadly, 'no harm in any man as likes to stick at it. But – be fair to thesel, John – kick up a bit!'

The challenge was met and after a direct and abrupt confrontation with Pennington first thing the following morning, John got his two days for the following weekend.

The hunt met on this Saturday morning outside Kirkstile Inn. The yard was full of hounds and the forty or so dogs sniffed and scuttered around the outbuildings incessantly. They would be loosed at nine o'clock. Hardisty was in the pub taking his nip of whisky with the landlord, and Isaac – greeted by all and besieged by the dogs so that he had to wade through them to the door – went in for 'a bit of the same'. The bar was full, though few of the men were drinking, and John, tingling from the walk across the fells with his brother, sat down delighted to see so many new faces, luxuriating in the knowledge that he would be two days away from the farm, from the cottage. Yes, even from Emily and the baby. As he looked around and grasped the glass of spirits which Isaac put in his hand, he considered himself in rare company.

The men were dressed in their working clothes, patched jackets dangling open, stained waistcoats lacing up their chests with tarnished buttons, boots and leggings and corduroy, hands thick as bricks, caps containing faces shining red from their beating with the weather. One or two had terriers which would be set down the holes, and John saw something he had not often seen – a bitch terrier and her pup chained together by a short length which led from collar to collar; they would run together all day, and every day until the pup had learned how to work with the hounds. He was like that with Isaac, he thought.

He was soon introduced to the company by his brother, a deceptively easy operation for the prevalent names were Joseph or John and convenience had bred from these such a confusion of Jos, Josters, Jobys, Josses, Joseys, Jontys, Jacks, Jackies and Tonts that the nicknames would have made things simpler – but those could not be assumed by John that came from intimacy or distant recitation only. Though he loved to be in this company he could not rid himself, however he sprawled in his chair, of the belief that what was natural for them was, for him, a treat. As if to emphasise this, the excitement had drawn all his boyishness on to his face and he felt over-young among them – while Isaac, not much older in years, stood there with his foot on the bar-rest planted, part of a generation altogether more substantial and assured than his own. And though he was away from Emily, John could not help remembering her face as she had kissed him that morning, the sleeping child, its arms flung out over its head as if floating in the cradle – thinking of them as if he had abandoned them, not merely left them for a couple of days – so that as he sipped his whisky and listened to the steady mutter of dialect around him he was irritated and bewildered by a sudden desire to return to his home, to reassure Emily that he loved her, to be with May, to tell them – what, he did not know. Nor could he understand his certainty that although there were men here no better placed than he, yet he would never be able to take leave of everything in the way they did: never be able to be out after his sport leaving his wife and children and work to look after themselves. For these reasons also, he was glad when nine o'clock approached and the huntsman moved out, the whipper-in called the dogs together so that they herded as a pack and moved, a jostling phalanx, up the lane. The horn sounded and the hunt began.

They went over to draw Holme Wood, a fox having been noted there on the return from a hunt a few weeks back, and John and Isaac stood outside the wood as the hounds streamed through the trees, their bark echoing the axe-blows which came across the valley from the wood at Mosser. The day was grey but there was nothing to prevent the scent rising strongly and the hounds were as skittish as kittens.

John looked around him. Everywhere the fells rose, their yellow-green winter grass cut across by the dark bracken, the scree grey, a dull glint of mineral which would later glitter under the sun. Even under such canopied cloud, the air seemed to leap at your flesh and bark its shins on your skin. Farms and cottages sat along the valley bottom and on the lower slopes as easily as rock-pools left by the tide; and from the intent scarlet face of Isaac to the top of the Mellbreak itself, the day was made for sport such as this.

Holme Wood yielding nothing, they moved on to a small planting at the foot of Little Dodd. The hounds clamoured – but for no more than a hare, and John laughed at the electric hopping of that animal as its white tail flashed up the fell-side. Hardisty called the dogs back to him and they went up the Mosedale Beck, right into the fells, their sides rising steeply. This was the time for conserving talk and energy and the two or three dozen men tramped steadily through the peaty bottoms, skirted the bouldering outcrops, said little, intent on Hardisty, scarlet, at their head. Before them the hounds fanned out until the bare hillsides seemed to breed dogs out of those cavities and clefts which pocked them. Heads to the ground, feet padding ceaselessly, long tails swaying gently, the brown, black-white patched dogs muzzled for the scent. They went the length of that climbing valley without raising more than a crow. Even the sheep seemed unimpressed, merely scattering a few yards distant and then standing to look on the procession, rigidly still.

It was after midday that the fox was raised – down towards Burtless Wood beside Buttermere. It turned immediately and ran back the way the men had come and John had a view – the fox racing across a skyline, clinging to the ground it seemed, tail straight up in the air to leave no scent. But the hounds had the view as well, and they were after it.

It gave them a hard run. Into Mosedale bottom where it crossed the beck three times, around Hen Comb, behind Little Dodd, back the other direction towards Kirkstile. They lost it for a few minutes there until someone halloed they had seen it slipping up the beck – and they were off again.

John seemed to swoop and roll among the fells as he followed the chase. The field spread out, the hounds themselves strung along a quarter of a mile, two or three of them off on a scent of their own – lost to the day's sport: one hound cut its paw so badly on a wall that it dropped out, the terriers scurried along, the tied pair, like a diminutive canine monster. There were halloos every few minutes and the men themselves became hunters, climbing the heights in anticipation of a vantage which would give them a total view and enable them to race down when the kill was near, cutting up the loose screes and perhaps finding that the valley they reached was already clear of the chase, making for the badger sets down at High Nook which the fox itself could be expected to make for (they had been blocked the previous night), suddenly, by the action of that lush red-brown fox, spread out over a full range of hills and valleys.

Isaac's plan was to stay with the whipper-in. A younger and faster man even than Hardisty who could cut off this and hedge that, he held down his job to a great degree by his ability to stay close to the hounds – even when they broke and raced as furiously as they did now. No man could keep right up with them on that ground – but as near as anyone could get, the whipper-in did. With Isaac at his shoulder and John, sometimes gasping in agony, behind. As if to find yet more use for his breath, Isaac yipped and hooped all the way along – his belly shaking with the efforts he made, the hills ricocheting with the barks and shouts, and on his face an unshakeable grin. 'What a day, lad!' He shouted back at John. 'O, look at yon stupid hound! What a size – eh? Did you see him lad? Did you see that brush – like a bluddy Christmas tree. Eh! Come on! Come on! My God, they're scalin' those screes. We'll slither down yonder, lad, like fish on slab. Yip! Yip! That big hound'll hold out. My money's on that 'un – Bellman it is. Go on boy! Look at him lift! Come on, lad! Come away! Eh! What sport!'

They killed him down near Holme Wood where they had started the day and the early winter darkness rapidly fastened over the sky; the tops of the fells were in total darkness as they arrived back at the pub, lamp-lit windows, the men dispersing across the fields to eat before drinking, a few crows settling in the tops of the bare trees, John's legs shaking unsteadily as he made his way down the twisting lane.

Isaac insisted on buying John the first drink – a pint of ale was demanded and Isaac thrust the poker into it before draining it in one.

'That's more like it!' he exclaimed. He shook his belly. 'Oh! It's swimmin' around in there like a good 'un, John, sailin' home, boys.' He bent forward as if to listen.

'It's a grand property you've got down there,' said the landlord of Isaac's stomach.

'O my lad! This is an investment! There's fellas would queue up to put money into this thing. Aa was once at Appleby an' a fella offered me ten pounds cash for this corporation o' mine. Give us the munny, Aa said, an' Aa'll feed her up a bit wid it. What they call *interest*, see. Thou can watch they ten pounds grow, Aa said. My Godfathers, he was a fool to back out of it! Come on then John – sup up! We must have lost twelve pints of sweat clamberin' up that Mellbreak. Same again!'

'They tell me Bellman was up there first,' said the landlord, opening the tap on one of the large wooden barrels which stood on a ramp behind the bar.

'He was!' said John. 'Thou should a' seen it go into that wood – eh, Isaac? It could have tackled a wolf! It led all the way – didn't it, Isaac?'

'It did, lad, it did. Here,' he handed over a pint 'stick a poker in that – it'll sizzle thee gullet a treat. Fry up his insides – won't it, landlord? Now then there's taty pot on if my snifter's correct.'

'It is.'

'Well, thou's got two clients here'll dig into it.'

'We'll have to wait of Hardisty. He should be back from his kennels in half an hour.'

'True,' Isaac smiled. 'He did a trick today I haven't seen for a long time, thou knows.' Foot on the rest, elbows on the bar, head squat on his shoulders, Isaac settled down. 'It was just when they came out of that bit of a wood, see . . .'

The taty pot was served in the kitchen. Eight of them sat down to it and a full stew-pot disappeared. Then eight apple tarts were brought in and two jugs of custard. Plates of teacakes, butter and jam, cheese and cakes followed. The landlady came in to watch them eat as one might go to a circus.

'Well, missis,' said Isaac, whose trenchering capacities had astounded her, 'that was a very good tea. Thanks are due. And if you've no objection – Aa'll have a pipe at yer table.'

He smoked and then snoozed for about an hour, head tilted back, mouth open, boots kicked out before him – hugely lodged in the round-backed wooden chair.

John would have liked to sleep – he was tired enough – but he could not. He was too excited, still not quite able to believe that he was to have another day off, still perplexed by his longing for Emily – if only she were with him, he kept thinking, and the fact that he had the thought irritated him more than the thought itself. So he interested himself in the quiet chat of Hardisty and the men around him, afraid of missing a single drop of that day.

When Isaac woke up, the pub was full, the men having had their supper and come in. In the bar above the open fire was a deep rectangular rise in the wooden ceiling, making a platform in the room above on which the band performed for the dance. The women and girls went up by a staircase which allowed them to avoid the bar but there was another staircase, a short wooden flight of stairs in the corner, which led directly up to the dancing room and trays of drinks were taken up by that route. It was here that the landlord recouped for keeping the Huntsman and his whipper-in free of charge – for the knowledge that the Hunt was at the pub brought people in from miles around, especially at the weekend. When John went outside into the yard, he could hardly get across to the lavatories, with the horses and carts, dogs tied to doors, girls swirling around the foot of the stairs –

Emily would have loved to dance! – a few early drunk men playing pitch-and-toss by lantern light. The enjoyment and laughter of such a crowd affected him greatly; after his constricted existence in the cottage this was like a blast from a new world; it intoxicated him and yet still, still, he did not know why, there was the feeling that it was not for him – that he had made his choice in marriage and a family and work and this was one of the sacrifices.

Back in the bar the songs were starting up and the men stood as a jostling crowd, Hardisty's scarlet a fiery hub. Again, as in John's cottage, it was brown which ripened all colours, the oak settles and beamed ceiling, the oak clock from which the dead fox hung down, teeth stiffly unclamped; brown was the predominant cloth for the suits, yellow brown the light from the lamps, amber the ale, red and brown the faces; and the dialect in its tone had a matching glow to it, so that as John stepped into the noisy arena, he felt ripened by the richness of it all.

Some of the men knocked the fox so that its blood ran and they collected a few drops into their beer. Isaac was squeamish about that and bellowed to John:

'Some of them would eat the bluddy thing raw if it would bring them a good hunt tomorrow! Don't thee try the blood, lad – it clogs the bladder.'

From upstairs came the sound of a fiddle and piano, and the ceiling shuddered, dipping like a spring mattress as the dancers got under way. John wanted to be up there with the music: the pounding of men's voices, men's faces, the congested hunt of men at their drink and their talk, stifled him. Yet to dance with another than Emily should not be imagined.

'We'll be up those stairs in a bit, lad. Shorten that long face. And don't look at thee breeches! It's nobbut muck. They expect it after a hunt – thou won't be out of place. Eh? Emily? Eh? Damn this pandemonium! Thou's goanna *dance*, lad, I hope! Not run off wid another woman. Eh! What's thee worry? Come away me lad! Come away! Give us a tootle, Hardisty! Huntsman – blow that horn.'

The sound rang out and Halloos sounded throughout the bar. Then from upstairs the dancers echoed it with their own Halloo! The bar answered, the dance once more replied – and the long hunting cry sounded between the two companies in longer and longer wails until it resembled no earthly cry but was like the sucking of wind and forging water in a cave.

'That's better! Grand! Grand! O, my lovely lads one and all!' said Isaac.

'A song! Give us a song, Isaac!'

'Ay. Tune that throat of thine to music.'

'Use your bellows, Isaac. Blow us one up.'

'Here we are then,' Isaac announced, game for anything. 'Aa'll even put down me mug for it. We'll start wid a Tragedy. Very short.' He coughed and held out his hands, the whites of the up-turned palms suddenly making vulnerable that stout cask of him. He recited very slowly.

'There was an old woman had three sons,
Jerry, James and John.
Jerry was hung. James was drowned,
John was lost and never found:
And that was the end of her three sons.
Jerry, James and John.'

'More! More!'

'Right lads. A comedy. A bit longer this. Needs a push in the chorus region.'

'There was a jolly beggar,
He had a wooden leg.
Lame from his cradle,
And forced for to beg.
And a begging we will go, we'll go, we'll go;
Come away lads! And a begging we will go!

A bag for his oatmeal
Another for his salt
And a pair of crutches
To show that he can halt
Away lads – And a begging we will go, we'll go, we'll go;
And a begging we will go.

Seven years he begged . . .'

By now the ale had run out and back again through every vein of John's body, and his cares were flushed away. This was the life! He beat time with his mug before him and as Isaac called to another man and then that other to another, the fumes from the ale and the steam from the men infused the singing with such a density of pleasure that he felt he could curl up in it for ever and wish never to be disturbed.

'A speech, Hardisty, a speech!' someone shouted. 'Give us a speech, give us a blow, give us a song, and then tek us up those stairs, Hardisty – there's women like a hunt as much as any man!'

Hardisty nodded – solemn and starched with drink he was. Whiskies brought for him had been slopped into his ale until it was so spiked that one gulp would have set him reeling had he not made certain – his trick for drunkenness – that his feet were a yard apart and his bootlaces loosened. But it was his place to round off the drinking in the bar and so with momentous pomp, he went the three yards to the fox and nudged some blood into his mixture.

'Thou was a good'un, lad. A game'un.' This spoke most earnestly to the dead fox before he made his slow turn to the rest of the bar. He surveyed all. Caps askew, waistcoats unbuttoned, pipes growing out of faces, the landlord filling the mugs, the bar crammed and tumbling with men as stout and braised-faced as himself.

'A speech, a blow and a song!' he began, thoughtfully. 'Well, as for the song – that'll be John Peel, lads. It can be no other. He was our own man and he was on foot, me lads, like we are, and he lived and died his life for huntin'. And may we do as well, lads. We'll sing his song – the best huntin' song there is – and the greatest song ever written about any man, dead or alive. So that's the song.' He paused. 'As for the blow – well, I'll be askin' Jasper Fell to do that. If I blow now, lads, you'll all be splattered wid ale – because I've a skinful under me this night as could float an armada.' Slowly he half-turned once more, so that the fox was brought into his misting vision. 'As for the speech – I'll go one better! I'll give you a toast. And here it is. To the Fox, me lads, to Fox!'

After an hour at the dance, which went on until three o'clock, John began to sober up – but wish to as he might, he could not bring himself to ask a woman to dance with him. He joined in when they made two circles, one of men the other of women, to do the Roundelay – and Isaac even managed to get him up for the Hooligans which started with the men and women in straight lines up and down the room; but that was all. He did not feel sorry for himself, being happy enough to watch the others, especially Isaac, whose torn and mucky clothes and figure were carried on a most nifty pair of legs, while his gallantry, being rather drunken, escaped buffoonery only by a hair's breadth. John sat near the band and watched the man with the fiddle: the sound of it made him think of his grandfather – and he saw that he, too, must have enjoyed nights like this. As he could not come like Isaac, perhaps he could learn the fiddle and come as his grandfather had done: Emily would be fast asleep: May long in her cradle with her arms flung back: he would have to buy her a present to mark his absence . . .

Isaac woke him up and they went out. There was no hunting on Sunday and the plan was to use the night to walk over into Buttermere where, illicitly, there would be cock-fighting in the early morning.

'They're huntin' down at Lorton on Monday,' Isaac said. 'By godfather that should be real! There's foxes down there breed like rabbits.'

'Aa'm comin' with you,' said John.

'No, lad. Thou said thou'd be back a' Monday.'

'Aa'm havin' one more day's huntin',' John replied, doggedly. 'And Pennington can do what he likes wid his work. Aa'm havin' one more day.' She would have to accept it, he thought, and was irritated at his shiver of unhappiness. He was afraid to acknowledge the underlying thought that he might want to be rid of her.

'But thy missus'll be expectin' thee, lad.'

'Aa'll send a message. She'll understand.'

Isaac's worry ceased.

'Ah. She will! That's correct. She's a real 'un, John. Thou's catched a good 'un.'

There was not much moon, but the two men were not in a hurry. Isaac had a quarter bottle of brandy for when the cold hit them – as it did when they felt the night wind come off Crummock Water.

'Look at that lake, lad,' Isaac murmured. 'Just look at her. She's the finest thing thou'll see in a lifetime.'

They walked along the track, under the dragon-like crags, the lake to their right, the slow tread of their step building up a rhythm against which the sky, the line of fell-tops, the trees and walls, even that strange silver spread of water, could make no attack.

'Stop!' Isaac whispered. 'Listen.' He put his arm around the younger man's shoulders and they heard sheep scatter in a field above them.

'That'll be Fox,' said Isaac, beaming. 'Come away, boy! Come away!' he shouted into the dark. 'What sport, John, eh? What sport!'

NINE

Emily had been relieved to see John go. As he left the cottage with Isaac she felt happier than she had done for a long time.

Since the birth of the baby, she had been unable to cope with his restlessness as once she had done; at times she feared it might escape her altogether and turn into something which could harm both of them. Isaac mopped up John's spillings of mood like gravy off a plate and she believed that the two days would satisfy at least some part of the mainly unspoken chafing which threatened to bring him to despair.

There was so little for John to do except work. He had not the money nor – it now appeared – the inclination to join in with those married men from the pits who met at The Cross most nights. He had not the time to keep a dog or follow a sport. He had done most of what could or needed to be done around the cottage and though he enjoyed challenging Mr Pennington, it gave diminishing returns. While the way in which he was driven to work by himself frightened her. Sometimes he would come in so riven by it that he could neither eat nor sleep, and she had to pull off his boots, even help him with his jacket and more than once abandon him in the chair beside the fire – so cleft in sleep that she could not hope to disturb him until the morning. If only he would take it less hard. And not be so concerned that herself and the baby should be lacking nothing. She knew that to find the baby crying as he opened the door on his return from the farm drove into him, his face tightened with irritation – and yet he would neither explode into temper nor leave her alone for the few minutes needed to calm the child – but force himself to be pleasant, to relieve her of the baby, to shush away his meal until May should be quietened. And she could see his hands shaking as he nursed the baby. Yet at other times she knew that May gave him the same kind of peace as that which was on his face as he returned from a rare solitary walk among the fells.

Sally came over in the afternoon – bursting to tell Emily that she had talked to Jackson Pennington that morning. And he had said this, and she had said that, and wasn't it funny how some men were *better*-looking close up and others worse? And he had asked her if she was going to the dance the following week! *Asked* her. As if he wouldn't be bound to know that she was going – and so he *must* have intentions. There was a feverishness about Sally's delight which again riled Emily though she did not let it show. She thought that the younger woman was whipping herself on to affection, demanding a Great Passion as her right, greater than anyone's as she was so special. No, she calmed herself, she was just a little sad – though why should she be? – at seeing someone so free. But she would be silly to deny a place to her observation – and Sally *was* making too much of that most casual meeting. Probably, those eyes sucking at his face, poor Jackson had felt forced to ask her about the dance out of self-preservation! It was not that, though, not that! There was a coy vulgarity about Sally's appreciation of her new sexuality, a switching from superiority to over-humble inquiry – truly a fever, which slyly and whimsically mocked that love she herself had for John and May. She was glad when she left. Then she was sorry to have thought so badly of her friend.

It was pleasant to spend the long afternoon playing with the baby, no deadline to meet with a hot meal. She set May on the couch which her mother had bought them in a sale, and tickled her until both of them were laughing, tiny fingers and the softest palm imaginable tucking themselves around her forefinger and tightening there. She shook her hair loose all over the child and tears sprang to her eyes as the baby pulled at it. Emily felt that she could gobble the baby up with love. Sometimes she was so afraid of how much she loved her that she would neglect her for a morning – letting her cry on, not coddling her at all, being strict where she would have been soft – but that always ended up with rushing over to her and hugging her as if she had been away for a week. More often, she wondered that John might worry that there was any love left for him – so much was given to the baby: and then she saw that love was not a capital amount, limited and exhaustible, but a source itself which could feed many streams.

When May was in bed, then she missed John. She took down *Silas Marner* and skipped one or two of the pages of dialect which tired her. She wanted to see Silas alone in that cottage in the woods, the loom working, the gold growing into the earth. She could not read for long – the silence about her unnerved her. Her eyes looked at the fire and the logs' heat burned on her pale skin; her face was thinner since the birth. Soon she was in bed, but unable to sleep until she lifted May out of the cradle and brought her in with herself.

Sunday would bring him back again and the day had a point. She spent the morning cleaning, the afternoon baking, and spread the table with food more than John had seen since his wedding day. She had dug into her savings for this meal and got young John Wrangham whom she had seen in the fields to go up to The Cross and bring two jugs of ale. She expected them at about five.

As the minutes and then hours passed, the table appeared more and more forlorn. Nothing was removed, nothing eaten – but the meal seemed to diminish in size, the fire to glow less brightly, herself to turn from condoning even pleasurable annoyance to worry.

She did not stop to wonder at the knock on the door – Isaac might have come on ahead and he would have knocked – but flew over to open it, smoothing down her apron and, after lifting the latch, reaching her hands up behind her head to comfort her hair. It was Jackson.

Emily stepped back in surprise and this was taken as permission to enter which he did. To avoid unnecessary proximity Emily retreated further, to the other side of the laden table she had set in the middle of the kitchen. Jackson pulled off his cap and stood just inside the open door.

'It's a fine welcome, that,' he indicated the table, 'for any man.' He paused. 'I'll close this door if you don't mind. It's cool out.'

He turned to close the door, very deliberately lifting the bar over the latch and Emily shivered to see the blond hair waving down to his clean collar, the tall, best-suited back of him slender and at ease in her home. She put her hand to her throat where she had just that morning sewed a little frill at the neckline of her blouse – and wished she could tear off the frill before he turned to her. Her fingers tugged at it, then dropped as he once more faced her.

'Yes,' he repeated, softly, 'it's a fine spread.'

'He's a fine man!' she retorted, a little shrill her voice. She was taken aback by its sound.

'He must be,' said Jackson. 'He must be that, Emily, to have thee for a wife.'

'Why did you come?'

'Aren't you pleased to see me?' He smiled gently and she thought – he's drunk; that would help explain it: but he might be dangerous in drink; that would make it worse.

'You – you – are you drunk?' she asked, timidly.

'No.' He laughed. 'No, I don't need drink to fetch me here.'

'John'll be back soon,' she said, quickly looking at the clock. 'He said he'd be here at nine. In five minutes.' He was unimpressed. 'Isaac'll be with him,' she threatened.

'No he won't.' Jackson spoke very slowly as if to lengthen his time so. 'Word came to The Cross that they won't be back today. They're off to Lorton. They'll be back tomorrow.'

'Oh.' She felt a self slip off her, run off like water – but she recovered immediately.

'So you only dare to come down here because you know that neither of them's about.' She paused. He did not appear chastened. 'Maybe you didn't need drink – but you needed . . .'

'What?' he asked.

'I don't know. O please go, Jackson. Thank you for bringing the message. Please – go.'

'I'm hungry,' he said. 'Looking at that table's made me hungry. I think I'll have some supper.'

'No!' She made as if to dart across to him. 'No,' she repeated, stopping as she saw him move to meet her.

'You wouldn't begrudge a man some feed, would you, Emily? It's a long walk from The Cross.'

'It is not.'

'It seemed a day's journey, lass,' he replied, gently.

He calmly sat down and began to eat.

'Would there be anything to drink?'

Emily's throat was too dry for her to be able to let words slip through. She shook her head.

'What's that there?' He pointed at the jugs in the hearth.

'No.'

'I'll get it myself then.'

As he pushed back the chair she cried out. He looked at her and shook his head.

'I won't do you any harm,' he said. 'I won't harm your little finger.'

She put her wrist to her mouth to stop herself from crying again and he nodded before bringing one of the jugs over to the table.

'Sit down!' he said, sharply. 'I'll do you no harm! If I'd a wanted to force myself on you I could a done when I came in. Nobody could hear us down here. Sit down, woman!'

Emily sat on the couch on which she had played with May just a few hours before. She looked at the ceiling as if hoping to see through it and reassure herself that the baby was all right.

'Don't be stupid, Emily. I'll do nobody any harm. I haven't forgotten.'

'Neither have I,' she retorted, suddenly less afraid through this reference to that first time. It could be no worse than that. And she had survived.

Jackson pushed his plate away from him: it bumped into a plate of teacakes which tumbled down: he pushed harder and more scones and cakes spilled. The table was spoiled. A childish action.

'That wasn't very clever,' she said, gaining yet more confidence from this nervous display of his. 'And if John and Isaac aren't coming back tonight – they'll be back tomorrow,' she warned.

'Do you still want me to go!' he asked, uncertain now that the balance had inexplicably tilted in her favour.

'Yes. Yes I do. I'm married to John Tallentire and you've no business being here in my house.'

'But what can I do, Emily?' He stood up, a hand reached out towards her. 'I can't stop wanting you. I can't stop blaming myself for what I did to you.'

'Well, you'll have to learn to stop. And I've long ago forgotten what happened that first time. So can you.'

'You've forgotten.'

'Yes, I have!' She attacked. 'I've other things to think about, you know.'

But she had gone too far. The lie about forgetting what happened that first time was less damaging to herself than this over-reaching disparagement. For as soon as she said it, both of them knew that she *did* think about him – and Jackson smiled.

'You still think about me, Emily. However many other things there are.'

'I think about all sorts of people.' She paused. Then with a weak throat she added, 'I think about Sally It's *her* you should be visiting.'

'I care nothing for her,' he said evenly. 'Does that please you? Are you glad I care nothing for Sally? Well if that's a way – I'll go further. I care nothing for Mary or Martha or Janet or Jane or for anybody but Emily – and that Emily, you. But why doesn't that make you more glad? Tell me that, and I'll go.'

'I can't tell you.'

'But you must.'

'There's nothing to tell. I like you as much as a married woman can like a single man who's been kind to her –'

'– and terrible!'

'– I *can* put that out of my mind even if I can't really forget it. You've been kind, by staying away.'

'Only by that?'

'Yes.'

He stood silently, looking into the fire, dejected once more.

'Don't you see how impossible it is?' she asked.

'I see now.'

'But it was impossible any time. I'm married, Jackson.'

'But it doesn't matter! I don't give a damn for any marriage.

It doesn't change a woman – just gives her a little ornament to dangle in her hand.'

'If that's what you think I'm sorry for you!'

'Yet if you had said any different,' he continued, as if she had not spoken, 'then you wouldn't be what you are. And what you are I love, Emily. There it is. Love.'

'Please go,' she murmured. 'O please, please go.'

'Come with me.'

She shook her head and would not speak.

'And I believe if I stayed and talked and talked,' he said, more loudly than before, almost bitterly, 'and talked and talked to you, and told you enough times I loved you I believe I could wear you down this night, Emily. Even you.'

But she sat rigidly still.

He took up his cap and swept some of the scones off the table. 'Say something!'

She stayed silent.

'My God, I could come across and beat you away with me. *Say* something!'

'Go.'

'You'll give me nothing? Not a kiss, not a kind word, nothing?'

'No.'

'Damn you, Emily! And damn your precious marriage!'

He went and the slam of the door woke May to whom Emily ran, crying as unhappily as her child.

TEN

The subdued and nervous mood in which Emily greeted his return matched John's anxiety. Neither told the other that there was a flaw in the love which had never till now threatened to lose the chance of regaining what had appeared to both of them as an original perfection. John said nothing of that night after the dance when he had wanted to be rid of her and the thought of her for the first time ceased to be there. Emily did not mention Jackson and buried her lips in John's neck to forget, forget that perhaps Jackson was right, she knew that he was right, had he stayed on and on, she would have given in – blaming weariness maybe, but still, O John, she would have given in. In this false mood they told each other that they were happy.

John was relieved when Isaac left – though the sight of his striding off there on his own made him sad at the time. For with Isaac he had lost himself. With Isaac he had thought – why *not* just jump up and leave Emily and May for weeks on end? Why *not* spend life after sport? Why not dance with other women? Why not go off with them? Why work? Why love one alone? But then he realised that what could be limited in Isaac, by the grip he had on his own affairs, would spread further and further in his own softer hold; feared that by following Isaac he would grow to imitate him and knew that he would make a mess of it and end up as nothing.

But being with his brother had defined him for himself a little more. He had been away from Emily and his home – and two days was enough. He had not enjoyed the Monday hunt at Lorton; all the time he was longing to be back. Back to his work, too, for in the end he felt that hunting on a Monday – a working day – not a holiday in anybody's book – was a waste. Of what? He did not ask, but waste he felt in the day, the hounds, the walking he did, the talking, in the drink at dinnertime, on the fields he walked through and in himself from his dragging legs to his disapproving reflections.

More than this the possibilities spread before him by Isaac made him afraid that the way he had chosen to live – for he had a choice – was most insubstantial, being so easily threatened. This led him to attempts to attack the origins of the fear, to work even harder, to stick even closer to the cottage, to sign on with Pennington again at Whit and again the following November.

Emily, who had been more unhappy than she thought she would be at Isaac's departure, was more than compensated by the relief she felt when, about the same time, Sally told her that Jackson had left home again, 'this time for good,' said Sally, 'he told Jo Dalzell he would never come back again. Never!' And if she felt so happy – and she did, she sang all that day and was lapped in a sweetness of temper she could taste in her mouth – then everything was surely all right again, she thought.

Mr Pennington made a short comment on Jackson's exit and drafted back another son.

In her release of enthusiasm, Emily made her first constructive effort to get into the village. Before now she had excused her disinclination, first on account of having to put the cottage in order and later of devoting all her time to May. She had even begun to blame John for bringing her to Crossbridge – and all Sally's chatter could not make up for that net of relations and born friends she had found such unacknowledged safety in at home. At one stage, she had worried him into considering a move down into the Wigton area – 'not Wiggonby itself,' she said, 'though if you could . . . but somewhere around there, John, to be nearer.' 'Nearer *my* lot an' all,' he said. 'Aa thowt thou wanted rid of them all as much as me. There's no need for a great gaggle of friends, Emily. We can stand it on our own, can't we?' Nevertheless she had worried him with her suggestions – and now, when a few months had stamped the certainty of Jackson's disappearance on her and, most finally, she heard from Mrs Pennington that he had gone to London and joined the army to go abroad – now her enthusiasm pushed out its waves to unclog all the silt that had checked her love. It was all that she wanted. In earnest of this, she made her efforts to be more part of the village.

What she enjoyed, however, were those occasions when everyone was part of the crowd – the day of the Club Fair (called a Walk) when the band played all day in the field behind The Cross; or in that Autumn the time the Potters came and stayed for a month – selling their plates and china by organising fêtes and sports, competitions, raffles, socials, Nights of Daftness when the men would line up with their hands tied behind their backs to try to eat a teacake dripping with treacle and hanging on a string, or push their faces into a barrel of water to eat the bobbing crap-apples; she liked to go to the concerts at Martelmas and take May to the children's do at Christmas eve – willing and happy to go anywhere where there was a crowd and she could nod without having to stop and talk. But for the more personal matters, being in the chorus at the concert, serving in the pub as many of the young women did on the nights of the harvest supper, or accepting the invitation to tea sent by the vicar's wife, so regulating her visits to the shops that she met the same people every time and thus was slowly absorbed into and identified with a particular group – for these she had no taste. Perhaps not having done it right away made her feel awkward, as if her action was saying 'I was waiting to see if you were good enough for me,' or, worse, 'I thought I could manage on my own but I can't' – whatever it was, she felt that she obtruded into any group she met, while in a crowd, she was as happily numbered as the rest. More certainly, however, her meetings with Jackson had left her with the fear that somehow knowledge of them was carried around the village: that Jackson had said nothing she could have sworn – for Sally's ears would have pricked at the slightest wind carrying that name and yet she brought no gossip, not a suspicion. Still, Emily would not be sure, and this made her most wary.

In the winter John bought a hound, but sold it soon afterwards and got himself a concertina. He would play on it every night, no matter what time he came in or how tired he was, he would go upstairs and play and sing to May, and as she heard the thin, lightly-crushed sounds of the concertina and May's small voice laughing and singing out of tune, then Emily felt that such happiness as she had known before was but a girlish affair compared with this.

That summer she was pregnant again but she hardly felt the child, it was so small inside her. Seth came up to see them a few times and she was amused at the contrast he made – so white and serious – with Isaac, but happy to see John talking to him and watch the brothers as they left her comfortable (after the four of them had walked together to Cogra Moss) and went off to scale up the screes on Blake Fell, John pressing Seth to physical action as Isaac had pressed him. Then she would look at the small, perfect tarn in the hollow of the hills and switch from that to the men and then to May stumbling along beside the fence, falling over the bull-toppins or reed-tufted grass. Two boys were splashing in the cold shallows and a man had waded out almost to the middle to fish: she could see John and Seth scrambling, black figures on the slatey screes, and felt the child inside her so quiet. So different from May, as peaceful as the hills around.

But as the time for the birth came near, she could no longer be as peaceful. The child hardly plumped her even, and when she felt a movement it was so slight, so faint that she worried. She retreated from the village and once more allowed the fields which cut off her contact with it to become her boundary. She demanded that John take her down to her mother and then, after he had gone to arrange it with Pennington (for which necessity she despised him at that moment), she would cry and say she was sorry, being silly, of course she wanted the child here, in her own home, with him. She would go to bed with May and let him come in to a fireless kitchen, no supper, no welcome – and then, after listening to his clumsy efforts, rush down to make reparation. The hills which she had looked out on and loved angered her by their unchanging, unyielding, uncomforting aspect. She woke at the first patter of rain on the tiles and felt the pellets of water drum on to her motionless belly.

Ephraim was born in November. The birth gave her little

pain, but to make better the malformed, spindly body of her child she would have endured anything. The doctor when he arrived the next day confirmed the midwife's private opinion; that the boy would be lucky to live until Christmas.

That he lived longer was due to the total subjection of herself which Emily made before this child. Throughout the winter and into the spring the cottage was concentrated around that poor body whom the slightest chill would threaten. John took May out of Emily's way whenever he could, but the action was barely noticed as he and May and all about her was barely noticed. Ephraim, Ephraim – she prayed and nursed and willed him to live and grow strong. There was nothing John could do – the bond between the mother and the sickly child filled the cottage and no other feeling could penetrate.

John worked but the work lost its meaning to himself. It was necessary for the money for Emily and the child, but that had not been the wheel which had driven it to become such a provider of life. The work changed its nature and became a weight to be shifted; or he would be crushed under it. What he had thought undeniable did deny him; his labour yielded nothing.

John spent the night of his twenty-first birthday watching over his son while Emily lay forced to sleep on the chair beside them. He kept the fire going and milk ready. A scattering of hail tattered across the window pane. His boots stood before the fire, growing and shrinking before his eyes. Emily's hands were shut and her head sat brokenly on her shoulders, pulling against the shawl he had put around her neck. Afraid of her now, even the help he gave was offered guiltily, almost shamefully intruding on his wife and the baby.

The boy died in June and they buried him on a bright clear day with the noise from the haymaking and the sight in the distance of the big marquee rising behind The Cross for the Club Walk. Emily was frozen at the small grave and she did not return his look but kept her head bent to the ground as they walked down the short path to the church-gate.

He promised her he would leave Crossbridge at the end of his term, in November, but 'It's too late,' was all she could reply.

Days later, on a hillside, looking down at the shut door of the cottage he felt himself to be spent of all life, love between Emily and himself blighted by a birth which should have nourished it.

ELEVEN

By the end of the summer John was desperate. He could make nothing of Emily, and himself he hardly recognised. Only the work thudded through him with any comprehended regulation, and that now beat inside his body as loudly as an amplified heart-beat, straining to burst.

He finished at tea-time one Saturday afternoon and set off for Embleton to see his grandfather. The twelve miles was mostly downhill and he went quickly and easily, his back to the fells, before him the plain and the sea. There was no clear idea in his mind as to why he should want to see the old man or what he would say to him: he had thought of taking May with him as if to use the child as an introduction – but Emily would not let her go. He wanted to talk to someone, perhaps even just to touch them as sick people needed to touch a saint for a cure: there was no one else he could turn to.

The day was windless, a long white harmless ridge of cloud above the Solway, trees in full leaf, cattle and horses grazing in the field, the sun warm on his face, it would be light almost to midnight even now and the cheerful clop of the horses that passed him, the chatter of two young women holding their hats, long skirts covering the pedals of their bicycles, a vicar in a trap with a bull-mastiff sitting unmoving beside him – all mingled with the ease of the descent, the appeasing rhythm of a walk to lift John's hopes sufficiently for him to look out from the shutters he had drawn on himself and breathe the balm of the long Edwardian afternoon. Privileged. For in an order in which privilege plays such a striking and important part, even those who are its props can yet occasionally be touched by a belief that they, too, are privileged. So, as John walked down to Embleton, he felt that a grace had understandingly permitted him the few hours off, that providence was working for him in the steadiness of his health, the roof he had for his family, the grandfather he would see; that luck was with him, waiting at the end of the golden afternoon.

He knew that the old man had retired on his seventieth birthday and been allowed to stay on in his cottage at a reduced rent. As he approached the place he thought of his last visit and his legs lifted briskly in anticipation through that memory.

There was a silence after he stepped into the cottage, one so marked that it belied the existence of the querulous voice which had bidden him in. John saw his grandfather in a deep chair by the fire. The room was away from the sun and the fire emphasised the shadows, brought coldness to them.

'Well. Who is it?'

'It's me, John.' He stepped across to his grandfather. 'John,' he repeated, wondering why he had done so.

'Have you seen Alice?'

'Grandma? No.'

'She went for some shopping.'

'Yes?'

'She should be back. Go and look out of that back door for her.'

John did so and returned.

'She isn't in sight.'

'Well she should be.' Then Harry looked carefully at his grandson. 'Will you be wanting your supper?' he asked, sharply, then added, 'it's not as easy when you're not working. Shut that door, will you? I'm starvin'.' This last order was given apologetically, as if, conscious of his rudeness – though unable to check it – Harry wanted to be unregarded for a few seconds.

'Thank you. Sit theesel down. Family well?'

As he skipped through the hoops, the old man returned his gaze to the fire and kneaded his hands over it, as if to press its heat into his veins by main force. John answered and rolled back his stock of counter-inquiries, all the time shrinking inside himself; he realised he had come to be given amulets, but the charms were not to be had, the spirit gone.

There were two occasions only during that uneasy visit when John felt his grandfather to be as he had once been.

'Well, they've retired me, John,' he said, suddenly cutting across an answer he had demanded as to the stock on Pennington's farm. 'They used me up and cast me off. Like the chaff, John, sent away from the barns to be burnt.'

'But . . . But thou's bein' well looked after, Grandfather.'

'Who wants that?' The old man's volume and authority returned in the voice which threw out that accusing question. 'Aa can still work. They know that. But it's – "No, Mr Tallentire, thou must retire." "Yes, Mr Tallentire, we want thou to have a peaceful old age." They didn't kick me out, John – Aa could a' kicked back then – they Mothered me off the job! Whativver Aa said against it – they laughed – mekkin' out Aa was a comical old character as couldn't think of what to do widdout his work – and wasn't that so *very* comical! But it isn't a question of fillin' time, lad. Nivver was. Not to my way. Aa can't be interested in piddlin' aboot like a soft-bladdered old nag. Aa'm nothing widdout work. Nothing! No man is.'

The other time was after supper – during which Alice had passed things to Harry in such a protective way as caused the old man to groan and look silently at John, as if saying – 'Look! They've convinced her as well,' and John had been forced to assent to the significant nods and looks of his grandmother – a meal in which the clatter of cheap forks on thick china dominated all other sounds in the room and a light was unlit beyond the time of tolerability and left unlit into regions of miserliness – then, thankfully after John announced that he would set back for home, Harry walked with him as before, but this time stopped at the gate.

'Thou mustn't upset theeself about that boy that died,' he said. 'Aa can see it's botherin' you; don't protest. "The Lord giveth and the Lord taketh away," John – and if thou's not as strong in Him as Aa was – and am – then that's a truth can still be spoken.' He paused, and John waited, attending for the word as if his future needed it. The moment seized him. 'Besides,' the old man concluded, abruptly, 'it might be better nivver to be born. Good night.'

He turned away and John let the door bang his grandfather

back to the fire before himself turning to go. Emily was asleep by the time he got home and despite his soft-footed care, she woke up and her accusations drew a hasty reply from him. Once more their words hurt each other.

Emily went nowhere for consolation: her only regular visits, apart from a resentful shuffle around the shops, were to the churchyard, to Ephraim's grave. She went weekly on the afternoon on which he had been buried and trimmed the small hummock on her knees. May would be left with Mrs Braithwaite. The vicar once tried to lead her from the grave into the church but was given short shrift.

In so far as her mood broke on to the surface of her life at all, it appeared as slatternliness. In her looks, her clothes, her behaviour, the way she kept the cottage, the way she let May run about in clothes long dirty – there was that willed carelessness which incited attack if only to rebuff it.

In October, John told her that he had given Pennington notice he would quit at Martelmas.

'Well, you can go and tell him you're staying,' she said.

'We said . . .'

'*You* said. Maybe I did. But whoever did doesn't matter. I'm not moving from this place.'

'But I could be hired near your mother, Emily. Somewhere you'd have people you know about you. You wanted that.'

'I don't now. I wouldn't care if I saw none of them again.'

'Don't be like that.' He was still too bemused by her reaction to find any anger to match hers. 'Don't be like that, lass,' he repeated.

'I'm not a lass!'

'O, don't be so touchy, Emily.'

'Leave me alone.' Then, with a sudden stab of bitterness. '*You'll* never touch me again – that's for certain, John Tallentire.'

'What do you mean?'

'You know. And if you weren't such a day-dreamer you would have guessed before now.' She paused. 'I'm married to a man who'll stick in his rut 'til it buries him. And he'll not even notice he's disappeared.'

'Less of that!'

'Truth hurts, does it?' From her expression it was she who looked more wounded than John by the 'truth' she darted at him.

'No,' he answered, eventually, 'it doesn't. But how it's said that hurts, Emily.'

He wanted to go out but did not care to think of her being alone. His back moved against the back of his chair and he pressed until he could feel the wood cut through his jacket and batten on his shoulder blades. He could not look at her, yet he could look nowhere else for longer than a moment and his eyes made ceaseless forays around the kitchen, as if memorising everything for an inventory.

'Who would look after his grave if I went?' she asked. As if to emphasise the limits of the concession her sentence had contained, she stood up and went upstairs to May.

He did not follow her and soon, from the silence, knew that she would not come down until he was out of the house.

In the pub a glass was a mask for every man's face. He began to drink. In the pub he could stop his crying by drowning the tears before they reached his throat. In the pub he could buttress his solitude with the props of other men's lives. He was there on that night soon after Christmas when Jackson came in, lean and settled in his uniform, home on leave.

John had dulled himself to Emily, but he would have needed to blind himself to miss the change that came over her now. She took out all her clothes to clean and brush them; bought herself a new skirt; she had the house pretty once more, none of it for him. He prised open her new self – noticing that there was a flamboyance in it which was strained, an eagerness which was disconcerting – finding some relief in that she was *not* as she had been with him. There was nothing he saw to charge her with directly. Nor dare he confront her in any way. Afraid of hurting her. Afraid of that startled tension which, he thought, could snap her if wrongly broken. As near as possible, then, he did blind himself, alternately despising himself for it and reasoning that it was the only way – she must be let work out her own life: interference from him would be asked for – and given – when needed; he must be available, no more.

That his love had come to this demoralised him. That their

life could come to this. Though now he was too concerned to keep up his present defences to allow the full effect of the reduction to be experienced, he knew it was there, waiting only an opportunity to set on him.

Emily waited for Jackson to call on her. From the minute that John left the morning cottage she was ready for Jackson to call on her. It seemed to her that only he could lift her from the torment of her grief. She refused to recognise that she was inserting more into that faith than its slender basis in her affections could sustain, nor did she let herself think of consequences; her faith was too bound up with fantasy for that. Jackson would save her – she believed that, had felt the knowledge certain from the moment she had heard of his return. Then her body had quickened as it had not done since that age before Ephraim's birth – and, the weight of inertia lifted, she had seen a way to breathe again, again be herself, rid of the despair which was destroying her.

But he did not come to the cottage.

She saw him across a field as she was returning from the shops – he waved, shouted a greeting and walked on as he would walk on from any other woman in the village.

She began to plan so that she would be forced to a meeting with him. She had been too severe, she thought, and he was too honourable to take advantage again – or too proud to come again. Yes. She must go to him.

She went to the Penningtons' for water and, as had not once happened before, used the trip as an excuse for calling on Mrs Pennington whose surprise was covered by an immediately accepted invitation to come and look around the house. John found her chatting to the farmer's wife in the cold flagged scullery and avoided her eyes, embarrassed for her. When Jackson came in, flanked by his father and his younger brother, the three men passed the scullery with a bare nod of acknowledgement and made for the table – for which Mrs Pennington had also to desert her. Emily had no excuse to accompany the other woman's flurry.

John was waiting for her in the yard, holding May by the hand. In his other hand he took the bucket of water and set off in front of her, not looking back though he could feel her body trail behind him, stinging with confusion.

The leave-time passed away until there were only a few days left and yet Emily had managed no more than a brief, pointless conversation with Jackson – one so artlessly and openly begged for that not only John but a number of others in the village observed it. Knowing that his wife had thus become the new juicy lump in the stew of gossip, John did not go that night to the pub. For which she accused him of never leaving her alone. Of pestering her by his everlasting company. Of torturing her by his silence, of murdering her by that never-gone look in his eyes. *She* would go out if he was determined to stay! It was her turn, anyway: her turn for a long time.

He let her put on her coat and watched each button pushed through its hole. He saw her try the shawl and then throw it away to take out the new scarf she had bought for her hair. Into the dark brown gloves her white fingers went like foraging strokes of light and the hooks clipped shut, one, two, three. Only as she went for the door did he move. And she stopped. Still on his chair, he looked at her without equivocation: she would not leave him that night. She ranted – he did not move. She laughed at him, still he watched her, and when she ran for the door he grabbed her wrist and held her, let her free arm beat on him that locked her, forced her back towards the couch into which she dropped, suddenly lifeless.

On the day following, her determination obsessed her. She took May to Mrs Braithwaite, took no notice of the unblushing curiosity on the other woman's face and went back to watch until she should see Jackson go out on his own. When he did, she followed him and caught him as he turned out of the lane and made for the pub. Despite helping his father he daily let it be seen that this was freely done – and his midday drink was one of the signs.

'Let me talk to you,' she said.

Jackson kept walking and smiled awkwardly at her.

'You'll have to come and have a pint then, Emily. I need me whistle whetted. I don't know how your man sticks at it all day and every day widdout a drink.'

'Please. Stop and talk to me.'

No one was on the road but Jackson was impelled to look around him by the urgent pleading of her voice: as if such nakedness should be seen by others as well as himself, covered by a company. Alone, it was too harsh for him, and he turned from her, wishing the lonely road crowded so that she would not go on.

'Don't look away, Jackson.' She caught his hand and held it tightly. 'I'll come into the pub with you. I don't mind. I'll watch you drink.'

He stopped and saw such agitation between wildness and servility in her face that he dared not answer. Anything said would be sucked into her and he himself with the words. Her mouth was a pale mark across her paler face.

'Go on. I don't mind. I won't be afraid in the pub with you there.' She paused and pressed both her hands on him. 'You've lovely warm hands. Maybe I will have a drink. What should I drink?'

'I'm going to set you back home, Emily,' he said eventually, his tone forced – light. 'You don't look well.'

'Oh. Do I look terrible?' Her hands left his hand, flew to her neck, settling there like broken wings. 'I can look nice when I take time to get ready. I suppose you're used to nice-looking women. You must have seen hundreds of them. Tell me about them, Jackson. Oh! don't be afraid. How can I be jealous? I'm a married woman.' She laughed, and the sound drove his head back. 'I mean, I only want to talk to you.'

'We can talk – let's go back and talk. It's cold here.'

'Back?'

'We could talk somewhere warmer.'

'Your hands are warm enough.' Then she looked at him slyly. 'You mean you want to come back to the cottage? I don't know whether I can have that.'

'Well then. Let's go to my place,' he replied, heartily. '*Your* hands are frozen.'

'I just want to talk.'

'I know that, Emily. Come on.'

Cautiously he took her arm and went back the way they had

come. She clung to his arm and he wished all his force that *some* feeling could go out of him to comfort her: but he had none for her, nothing but pity. And that, to her wrecked bewilderment, was a lash.

'Well, I can say I've walked out with you,' she said as they went into the lane.

'Yes. Yes – we've walked out together. A stupid private soldier and a pretty young married woman.'

'Don't joke, Jackson.' She leaned her head on his shoulder. 'I know you don't love me anymore.' Her head jerked away from him. 'But I thought I loved you. I want to, Jackson.'

'We're nearly there.'

'Don't talk to me as if I was a kid!' She broke free of him. Then once more she took his arm. 'I'm sorry. You're being kind, aren't you. I'm the one who's stupid, Jackson. Worse than any kid.'

It was with Emily still holding on to his arm that Jackson reached the farmyard. Pennington and John were wheeling turnips over to a byre. John lifted the spade from the barrow and went for him. He saw Emily's mouth open but heard none of her shouts – pushing her out of the way, knocking her down as she clung against him.

Jackson had run over and grabbed the other spade. He, too, shouted – but John concentrated on making firm his grip as he walked forward. The two men swung the vicious weapons like axes. John grazed Jackson's cheekbone and charged at the blood. A short chop hit his neck and he dropped senseless.

TWELVE

He tied the bed on to the cart and knotted the coarse binder twine tightly. Everything could be fitted on except the settee which he had taken down to Joe Edmonson's when borrowing the cart. He had said that he would collect it sometime but knew that he would not.

John worked very slowly, his fingers deliberating each time they touched a piece of furniture, the object eased along, even the chairs lifted only a necessary couple of inches from the ground so that they would not be scraped. Though it was mid-morning, the sun had made no entrance and sheeted clouds blew over the fells lending their metallic coldness to the wind which bit into the man's hands: the big central vein of the back of his left hand swelled up, purple puffed under the raw skin, a hard blood lump from wrist to knuckles. Looking down from the top of the fells, the cart could be seen small outside the door of the cottages: a capped and corduroyed figure slowly moving in and out of the door with the possessions which, once removed from their place in the small room, took on a strange double aspect; looking at once too many objects to be hung around the neck of any man and yet too few to support him in all but the most trivial afflictions. Seen from that height, the winter fields and trees bare about him, life coming from the chimneys, the whine of the overhead loop with the ore, the pits themselves – all hidden, burrowed as any hibernating creature – he looked minute and forlorn, his gesture of leaving purposeless, and the white linen, which was placed on the top of the cart and was ruffled by the wind, seemed a flag of distress or surrender.

When the job was done he went back into the cottage and squatted on his haunches to look into the dying fire. The door open, the cold found the small area as a trap and his feet and body stiffened against it; but he did not move. Emily had taken May away, he had not asked where, and he waited for their return to prompt him once more.

She had gone to collect his money from Pennington and the Friendly Society and then walked down to the churchyard to look as she thought might be the last time on Ephraim's grave. In her movements and her expression there was dreadful briskness which needs but a light blow to fall off and reveal the desperation it defies, that shell of pride whose hollowness reverberates at a touch.

Jackson watched her leave his father's farm – but remained where he was, guarded by the window. He was no longer afraid that she might cling to him – her step allayed that fear – but yet another circle had turned, and as he saw her now, white-faced in the shroud of the shawl, May trailing behind her holding a disregarded hand, he saw his loss of love for her as the blindness of momentary conceit. He wanted her to stay, to talk to him – he wanted her to love him – but he could not move. She had gone through her feelings for him – or they had been sealed off within her. She would, he knew, look plainly and disinterestedly at him and he would have nothing to say.

In the churchyard she felt panic. The grave was so small and there was no stone. It could sink or be grown over so easily. She looked around the tilting headstones, carved with the names and times of men's lives, and thought that the grass was better than such pitiful chippings, yet this did not reassure her. If she did not mark it well now, then she would forget it. She went back to the gate and looked up at the church, filling her eyes with all details so that she could find her way back without fault in any dream.

John waited until she came into the cottage and then he stood up. He was ashamed that he could not look at her – ashamed because it was such a petty, half-way thing, neither revenge nor understanding being in it, merely a weary spite – but he could not. And whenever he talked to her, the words came through a threat blocked by tears forced back from his eyes.

'Are you ready now?' he asked, quietly.

'Yes.'

'We'll go then.'

'Yes.' She paused. 'You must have *some* idea, John. You must know where you want to go.'

'No,' he said, head bent making for the door. 'I don't know.'

She did not press him, being as incurious as he was about where they would land up that night and what he would do. Only May, silent between their deep retreats, had brought her to the question. She would know soon enough.

Emily heard him lift the handles of the cart and begin to push it out to the lane. Two of the pans jangled mournfully and the wheels bumped slowly over the track, dragging behind them the slow step of her husband. She shivered on the bare flags of the kitchen and yet could not leave it until John had turned the corner – then she turned and was swiftly out, ushering May before her, slamming the door as abruptly as the wind, wrenching the key in the lock.

Pennington was outside his gate waiting for the key and she hurried to get in front of John so that he would not have to stop. But Pennington barred the way, and the pile of possessions slid to an angle as John set down the cart.

'Sure thou won't change thee mind, eh?'

'No.'

'Aa don't know,' said Pennington. 'Just a bit of a fight. Our Jackson's always been a stupid bluddy man. He'll be off where he belongs again on Saturday. Aa means – what the hell – Eh?'

'No. We're off, Mr Pennington.' John picked up the handles and pushed ahead, this forcing the older man out of his way.

'Aa'm greatly put upon by this,' said Pennington, as the family went past and away from him. 'Aa could sue thee, John Tallentire, but Aa's not that kind of man. Eh? Is'te listenin'? Thou can start again this minute.' He raised his voice as the small procession left him alone and went further up the lane. 'Thou always got thee money on time, man. Didn't thou? What else dis'te want? Eh? Answer me that! Eh? Answer me that!'

At the end of the lane he went straight on, down towards Cockermouth, away from the fells.

The hedges lining their route were bare of leaf and bird and it was only May, soon sat on a chair on the cart, whose pecking head and chatter brought lightness to the dour journey. John between the shafts, Emily a few paces behind him, each in limbo, shades of themselves never to stop, it seemed, this aimless walk.

John avoided Cockermouth and avoided Embleton. The early night came and still he did not stop more than for a few moments now and then to rub his forearms – he would not draw in when Emily offered him bread but ate the food standing staring at a cottage across the fields. He was relieved that it was dark. They came to Bothel and passed the place where Mr Errington had offered refreshments to his blushing companion and Emily was so tired she could have fallen to sleep on the road itself. No moon and the wind colder, gusting the trees, silencing the huddling sheep in the fields, whining through the hedges. May was asleep in the chair, covered by a blanket, strapped to the chair-back by a length of rope. Sometimes, when she had been troublesome back in the cottage, John had used the same rope to tie around her ankle and the table leg so that she moved only a yard or so from the care of the table.

He wanted not to stop ever. To do so would mark a place, and he wanted no connections. The jobs he would have to do would throw him into a certain intimacy with Emily – which he could not bear to think of. Moreover, he felt that without the weight of this cart before him, without its frame he himself would fall, be able to do nothing in the world but lie there, inanimate.

'If you go much further we'll be at your father's place,' said Emily. 'Maybe they would put us up.'

'We'll not turn to them.'

She hesitated.

'We'll have to stop soon,' she said eventually. 'Or I'll just drop, John.'

'We'll stop when we can!' He shouted. 'Stop whinin'!'

The anger stoked his energy and he raised his pace. After some minutes he noticed that all was silent behind him, her following footsteps gone. He set down the cart and looked back – to see no sign of her in the black night.

He clenched his fists as a spurt of fury threatened to loosen his mouth to accusations – words he wanted to check, fearing their flight. Finally she caught up with him and stood, a few yards off, a shadow in the dark, swaying.

'Get on the cart with the babby,' he said.

She nodded but did not move.

'Come on then! Get *on*, woman!'

'Yes,' she replied. 'Yes, I will.'

But still she stood.

'Let's stay here, John.'

'Don't be stupid.'

'I can go no further.'

'Yes you can – try.'

'I can't try.'

He went to her and for the first time that day looked full into her face. The skin pulled at the bones as if to find their cutting edge. Her mouth was tight, lips pressed together firmly as if afraid ever again to relax to a spontaneous expression.

'I'll lift you on,' he said abruptly and picked her up, feeling her body hard underneath the swathes of cloth, the cheek frozen which rested on his own for a moment before pulling away. She said nothing but allowed herself to be set on the cart, covered with the other blanket, wedged beside her daughter.

'I'll look for somewhere,' he said.

John took the next turning off the main road and looked out for an empty shed or cottage. At that time it was not too difficult to find abandoned cottages pocking the countryside like craters on a battlefield and after a mile or so he came across such a one. The windows were broken – but boards half-hanging from them showed that there had been squatters there before. The door was open and inside there was sacking on the floor, stinking of excrement. Hooks hung from the low, cracked ceiling, there was a hole in one of the walls stuffed up with wood and paper.

He threw out the sacks and secured the windows – and then his energy was spent. The bed he brought in with more sense of effort than he had showed along the whole way. Emily helped him with the rest of the furniture. John realised that he should have found wood and made up a fire, should have prepared against the cold of the morning, helped by more than the lighting of two candle stumps to bring some warmth into the place. But he was without any impulse to it. That mood which had once seized so malevolently on him now merely touched him – and he went under.

The life he lived for the days and weeks following could best be called an under-life. Too much for him, he neither fought it nor ran from it but crept down into himself away from it. His day was set from the first morning when he looked at Emily making the fire. He watched until she was finished and then went to the chair beside it, sat and stared into it. Saying nothing when bread and tea was put before him, making no effort to help as she dragged the furniture into a more practicable position, never moving to be out for wood or to look around. He washed and shaved once a day – did it when he was alone in the room. To May he was indifferent but he was not angry with her when she scrambled on to his knee or made a noise. He went outside to defecate and saw nothing but the short track. One thing he did do – he laid on the table all the money he had in his pockets.

When, about a fortnight after they had come, the owner came, John was alone. His silences were such as the man expected and once he had made up his mind that no money would be got out of these new squatters he made the best of it, as he had done often enough before, the cottage having been empty for years. He noticed the fire and scored that up as something for himself: the damp would be held back a little and so the cottage would be in some condition if ever he wanted to let it again. It was too distant from his own place to be of the smallest use to him and already too derelict to be spoiled. So he left not unhappy at having the place inhabited and rather pleased to be maintaining a squatter whom he could own and display in his daily talk.

The only comfort about the days, to John, was their end. Then his terrible blankness could be used in sleep. In a short time he had exhausted such thoughts as he had on the reasons for this condition. He now thought himself a stupid fool for ever believing in love, and deserving of all he heaped on himself for holding to that faith so fiercely. He did not blame Emily – for he scarcely considered her now; no lift of her voice, no action of hers, no sight or touch of her impinged even slightly on his retreat. Occasionally on his inward eye would flash a picture of her and himself as they had been – and then his face would tighten, draw as if for tears, but the lines would be hard, squeezing out the memory, rejecting it as foreign to his state. Even more fiercely came memories of those days he had spent knowing that Emily's thoughts were all of Jackson: that painful suspense would now quicken to such a bite of hatred as shuddered through his body until he moaned for it to cease. At such times Emily would touch his arm only to feel her fingers shivered off. John knew that his circumspection had been out of care for Emily: unable to understand her, he had thought that only by going her own way could she be saved from herself. But he also called himself coward.

Having known such a passion as could make a sight alone fill with contentment, one that drove into him until it seemed that everything shone through love, he was now in darkness. He could see nothing but shadows of former shapes and was no more inclined to discover their substance than that of ghosts.

And he thought that the god he had made of himself at work was little but a function of his desire to serve. To a function he had given his spirit. To call what he had done more than a mechanical drudgery was to glorify it. Demanding satisfactions in it he had found them – but such as had ceased when the self-erected purpose had fallen. His work had been a labour to himself and had over-leapt the rewards of absorption in the results. It was his skill and stamina he had loved, not the growing barley or the safely delivered lambs. That in himself he had sought, that was right, he knew; but so to impose yourself on the world is to challenge it to return your force, and the disruption it had returned carried in it the wreckage of labour, flotsam of days and tasks, useless-seeming now – he thought of them with amazement, fingering their recollection, unable to imagine the form which had held them in place.

Finally, with no self-pity, he saw himself as a man whose life would never be fit for anything but manual labour. Whatever was required of the meanest talents and the most blinded mind would be required of him. He remembered what Seth had told him of the farm labourers not many years ago joining and marching for their unions so soon to founder – but the image of those men and their meetings at night on the cross-roads, lanterns shielded from the wind, women and children with them as they listened to their fellows saying 'it cannot last', 'it must change', and thence going to risk eviction and transportation for fifteen shillings a week – such conjoining and faith in a future was not able to draw any hope to him. The conditions might change but the situations would be the same: he would fill in the holes in the ground and then stand aside as the pyramid rose.

These reflections fragmented, elusive, flickered on the walls of the cave in which he now lived.

Happy to be a blank in darkness.

Wishing neither to give nor to resist.

Sat there at the side of the fire, still as a painted man. Old. Shoulders bent, body hunched, petrified by the unyielding reflection of the thing he looked on. In this pagan and beast nothingness, he was immovable.

It was Emily who acted. She was out looking for wood in the morning, fetching water from the beck, spending the little money on the cheapest flour and lard. They ate flat-cakes and drank water when the tea ran out. She kept to the one room as if fearing that an attempt to get him to move upstairs would destroy the last of the small contact they had. Sometimes she was lucky and could persuade a farmer's wife to let her help with a day's washing: she sold her two dresses and with the money bought wool and sold the socks and pullovers she made. For two months they managed on less than seven shillings a week – and then the savings were almost gone. She sold the chairs John had made and bought two hens so that May would have eggs. For one week she had herself hired for stone-picking and took May to help her clear the seven acres for five and threepence. At all costs to herself John must be allowed to come out of that empty waking nightmare on his own. She worked to keep him and May alive, and the fundamental nature of such work restored her as, she hoped, it atoned for what she had done. So as John grew worse, the cumulative effect growing on to him like a scaling disease, she became firmer. The despair

which incomprehension had rotted to a frailty like madness was
put away from her and she thought of nothing at Crossbridge
but Ephraim's grave to which now she could not bring herself
to return.

Once Isaac came by, bold as ever, driving a flock of geese.
Caught out at the end of a good run, droving had been the best
he could find – 'lasses' work,' he said, beaming that he was doing
it. The geese were like a drift of snow, magically carpeting the
brown track.

Their sound did not bring John from his seat, nor did the
information that his brother was there. So while Emily looked
after the geese, Isaac went inside.

John was more pleased to see Isaac than he would have been
anyone else. But his pleasure was soon spent, having now so
little to nourish it: like his appetite, his doings with the world
had grown so meagre that a peck served where a bushel had
been needed before. Isaac could make little of this exhausted
replica of a brother and, it not being in his nature to give more
advice than the call 'Get up, man! Come away!' he was soon
baffled. John's unhappy appearance, the bleak cottage, the distant acceptance of it all by Emily – all this unnerved him. The
best he would do was to wring the necks of two of the fatter
geese – for which he would himself reimburse the farmer – and
hand their hot, downy bodies to Emily before passing on.

His visit, though, changed John. That passing touch which
seemed to come from another world touched on him and, weakly,
he began to struggle from the bottom of self into which he had
been pitched.

He walked out a little the very next morning – looking at the
dull, featureless fields, feebly scanning this bare no-man's-land
into which he had brought himself – neither fell-land nor plain,
neither lush nor formidable, poor land. He was soon tired. Emily
hoped that he might be getting himself ready for the Whit-hiring
now only a fortnight off, but soon she saw that even if he had
the intention he had not the strength. He was as white and
fragile as a convalescent. All that was boyish had gone for ever
from his face, replaced by lines which age would trace deeper
from then on; his cheeks sunk deeply so that his mouth was

raised up on his face and stood out from it, a most fragile challenge to the world.

He watched his daughter playing. The child had found games to fill her solitude and he watched her as she built and destroyed, chatted to herself, ran after the birds. He carved a doll for her with his pocket knife.

Then Joseph, his father, came. Up the track and into the cottage and no less directly to the point.

'There's a place for thee at Wiltons,' he said. 'He missed gettin' a good man at Wigton. Got landed wid a stupid calf as couldn't work off steam. Thou can tak ower frae him on Sattiday.'

'I won't go,' John replied.

'Well, thou shall have to do summat, my son. This pig-sty's no place for a man. Thee wife's next thing 'til a beggar. Thee dowter looks like an orphan. *Thou* looks like workhouse fodder. Thou shall hev to do summat. Yer mother's sick wid' worry.'

'Don't bring her intil it. Thou means *thou's* shamed. That's all.'

'All! Ay lad, Aa's shamed, but *thou's* bluddy near ruined. Now – theer's a job, he'll give thee fourteen bob a week. Tek it. Git out of this muck-heap. That's what Aa kem to say.'

'And now thou's off.'

'Ay, that's correct. Aa knows better than to stay to reason wid thee lad. A fool can't see his own good. But think o' thee wife and dowter. That's all.'

'Emily hasn't said anything.'

'Then she's dafter than thee. There's no credit in agreein' wid weaklin's.'

'So now thou's off,' John repeated, deriving amusement from that which annoyed his father.

'What the hell dis'te expect? A carnival? Thou's bluddy lucky Aa kem, lad. Ay – Aa's off! Aa'll catch diphtheria sittin' in this byre. What the hell, man! Is this as good as thou can manage for thisel?'

'It's little enough different to what thou's got.'

'If thou think like that – thou's mad as well as daft. There's no question.'

'And that's that! Eh?'

'Yes.'

'Come in – orders and out. Job done.'

'And wasted by the sound of it,' the older man replied, almost jumping from one foot to the other, so furious was he against his son, so irritated by what he regarded as sloth, so keen to be gone that it might be thought he was afraid that to stay would tar him with the same pitch.

'Go then,' John said.

'Ay,' Joseph hopped about – John laughed. 'Tek that smile off, you useless effigy! So the poor little lad got blocked wid a spade. O dear me. Thou needs hittin' wid another to knock t'sense back in. Ay, laugh away, you bluddy ignorant pile. *Thou* was gonna be "on thee own", *thou* could manage – ladida – bluddy mess! Useless! Ay – laugh away. God,' he drew back his arm, 'I would brain thee if Aa thowt it was worth it.'

'Thou can't brain thesel father. Never mind me. Tell Wilton thanks – but no.'

'No? What's 'te mean – no?'

'Well, father – thou can work it out as thou runs back home. It's only got two letters so thou should just about manage by Red Dial.'

'Oh! Oh now! That's it. That's it! Good-bye my lad. O yes! Good-bye!'

'And now thou's off.'

'What in hell's name dis to keep wailin' that for? Ay – Ah's off.'

'Father,' John paused. 'Thou never asked one question – never wondered one thing. Dis te not *want* to know what happened?'

'Aa do not.'

Yet Joseph hesitated.

'What'll Aa tell folk?' he asked, eventually.

'Tell them the truth, father. Tell them thou found me a squatter and near enough a pauper and daft enough to turn down a grand offer frae Wilton. Tell them May looks badly and Emily looks worse – and tell them not to look up from their own feet, because if they do they'll see the same thing I see.'

'An' what's that?'

'*Nothing*! Between here and high heaven – Nothing.'

'Aa'll tell them thou's mad daft.'

He left and Emily, who had listened outside, rushed in and hugged John. He held her up and kissed her flying hair.

'Nothing at all,' he murmured.

PART TWO

THIRTEEN

John had taken work in the mines. It was, Emily thought, like coming in from the wilderness.

The town boomed against her senses as the sea sounded along its shore. This move from the countryside to the town – even though the town had a population of no more than eight or nine thousand – was the more dramatic as neither John nor herself had lived anywhere larger than a village: the effect of any subsequent move even to a city would be much less than this first impact of town life.

In the beginning it had seemed to her like a ceaseless carnival. Though approaching the end of another pregnancy, she would still go with May, and Harry – born a few months after their arrival in the town – drawn to the centre to watch the people. She thought she would never tire of that. Streets full of shops, each jostling the other for trade, pushing out on to the pavement with boxes of fish, slabs of meat, sacks of vegetables, an ironmonger littering the street with his implements, cobblers in their windows hammering and peeping, clothes shops deep-blinded in shaded respectability, tripe for sale, pigs' trotters, sheep's heads, a rich cave of carpets – and on market day the stalls stretching up all the side streets, a plantation of canvas and boards loaded with booty for plunder – white pyramids of eggs, geese dangling by their feet – and a swarm everywhere, a restless crowd of women and children, the children scattering around about their mothers like disordered planets, the women scarved and sharp-eyed, by their looks equipped for any bargain, swooping along the shop fronts and trailing by the stalls almost scenting out their goods, so eagerly were the faces pushed forward. In the beginning, Emily had clenched her purse tightly, afraid that once opened, all would go, be bound to, so much there was to be bought. One street's length had exhausted her – the unknown faces rushing past, none carrying a history for her yet each so like herself – she felt the helpless exhilaration that many feel when they settle in new places. That everyone was new excited her, that she had no part in their lives unnerved her. For two or three years, until after the birth of Alice, the sounds and smells of the few streets in the town's centre spun her into this web. Just to go shopping was an outing for them all.

In the first decade of the twentieth century the town, like many others, ran with the juice of many pressings. There was the elite – doctors and solicitors; above them the men who owned the mines and the tanneries and the bank, living outside the town but still dribbling a last flavouring on to it of the aristocracy and gentry. The church was strong but the chapels were fuller. Temperance Halls were as busy as the pubs. The Salvation Army played on Saturday nights and all day Sunday. There were football teams, a music hall, a new bath-house, horse-sales, boy scouts, a workhouse, a cottage hospital, lodgings, slums, schools for the now compulsory secondary education, reading-rooms – and between all this, between the hills which rose up on the shore, physical pincers of the society, were the miners, clogged along the cobblestones, black droves to and from the shifts.

At that time, the West Cumberland Coalfield produced over two million tons of coal a year from forty-three collieries: almost nine thousand men worked in pits. Tell anyone that the pits would be closed by the second half of the century and he would not have listened, let alone believed. West Cumberland sat on coal; if you dug too deep in your allotment you would break into a seam. And not content with the land, the coal ran out under the sea where here it was mined further out than anywhere else in the world – some of the men walking four miles under the water to reach the facings, hewing below a depth of over 200 fathoms. The Earl of Lonsdale had leased the mines to the Bains who had introduced new machinery, doubled the number of men, opened further seams – and below a hundred square miles of earth and water the miners drove shafts, seams, roads, ripping the coal from the rock and limestone.

John had found a cottage to the north of the docks, in a settlement of terraced houses that ran almost to the edge of a cliff. Below were the coal-dusted rocks and along the shore – north to Maryport – the wheels and workings of the pits like beacons in their aspect but in purpose more resembling the Roman mile-castles which had once guarded the coast – for like them, the workings were both a mark of power and a defence against privation.

He was not as beguiled as Emily by the glamour of the town. He saw more of the empty steep streets as morning rain soaked on his way back from work under a sea that had not spotted him. Where Emily saw the liveliness of the women, John's impression was of their gauntness. The hollowed faces and bone hopelessness of the people Picasso painted at this time were portraits of a continent of the industrial poor. Emily felt the benefit of John's higher wage now that he was out of his apprenticeship: to him, though the extra cash in hand was pleasant and welcome, there was strangely less plenitude about him than there had been on the farm – for all its grinding labour and ignominious pay. When he went out of his allotment to walk along the cliff and look down at the fishing boats, the lights of the town, the sea – even then he felt an absence, for despite the movement of the sea, or perhaps by contrast with it, the shapes beneath him seemed static and angular. He could break it up into squares and triangles, hard solid forms – in a way which was impossible on the land. As if the weight of men below the crust threatened the surface. So that the houses ran in battle-lines, the larger buildings in the town centre making a fortress. Ready to repel an attack from the exploited riddles below. While the cracked walls, the tall chimney broken like a bottle-top, a waste of land between terraces – a void like a scar suppurating – the rampage of a Saturday night showed the danger to the town of this strain. And it crumbled to small, racing bodies as the wail of an accident sounded from the sea's edge.

Having made his decision, however, he was not going to let such vague misgivings spoil it. It was, he thought, no more than a hangover from that terrible time of blankness (which to remember made him shiver) – and besides, he had then made his discovery, then found that existence had no needs but a little food and shelter, then felt himself as near the bottom of things as he could be – and survived. That he was stuffing much of his instinct down his throat was painful but it had to be swallowed: for no matter how much he 'liked' the new life, he could not feel for it as he had done for the old. Those innumerable recognitions which mingle around you as you work at something you have done from childhood, the visions that they form, one layered on the other as fantasies, day-dreams, proper hopes and impressions which constantly advance and recede around you – they were gone.

His grandfather had died a few months after he had last seen him: his son Harry was named after him. At the funeral only four of the old man's sons had been able to come and John had been a pall-bearer, walking behind his father. The funeral was attended by over fifty people including those who had employed him throughout his life, and John had felt as old as his grandfather when one of his uncles had thanked the Latimers for 'letting his last days be so peaceful'. He knew that the old man had deteriorated even from the state he had seen him in, and that added to his determination to break from work whose nature so bound men that they could not survive in any way without it.

Now at twenty-six, John was well on that plain which, in his life, was like a table-topped mountain between the rapid steeps of childhood and the swift drop to the grave. If his mind was not made for the mines, his body was, its comparative shortness an advantage in the pits – sometimes he had snuggled into seams no more than eighteen inches high, stripped and running with sweat, lying on his side to hack out the coal, being more than ready to go on into a double shift for the extra money. He worked in Seth's gang but Seth was a cutter and John's marrer was a man called Fred Stainton who had been in the mines since his thirteenth birthday.

That great rush towards work – which had been an expression of himself as much as an act of labour – was now gone. He did not mind it – though he dreaded to hear the cough of some of the older miners and broke his temper regularly as he tried to scrub the black mineral from his skin – but he had no love for it. On the farm, doing the job well had sometimes given a satisfaction other than the job's completion; here, the mark of a job well done was the quantity of coal dug out. There were men who worked as if their lives depended on their skill – some of the big hewers who cut down coal as remorselessly as lumberjacks topple trees – and men of all ages who would take pride in the making of a pack wall or a gateway and lay out their tools like master carpenters, pointing out the old shafts which led to the great columns of coal, twenty-five yards square, which had formerly supported the workings as grandly as pillars in a cathedral. John could not match them – nor did ambition rise as substitute for affection: Seth disparaged his brother's willingness to stay an ordinary collier, but John wanted no more. Only when he climbed into the cage to be pressed against a crowd of thirty or forty men and drop down into the earth, or in the shed when he lined up for his wages and felt each man ready on the same mark – only at such times, being an anonymous member of a crowd, did he feel the smallest enthusiastic stirrings for the work he did and the way of life it dictated.

Seth, who had helped to set him on his feet when he first arrived, had put him on the list for one of the company's cottages. After a few weeks he had got one – such cheap shacks were a small investment for the money that could be made out of them – and John had moved in, with little more than the bed after Emily's forced sales. It was one of the cheapest of those cheap barracks – necessarily so as he was on apprentice's wages to begin with. Even those, however, were higher than the man's wages he had received from Pennington. The settlement of which their terrace was a part was known as 'The Tops'. An easy target for justifiable sarcasm. Anyone looking on the miners' cottages from the air would have seen regular stitches of roof and alley. No differences could have been imagined between them. All had back-kitchen, a kitchen and parlour downstairs, two bedrooms and perhaps a minute extra – little bigger than a cupboard – upstairs, a backyard with a lavatory and coalshed. Alleys ran between the dark backyards like stony river beds after a drought. Washing was strung from wall to wall on

Mondays, filling the dry rivers with skeletal linen. A step or two led from the front door to the street and there the children or their parents would sit and watch the world go by on sunny days. Yet within the town there *were* differences – between Kells and Ginns, Bransty, Hensingham and Mirehouse. And 'The Tops', as would be said with such a blindness to the effects of repetition as made originality appear a waste of time, a thing for the children and those without self-confidence, 'The Tops are aboot the Bottom!'

Built before the great expansion of mining at the end of the century, they more resembled those plain agricultural cottages that John and Emily had lived in; but two up, two down, bigger. Some were scheduled to be pulled down – and already halfway to it from the assistance of those who used them as quarry. One terrace was called 'Rat Row' and the men would take their dogs down there on Sunday mornings to bet on the number of rats which could be killed in an hour. Potters lived in some of the houses and treated them with the same respect as they treated any property – open or closed – without their caravans. On the same terrace as John lived two families, the Wylies and the Stobarts, whose drinking and thieving was about to end in their eviction. Yet after John had made certain that Emily was not frightened by it – which she was not – nor worried for the children, he settled down well enough. Like most districts with a bad name, its differences from the others were far less than its similarities.

The parlour was to Emily as the allotment was to John. He had rented a big chunk no more than five minutes from his door – along the back alley, across 'the waste' to the small sub-branch of the Co-operative, and from there past the chapel down a little path to a flat piece of land on the lip of the cliff. It took him most of the first year to take the stones off it and break up the ground. He managed no more than a few stitches of potatoes that time. And Emily had got a pair of armchairs for the parlour. Over the next two years, it became a race – he down there most nights when he came back from work, she gambling on the sales like a professional punter. She had to win, for as soon as he got the allotment 'something like', he was away with plans for building a small shed and planting some shrubs – whereas once the parlour was completed – including a piano which had been bought for ten shillings 'and taking away' – it was set, to gather as much dust and silence as any sanctuary. The space in the house, the children about her and the neighbours' business so often made her own, left her with little regret for the village. The time when she had placed herself entirely in John's moods, when they had spun together so that the world about them was no more than a whirl of colours, undefined compared with the power of their own motion, was gone and she was glad of it. For the first time there was something in her which could not be touched by him. While John thought back on that time as one of wonder and intense life, she regarded it as a storm, thankfully blown out.

Though he had regained his temper with his self-respect and she could still feel the tremor of that compulsion which had led her towards a fever of intolerable longing, they were easier with each other than they had been, neither the dead affair of Jackson nor the body of Ephraim turning an accusing face to them, and each too, now aware of the consequence of sinking to that dying selfishness which exhausts those nearest.

The days went in no certainties. There was no great aim, no investment made in the future, no life carved out with care for the calls of a tyrannical conscience or a driving will. At one of Seth's meetings, John had been turned to and described as 'an ordinary fella' – to mark him off from the union members – and he had felt it accurate and no slight. Emily, too, made no extraordinary demands for herself – neither barricaded her doors against all-comers nor lived as much in neighbours' houses as her own, as some of the women did. When a woman was ill, she would take in one or two of her children, just as May had been lodged out at Alice's birth. She did not go to chapel but gave money to the Salvation Army and May to Sunday-school. She neither drank nor smoked, nor was she extravagant, though she would pinch for herself to get fancy bits of things for the children. The supper was in the oven when he came home and she shoved the children away as she washed his back in the tub before the fire. The Co-op served her for most of her shopping, the stalls at the market for the rest. She settled in and settled down and in those first few years let the routine of house and the demands of the children take her over. What with John entailed rejection and suppression, in her seemed to fit without cutting.

On Saturdays she went to the market, that portion of the previous days' earnings left for the spree itching in the bottom of her purse. She always got sweets for the children and John, for herself she liked to get a little fruit – grapes when there were any – or a bought cake – cream sandwich or vanillas. After tea John went to the pub.

She sat in the rocking chair – smiling at the image of John there just a few minutes before, Alice on his lap, May on the rockers at the back, Harry straddling an arm, John's arm circling the baby and strapped in the concertina as he rollicked the four of them half-way across the kitchen.

> 'Gee up jockey to the fair
> What will you buy me when you're there?
> A silver apple and a pear
> Gee up jockey to the fair.'

– and with all his voice shouting 'Whoa-there!' and 'Faster boy!', the children hanging on as for life and then released in a squall of laughter. Now Emily sat, the bread fresh out of the oven, the supper ready for his return, all the children well and in bed – trying, as she sometimes did, to get into a book but alerted at every sentence by an echo in her mind which the words caused but could not catch. She was determined not to waste her time on sleep – Saturday being the sole evening on which she could be absolutely certain of being alone – her children not old enough to have friends come around after seven and the women along the row either preparing against the morning so that they could slip to chapel, out drinking, or, like herself, hugging the luxury of a week done, these few hours the slow calm when one week was ended, another yet to begin.

She was irritated by the knock on the door, and made uncertain by its being at the front door. Pulling off the apron, she folded it up neatly without stopping to do so, laying it over the back of the last chair as she left the kitchen.

'Are you Missus Tallentire?'

'I am.' Seeing the caller was a woman carrying a child, Emily was relieved enough to open the door widely, but not yet so confident as to take away the foot that was wedged behind it.

'I'm Sarah.'

'Oh yes.'

'*Sarah* Tallentire. John's sister. Don't you – well you wouldn't. Aa wasn't left school when you got married. Can I come in?'

'Of course you can. Here – let me take that baby. What an awful thing you must think me standing here without saying anything. Come in – do. Bang that door, would you, Sarah? The snib's funny.'

'Oh. It *is* warm in here.' The younger woman, relieved of the child, set her large basket down on a chair and rushed to the fire. In the impulse of her movements, Emily recognised John and, even stronger, May. All of them had that black hair and the small hard blue eyes. 'Bread!' Sarah exclaimed – like a girl, clapping her hands over it. She could be no more than seventeen. 'Ooh! Can I have some, Emily? Can I call you Emily?'

'Of course you can. But have something better than bread. I've a sponge cake in the back-kitchen.' She smiled at the baby.

'Oh. Lovely.'

'What's she called?'

'Veronica.'

'That *is* unusual. But very nice. Here – I'll put some cushions on the settee so's she won't fall off. Would she like some milk?'

'She might. I'll be happy with the bread.'

'No, no. Sit down. You can't have just bread. What am I doing letting you go hungry like that? Sit there – up at the table where you've got some room. I'll put the kettle on. Now make yourself at home.'

From the back-kitchen, quite guilelessly, Emily shouted.

'And who's the man?'

'A navvy.'

'Where does he work?'

'I don't know. He *did* work at Wigton. He might be in Timbucktoo now for all I know.'

'They get around, do they?' Still from the kitchen.

'They certainly do,' said Sarah – giggling and then crying.

Coming through to the kitchen with the sponge cake on a plate, Emily bit her lip for an ignorance which, though unavoidable, had yet not been guarded by sufficient sensitivity to prevent the pain caused to the girl. She needed no further elaboration of the situation.

'Well,' she said later, having helped Sarah to a quick enough recovery and watched her make a rapid raid on the meal – the sponge cake reduced by over a third. 'You must stay here 'til you get settled in a bit more. You can sleep with May, and Harry can come in with us, that'll leave his bed for Veronica.'

'I knew you'd be kind!' The younger woman launched herself from her chair and flung her arms around Emily's waist, treating her who was but a few years older than herself as one capable of bearing every responsibility which she herself would not carry. 'I knew it was no good going to our Dad. He'd have taken us in – but . . .' She pulled back her head and glared at Emily. 'But my God we would nivver have heard the last of it. So I thought – Aa'll just get on that train – and I did, Emily – it goes right to the sea from Flimby, you could lean out and catch a fish – Ooh! It made me seasick, to look at it – and you should have seen this one young man in the first-class compartment – Aa'm sure he must have been a Duke, or a Sir – anyway – *Some*body – his *clothes*! – I could have pulled them off his back and got into them meself – oh! such *cloth*! – and there was a woman took Veronica when she started to cough so that was nice – and I says, "There's our Seth and better, there's our John and his Emily – they'll take us in." So I came. I am *glad* I came.' And Sarah stood up, calmly turned a small circle and went across to the mirror.

'Haven't you got a big mirror, Emily?'

'There's a bigger one in the wardrobe upstairs.'

'Can I go up?'

'You might wake the children, dear.'

'Oh. Oh well. When Veronica cries I just put my fingers in my ears. They'll cry for ever if you give in to them, you know. Then you're finished. Do you like this brooch?'

'Yes. I noticed it. It's lovely.'

'There's supposed to be a real garnet in it somewhere.' Sarah squinted severely down at her blouse front. 'God alone knows which bit it is. You can have it if you like.'

'No. Whatever for? You keep it.'

'No. I don't *really* care for it.' She unsnipped it. 'It'll look better on you, anyway. Your hair's not so black. Try it on. Go on. Don't be silly. *Keep* it. With my hair you need really bright stuff – otherwise it isn't worth it. There. What did I say? You suit it beautifully. Go and look.'

'It *is* pretty,' said Emily.

'Makes you look younger,' Sarah added.

'But it's too good.' Emily snapped it off as decisively as Sarah had done. 'You must keep it. No! If *you* don't like it – keep it for Veronica. I'd better get that little girl some milk – does she have it sugared?'

'As it comes. Is this a photo of you and John?'

'Yes. That was at Crossbridge. Our first year there. A man called Joe Edmonson took it.'

'Makes you look very young!'

Emily went to fetch the milk and from the retreat of the back-kitchen dared to ask a question that she would have avoided face to face – would have avoided altogether before a less volatile woman.

'How is it we didn't – know about all this, Sarah?' she asked.

'Oh. Well, I ran away with him – see.' She shouted – as Emily was out of the room. The volume gave the words a cheerful, even singing, air. 'And – well Mam guessed but I had to say something so I told Dad I was married. We lived at Garblesby and he came to see us once – just when I was gonna pop – and Jerry knocked him down. What a fight they had! My Jerry said that we were married – but Aa suppose Dad didn't believe us because he didn't tell anybody. He just nivver mentioned it. Then when Jerry went away, I went home – you should have heard the old lad *swear* – mind you, he daren't hit me 'cause I kept tight hold of the baby, see. So I went off again. I'm glad to be out of his reach.'

'How old were you then?' Emily asked, totally unable to resist her curiosity even though she tried to make of the question the merest passing remark as she brought in the milk to the child.

'Fifteen when I left home. Sixteen when *she* came to spoil things. Oh! I mustn't say that. I didn't mean it, darling. Here, mammy'll give you the milk, won't she? Won't she then? Is it too hot then? Well, *don't* puke it up just because it's too hot! Wait a minute, can't you?' She turned to Emily. 'It's too hot,' she said.

Sarah was fast asleep in bed by the time John came back. He was short of being drunk but the ale and the company had done a good job on him and Emily had no difficulty in accommodating him to the situation – particularly as she felt no obligation to repeat all that Sarah had said to her, nor were her own conclusions firm enough for her to do anything but override their reservations as mean and ungenerous.

'Of course she can stay for a bit,' said John. 'She'll be terrified, poor lass, I shouldn't wonder – with our father carryin' on and one thing and another. Of course she can stay.'

FOURTEEN

'Don't worry,' said Seth. 'It's an open meeting. Thou needn't say a word.'

'Are you certain?' John demanded.

'Positive! And even so, you might pipe up summat or other, no?'

'No,' John replied, decisively. 'I would have nothin' to say. It'd be a waste of time listenin' to me.'

'Well. We'll see. I felt like that once. Everybody gets used 'til it.'

John had joined the union, but while regular with his subscription and as solid as the others were in his demand for the Eight-Hour Day, he was, as many were, uncomfortable when faced with Seth's fanaticism.

'Your trouble,' he said to John, 'is that you worked too long on that bluddy farm. At the bottom of you you don't care who you work for or what it is you're asked to do as long as you get your money and can think of yourself as bein' independent. And you think you were independent because you could serve your notice any time. But that's the least of it, lad. You've got Rights. You must claim them. And there's no God Almighty ever said you should sweat your guts out for somebody else's profit. You should have a share in the profits of your work. But you're that pig-ignorant – you can't really believe that, can you? You just can't *think* that you have as much right to a fair share in what you produce as they have. It won't drop, will it?'

No matter how much John protested, he knew there was some justice in Seth's accusation – and felt inferior to his brother both in his understanding of the situation and in the resolution with which he responded to it. Yet as he walked beside his brother now, down the hill to the pub where the meeting was to be held, he wished himself back in his allotment or kneeling in front of the fire making the brass ornaments he had turned to, talking to Emily or Sarah – in any place but this. With other union men he felt easy enough, but Seth had Fight and Unionism written all over his face: still a bachelor, he breathed Tom Mann, Keir Hardie, Burns and Pickard, and would have his brother as committed as he was: chivvied him for the slightest tone, not of dissent – for that he enjoyed, giving him, as it did, the opportunity to smother John with argument – but such as betrayed less than total enthusiasm; John had to be the prize convert, a showpiece.

Slowly, still amazingly slowly, the working classes of Britain were organising themselves into Unions. The miners had already the largest union and the most potential force. The Taff Vale decision at the beginning of the century had shocked them to greater urgency and in 1906 Union funds became immune from legal action. In that year also, about thirty members of the Independent Labour Party went into Parliament and although they were still the tail of the Liberals, the tail was starting to wag the dog. Old Age Pensions on a non-contributory basis were being fought for, workman's compensation, medical inspection for children, unemployment and health insurance – and the miners' cry for the Eight-Hour Day had grown into a practicable demand. All this is often represented as the 'inevitable tide', the 'logical' conclusion of votes and education. Written down so, it seems that the causes fought for were certain of success. Yet in that first decade no more than one man in seven was in a union; even within those trades which appeared powerfully organised there were many non-union men. Funds were in constant danger of running out: lodges could be strong one year and abandoned the next: there were differences which made large-scale co-operation very difficult; entire unions could perish – as did that of Joseph Arch's Agricultural workers, and only by the most painful efforts did George Edwards build it up again, years later, a man in his sixties bicycling to four or five hundred village meetings a year, himself alone setting it up. The forces against them were at least as well organised as they were and the police and the militia were easily called in to break local strikes. There were Bloody Sundays and bayonet charges, lock-outs and victimisation – the crude reactions of a disturbed bully.

And over all this, like the fog in Dickens' London, were the fumes of inertia – a mingling from many sources. For there were men who could not believe that anything could be done, could not believe that they could win more than a temporary victory which would surely carry savage retribution: others who had been hammered so hard that the smoke they gave off was dust only, blinding, clogging, deadening: others who did not care – had not in themselves that capacity for extending their vision of life so wide as to include humanity, preferred to be outside all groups however worthy, felt themselves uneasy and diminished in the corporate clamancy; others who would come and go with the wind and saw the Union as useful to their private purpose sometimes, sometimes not; and men of all kinds who saw no solutions in the Union, whose life was wholly private, seeing no relevance in any organisation to their sparrow's flight from dark to dark.

The movement was very far from being an irresistible force. As yet it was more like grit in the swarming jelly of a society which contained modes of life, still lived, from every age and circumstance of the last few hundred years, a society which could see it as but another mass movement – nearer in spirit and appearance to the Wesleyanism of a previous century (on which indeed it fed for orators and moral purpose) than to anything else they could comprehend.

Though Seth had been elected on to the committee, he had been given no distinctive post. As organising secretary he would have been effective – even as it was he would travel every street every night to distribute leaflets or collect for an accident; he would have been reliable as treasurer, competent as general secretary, dedicated as chairman. But there was something about him which would always deny him those posts. He was too ruthless in his decisions, he would call on strikes for everything, he intimidated the older men by his urgency and depressed the younger men by his calls for 'an endless struggle', 'never, never to stop until we've got everything – and *then* to go on to get more!' In an instant grievances would become bitter. He embarrassed people by the stare-eyed almost possessed manner of his speech which, coming from that white, too-soon worn face, had in it something over-excited, 'like a consumptive curate' some people said. And as in his most neat and sober dress – even for this routine committee meeting he had put on a clean collar and wore his good shoes, gleaming with polish – there was a striking similarity to the puritanical God's-truth-fearing of lean-backed low-church curates, so in the pasty glaze of his face, that black hair lankly despising any wave, the blood-nicked chin, razor too fiercely drawn, there was the relished brimstone of those men, shadowed jaws snapping at purgatory eyes hot for hell-fire.

This too, John was aware of and so beside his brother he felt both inferior, and protective. For there was no doubt that Seth had been overlooked for positions in the Union he could have expected; no doubt that he was not given the same sympathy as the other members of the committee; but little doubt, either, that the day was approaching when his zeal would choke him, stopper him in some way so that he would become a comical caricature of himself. Boys already imitated his walk; the crack about the consumptive curate had stuck: he was already a marker in argument – 'You'll get as bad as Seth Tallentire next,' they would say, 'Now if Seth was here he would have us marchin' to London over that!'

To himself, John explained his brother by reference to their uncle Ephraim. For after the accident with the crusher Seth had taken Ephraim to live in with him and looked after him for those five last years of life when everything had to be done for the maimed man – from feeding him to holding him on the lavatory. All Seth's pleasures were sacrificed in the service: he left the choirs, stopped going to concerts, gave up his whippet. It was during those years that Seth had become infected with this strident fanaticism which had eaten away the youthful muscles of enthusiasm and cancered him with revolt.

John had been to see them often during the first two years of his coming to the town. Emily would send teacakes or broth or some fancies. Ephraim particularly liked rock-buns, holding a shivering hand to his mouth, his slackened eyes weeping as he tried to direct his teeth to nibble the currants. The rooms in the large lodging-house were most barely furnished – Seth having not the slightest instinct for domesticity. There were two rooms and in them the two single beds stood as isolated as the day they had been brought there, sheets lopsidedly trailing, brown blankets fiercely bundled into the bottom to keep the feet warm. It was chiefly boys who occupied the other rooms in this lodging house, and the smell of bacon fat peeled off the walls. Seth had taken these rooms as soon as he had come out of his apprenticeship and never thought to change them for the comfort he could easily have afforded as a paying lodger in one of the colliers' cottages. There was a table and three chairs, a brown corner cupboard, a most hastily carpentered bookshelf which contained all his Union library and literature, even one or two strips of coconut matting – but none of this held together: like the objects in some still-life paintings, the possessions were self-sufficient, each one to itself, and a man seemed but another object among them, crossing the slats of light.

There, at a window which looked down to the well of a backyard, Ephraim had sat, all day. He could have gone to the workhouse but Seth would not have it. John would come and take across a chair and sit down immediately to get over the fear he felt at seeing before him the pulverised man: no less strong a description would be adequate, for the accident had crushed all but the essential juice of life out of him. He was now too small for his clothes, his bones seemed too small for his skin – cloth and flesh hung about him. The little control he had over his movements was spent in trying to retain dignity and his face screwed with effort to stop the dribbling mouth and eyes. One hand was less all fingers; he had not enough strength to move across to his bed without lurching, in pitiful burlesque of drunkenness, from one object to another for support. He spoke little, the words shaking him painfully – and in his eyes there was a hunger for life or death, not this existence he had, so that they accused all who looked in them. Often, when John came away he marvelled that any man could survive as Ephraim had done and marvelled the more at Seth's uncomplaining devotion. Only he winced when Seth, in one furious mood, pointed to the old man and shouted, 'Look what they did to Ephraim! Look at him!' – for then John could *not* look at him. Nothing could persuade Emily to visit him and the fact that the old man's name was the same as that of her dead son did little to mollify Seth, who always held it against her.

Then Ephraim had been found dead in the yard by Seth as he returned home from a shift. He must have thrown himself out of the window; there was no accident about it . . .

As they approached the pub, Seth became more cheerful and winked happily at John. The committee rooms were at the back of The Royal Oak but, early, they went into the bar. Seth went over to talk to the secretary and John settled down to watch some of the miners playing dominoes. It was a game he liked to play himself and he was content enough studying the way they dropped.

He was nudged up the bench as two men came over. Like most of the others they wore clothes similar to those they worked in – dressing up was, for most of them, a weekend affair. The pit boots were planted in the sawdust like coal scuttles. Soon, John turned from the dominoes to listen to them, for one of the men, oldish, his cheeks still retaining a faint apple redness, almost magically set on the yellow leather of his face, was telling the other about the interconnection of the seams between the different pits.

'Yes,' he said, 'thou can match them aa' up, if thou's a mind. Tek that seam at Cleator Moor – Five Feet Coal Seam they call it – well that's same as t' Mowbanks seam at Workington, and t'same again as what they call't Ten Quarters' seam at Ellenborough, Ballgill, Flimby and Broughton Moor. And that Ruttler Band at Ellenborough – well that'd go into t' Little Main Band at Workington and then hit 't Banrock Band at Cleator and Whitehaven.'

The list of names went on, and John was fascinated just to hear them. There was something mysterious and also grand in such a list: he remembered the calling of names from the register at school, the excitement which came from his mother when she set off in pursuit of a relation and plunged through forests of names unknown to him, the might which seemed to rise up from the Bible as the preacher read from the Old Testament until the air rang with names, visible and strange as a wheeling flock of wild geese. And in the relish of the old man's voice there was pleasure: John could sit all night and listen to these men talking, feeling less danger then from that nihilistic despair which his self-absorption had burnt into him than at any other time. Healed by this calling of names.

'Up, lad!' Seth said. 'Meeting's on.'

He went into the bare back room and sat on one of the benches which Seth had so carefully laid out earlier in the evening. There were too many. Nothing but a routine meeting, few had bothered to turn up. From the back, John kept looking at Seth – smiling to himself at the fact of his brother's presence up there on the platform with the committee – and then, as if shy, he would look away from him – embarrassed by Seth alternately slouching and stiff-bodied glaring, now beaten, now triumphant and both somehow out of place in the even reading of the minutes, proposing and seconding, short treasurer's report on the funds, a long question about Bain's new provisions for starting times, a complaint about the threat to raise the rent of the cottages ('outside our jurisdiction,' said the chairman – to be followed by such an expletive from Seth as covered even him with confusion and prevented him from making his point at all), the plans for getting in touch with other, more powerful areas (the Cumberland-Westmorland coalfield was not only isolated, as most of them were, but very small, comparatively powerless) and as men rose from the benches each bearing particular witness to the spirit of injustice, John left Seth alone and warmed to the quiet tenacity of the miners around him.

The committee rooms were available for many other organisations and no particular banners or decorations betokened the miners' cause. The walls were dark brown, the ceiling spread with wavering circles of tobacco smoke, gently layered on the cream paint: the platform did not ride across one end of the room like a stage but jutted out from the wall, a precarious jetty. The sacrifices that the men were prepared to make in merging themselves into an organisation seemed to have begun in the similarity of clothing. The common mark of the pit boots, the bow of the back as they leaned forward on the backless benches, like sailors bending into a wind. And as the talk went on – the voices echoing in the large room, each word thereby a challenge, flung out to carry beyond those present – he felt secure in the rightness of what they were all to fight for. The days when a man worked as if he was made for nothing else in the world, when he called by 'sir' and 'master' those 'set above' him – those days would never cease to cast their shadow over his own, but for his children he wanted it to be different. However much he had been in awe of his grandfather, to have followed him would have been blindness not forgivable by those following *him*. His grandfather had never seen, but for him who had there could be no looking away. Yes, he agreed with the man who was talking, it was not right that Bains should expect them to work up to the waist in water: yes, he agreed, when there were explosions in the pit then the walls should be inspected by independent observers before work was resumed: yes, it *was* criminal that they should use fewer props than was safe just because the company was worried about the cost of timber; yes, it was a scandal that the widows of the five men killed and the seventeen injured in the last William Pit disaster should be given such insulting compensation. These things should be put right. If only, he thought, he had the intelligence and the guts to see how they could be put right without recourse to actions in which he felt himself to be abandoned to the will of a mass less finely pointed than that of any of its members. But habit or squeamishness, selfishness or stupidity – he did not know what it was – prevented him from moving from the word to the deed with other than timorous, almost grudging reluctance. He would do odd jobs for Seth meticulously, and in the mechanical operation find some satisfaction: when men were to be counted, he was present. Yet always there was the unease – that he was there but not as totally committed as he felt he ought to be, not as completely convinced as the reasoning should have made him, marching, fighting even, but without the scent of the glory of the battle which was there, he saw, in the faces of others. Once, he thought, he would have been capable of it.

He kept such reservations to himself. In the town he was thought of as a solid worker and a solid union man.

He could never talk anyone else into joining the union though: was not capable of even attempting to do so. Yet surely, he thought, if he believed in it, he should have been able to do that.

Into these partly secret, partly guilty thoughts which had, as usual, drawn his concentration away from the meeting, came the voice of Seth, made raw by the cold response of his audience. John was aware that some of them disliked his brother to the extent of hating him.

'An' I say we should *force* them to join!' said Seth. 'Any man working down a pit as isn't in this union is a walking blackleg – yes you needn't laugh, Tom Miller, blacklegs aren't just brought in from outside – they live amongst us – no, Mr Chairman, not here – I accuse nobody at this meeting! I accuse . . . now yes – *all* of them should be in. They take the benefits that t' Union gets for them – when, I say, *when*, Mr Chairman, when we get this Eight Hours through – who'll turn on it! I ask the meeting – who'll turn on it? – and there's many'll benefit as haven't paid one halfpenny subscription to this Union – men who've just sat on their arses – yes I apologise to the Lodge,' Seth's brow had already risen to sweat, a gleaming band, yellow under the poor lights. 'So – who'll object to working eight hours a day?'

'The hewers will,' somebody shouted. 'They'll lose on it if they can't do their ten-hour stint. And thou knows as well as anybody, Seth Tallentire, that the hewers in Durham's *not* for it. Not a bit.'

'That's not my argument!' Seth exclaimed. 'You're muddlin' my argument. Hewers'll have to put up wid' it. They have too much their own way as it is.'

'That's reet!' somebody shouted. 'Aa'll tell Ted Blacklock that!'

'Tell him! And tell him that if he keeps puttin' my gang on them poor seams it'll amount to victimisation. He's worse than the bluddy company!'

'Order. Order!'

'Yes. Well – yes. Now – I've lost hold of me bluddy argument wid' all this talking.'

'Harken to t'lad!'

'No – no offence. But a fella should have a straight run . . .
Mr Chairman. He should be given that. If he gets tripped up . . .'

'His face lands int' clap! Like thine, lad! I propose we end this
meetin', Mr Chairman, t' business being finished.'

'No!' Seth exclaimed. 'I mean, with your permission. Let me
bring forward me point. I must bring it forward, Mr Chairman.'

'Well sharpen it a bit.'

'Two more minutes then, Seth,' said the chairman, severely
looking at his watch. Then he nodded to Seth more kindly. 'Give
the lad a chance, everybody. He's got something on his chest –
let him get it out – we don't want him to throttle hissel.'

'Thank you, Mr Chairman. Yes. Well? What d'you say? I
propose that we *make* everybody come into this union as'll stand
to benefit from it. And if they refuse – now listen – I propose
we refuse to work with them. Don't work with non-union
members.'

'Don't be daft, Seth. It's a free country.'

'No – it isn't. That's exactly the basis of your mistake. If it
was a free country – then we would be free to get what we
want. And we can't. So there's your answer on that argument.
But – listen! – we should not allow men who are not with us all
the way to be down there working. Because they're working
for the other side. Every man that isn't in the Union is for the
masters. That's it! Every man that isn't in the Union is against
it. And they know, they work on it – whoever heard of a Union
man, a man on this platform, gettin' any easy seam? Answer me
that! It's bluddy Ted Blacklock and his marrers walk off down
that road. And for why? Because the company favours them –
because it doesn't fear them.'

'And they're frightened of thee, Seth, are they?'

'No – well yes! Don't laugh. Yes! They are. Not of me – on
me own – no, not of me. But of what this Union might grow to.
They give in, they give in – but they give little away. We won't
get anywhere until we smash them! And to do that – every man
Jack of us must be in the Union. And women, I would have the
women in so that they could draw the benefits – and I would
have the children in, the day they're born – so that ivverybody's

in the Union so that we can take all over – education we can tek over, governing and workin'. I would do away with all companies – parliament – everything – only the Union that is democratically elected by the men on the spot should run things.' He had held his audience when talking about bringing all men into the Union, held them despite the laughter, the chaffing which chapped John's nerve-ends, for it was something with which not a few of them were privately in agreement. But even this small current of sympathy had overcharged Seth and now he lost them all as his voice heightened its pitch, the sweat broke on his brow and he stood, hands clenching and unclenching, tugging at the white cuffs which hung from the short sleeves of his suit. 'There should be *nothing* but Unions,' he said. 'For men can see what they get then – they can see who rules them – and nobody rules them because they rule themselves! The Union would organise the business – maybe not us are clever enough, but we can mek sure our next lot are – and from the cot to the cemetery a man – or a woman, because they're more of slaves than we are – well – listen! – they could carry their heads high – one more minute, Mr Chairman – there would be no injustices and no accidents, there would be no dying of want and no neglect or poor people – and the Unions would care for men's minds because they would *know*. The men would – what a terrible thing it is to have a stunted mind, more terrible than many a bodily affliction – yes! – the Unions alone, on their own, only them, the Unions should take over this country and lead it out to a better place.'

'There's a better place in that bar next door.'

'Propose we close, Mr Chairman.'

'Seconded.'

'Passed. Word of Next Meeting will be circulated.'

'Meeting over.'

The men got up and moved out, taking no more notice of Seth than if he had been a post. He sat there, flushed now, tense on his chair, sitting after the others had started to move, still bound to the words he had so painfully let go. Unoffended by the brutal cutting-off – the bruises which would rise later and be poked and further inflamed by him in the solitude of his lodgings – now a man rapt in a vision. And John, too, did not move, his face riveted to that of his brother, love going out to him in waves which broke before Seth's wall of conviction. My God he was a brave man, John thought, and he was right, right! But why, looking at him, did such a cold sorrow run through him like a deep undercurrent pulling below the warm waves, why did his love chill to such despair at that rigid sight? As all his loves froze now when greatest demands were made: the responses left on the other side of that death-trance in the squatter's cottage.

The room quickly emptied, he walked down to Seth and touched him on the arm.

'That was a good speech, Seth,' he said. 'A real 'un.'

'Yes?' Seth stood up, jerked to life. 'But I think I talked too much.' He smiled. 'You liked it, did you?' He paused. 'I meant it. It's true what I say.'

He walked to the side of the platform and came carefully down the three steps.

'Give us a hand to clear these benches away, will you?' he asked.

FIFTEEN

Sarah had been staying with them for almost a year when they went to the sea-side on a Bank Holiday.

St Bees was only a few miles from the town and in summer Telford's horse-drawn coaches ran a regular service there. It was a fine, clear day, fresh but not cold, and there were a fair number at the beach. Emily found a good spot. To her right was the cliff called St Bees' Head riding out into the Solway like the prow of a ship, fields streaming back from its very edge, full green sail. Behind her were the narrow, steep streets of the village, the public school which was quartered on the lush spread which ran back from the bay, as protected as the pheasant which Kipling mourned as being the 'Lord of Many a Shire'. To her left, the south, more cliffs, lower than the Head, with houses sheltered in the creeks before the land swung out once more to sea and made perfect the arc. And before her the level water, rolling in calmly under the windless air, merely washing the pebbles. She felt completely refreshed, her sensations filled from such a deep spring of tranquil solitude as made her relax entirely, the sound of the sea as a soft choir to her pulse.

Sarah drifted off towards the village on the excuse of looking for sweets for the children. Most reluctantly, she took Veronica with her. On several occasions she had announced that she would leave, could leave, should leave them on their own, that Veronica and herself were a burden, a nuisance, a pest.

'But where would I go?' She would invariably conclude. 'Just look at my skin! It must be the stink that comes off those slag heaps; or our John. Who would have a woman with a skin like that? Besides I'm useful, aren't I, Emily? Who did the shopping this afternoon? Who trailed down to the market? And I don't eat so much, not more than anybody else, do I? So I'll stay – I know you don't mind.'

Seth had offered to take his sister in with him – been eager for it, saying that a woman and child would make his lodgings something of a home: but Sarah had paid one visit only.

'Live in that place! You couldn't want to put me there, John. And that chair still sat there – and knowing Uncle Ephraim used to sit on it. I told Seth to throw it out. It's an awful place! No wonder Emily would never go. And there's nothing but boys and old men around. I know what would happen. Soft-hearted old me would be cookin' and washin' for the blooming lot of them with Seth saying it was all part of the benefits of the Union. No, thank you very much. He can find his own woman.'

The question of compelling her to leave – in some unhurtful way – had arisen many times in whispered agitation between John and Emily, the last to be downstairs, hearing Sarah above them land on her bed as decisively as a bag of coals on a pavement.

'But you can't put your own flesh and blood out on the streets,' said Emily.

'It's nobbut by a short head that me own flesh and blud aren't *walkin'* the bluddy streets. Don't start back – thou knows my meaning plain.'

'Well, she's a good-lookin' young woman,' Emily replied. 'You can't expect her just to park herself indoors, waiting to be asked.'

'Can't I? Might be better if she did. She terrifies half o' them and t' other half comes wid their tongues out.'

'John!'

'It's true! Now Alf Toppin's a canny lad – she put the fear of God intil 'im. He couldn't walk down a street where she was widdout flickerin' on and off. Like a lighthouse. Yes – No – Yes – No – I will – I won't – she does – she doesn't – at her – back up – I can – I can't – thou could see fowks crashing intil each other all over Lowther Street. He confused the multitudes. An' then Arnold Blacklock comes up – brass wouldn't be outdone on *that* mug – up comes the bold Arnold and remember how *that* turned out! I nevver thowt I'd fight for any woman but thee –

but it was that or be taken ower. And him wid' five children – five credited.'

'She's lively though,' said Emily, loyally. 'Good company.'

'Well if thou's prepared to put up wid' it – that's it! The lass has to live somewhere.'

'Yes,' Emily replied, sadly realising that her regard for that fact would force her to continue to tolerate a situation which often appeared intolerable. She could dull her ears to Sarah's occasional dirges, she *did* enjoy the girl's chatter – was shocked but not outraged at the way in which she chased men and was a woman fully capable of dealing with the gossip that sprouted up around her husband's sister – but the life of her own family was intruded on, trampled over, it seemed, by the restless paces of the younger woman. She was afraid, above all, for John who was mute before her, his outbursts absorbed in polite silences. She had feared the quick rut of his bad moods when they were first married; but now she wished them back, for at least there had always been a return, whereas here she saw a slow freezing, in himself, of himself from her, from everyone; their love was now a grey, protective canopy, hardly noticed from one week to the other.

She sat among the bags and watched him with the children. The beach was stony at its edges but further out long flats of sand were left by the sea. The tide had just turned and would take some hours to reach her. With Alice on his back, May trailing behind him, dragging a stick across the unscratched sand, Harry trotting and splashing through the small puddles, they were making for the fringes of the sea. John had made no concession to the conditions, and his boots, his cap, his heavy flapping jacket all marked him out as a miner – and she could see his like scattered along the shore, a dark company of regulars, resting for a day. She watched his walk, steady and easy, Alice no more than a feather on his back – and he stopped to pick up Harry, carrying both children, the same pace. At that moment she loved him and wanted to shout out, to have him turn and come to her in that way, with that walk. It seemed that the children would claim all that she loved in him – or all the love he could give – she could see it in his stride. As she had done in the churchyard on her last visit to Ephraim's grave, she noted them, concentrating to remember every detail she could pick out, John and her children going over the flat sand towards the ebbing sea. He was too far away to hear her shout.

As always, John had started off with the children full of what they would do together. When the impulse came to him he delighted in the children, they were then like precious memories of his own childhood and every sound and movement they made intoxicated him – just as another twink could see him morose and indifferent to them, even savage. What discouraged him, however, was his response when given a perfect day such as this: then, with all to expect, he could perform so little. He would begin by being determined to enjoy the time with them, almost snatch them to him and run to beat the day: then, by irresistible degrees, an inexplicable paralysis of interest would seize his enjoyment, stiffen his enthusiasm to a drilled series of reactions less and less controlled until he either collapsed into himself in self-disgust or wrenched himself away, abandoned them.

This day, he had tried to forestall it by inviting Seth to come along with them – the two men easily able to form a small republic fit to withstand any number of women and children.

'No. I'm gonna slam through this lot!' Seth had replied, indicating a large volume, a new one, as fresh in the middle of his brown table as a new-laid egg. 'There's not enough of us at it,' Seth continued, 'and I reckon I'm in a better position than most – having no family – to read. If I get a good run up of a morning, I can nearly always break a good bit of it down before night. Mind,' he winked at John, 'I'm no great athlete, I tell thee.' He rubbed his hands, 'there'll be some jaw-crackers and eye-bogglers in that – I'll bet. Oh, it'll be a reet do. If thou comes past here midday thou'll probably hear it – that'll be me, talking it out aloud to frighten it. No,' he added, sinking as suddenly from this rare pinnacle of frivolity as he had risen to it, 'no, I've promised myself a day like this for a long time. And there's no Union matters to attend to, nothing but folk rushin' off to enjoy thersels – and so they should. I'm all in favour, and many *more* like days say I – so I'll get crackin'! See John,' he concluded, a little sadly, 'when you know what's in these books – folk give you respect. They listen to you – See?'

John had not the heart to persist in persuasion.

Before reaching the sea he had decided what to do. He would not stand and listlessly let them play around him but keep moving. Feeling a little ridiculous at the pressure of determination necessary to cope with three children so much in awe of the sea that the lightest touch would have kept them spinning with delight all morning, he ran the last way across the sand, the two held children joggling about him like army packs and, having set them down, he took off his boots and socks.

'Tek your shoes off!' he commanded. 'May, come away from it wid' those shoes. Your mother'll kill me if they're ruined. Tek them off. We're gonna paddle.'

'Can I swim, dad?' May asked.

'Thou's no bathing suit. Anyway – it's ower dangerous for swimmin'. Swim in a beck if thou must. Not here.'

'But I don't need a bathin' suit. Jessie Collins swims in her knickers.'

'Dis she?'

'Yes.'

'Well, see how't paddlin' goes. But Aa'm no great swimmer, lass. Thou'll be on thee own.'

'Thou means, thou can't save me if I drown?' the little girl asked.

'That's correct.'

'Well, maybe I'll swim just at' edge. Where it's shaller.'

'Git them shoes off!'

Alice was too small to be left for long and soon John was holding her again, wading through the shallows, feeling his toes spread over the sand, the spray fleck his white skin. Like May, she had been little 'trouble' – to himself, that is, meaning that he had not been woken up more than a few times, could manage her quite easily – but she was much prettier than May. Harry had been a bloody nuisance: in the first year he had cried almost every night – until John had been forced to go into the other bedroom: it was that or collapse at work. And for the first time, he had seen Emily beaten by one of the children: she had carried little milk and after a few weeks the feeding was torture to her. There was a woman a few doors away who had given the child milk but always he wanted more, his mouth strained open like a ravenous chick, head leaping forward from the neck to clench the gums on the teats. It was only then that John began to compare his wife's lot to his own. She had a hard life, yes. But so did he, and that made it even. It was not a matter of discussion, but something accepted by both of them. Moreover, Emily would have been in no way able to provide for herself and the children without him. Yet with Harry, when he had come home to find Emily making his tea, the boy on her arm, her action the flakings of energy, her body moving with such dilatory fragility as threatened to stop and sink to liquid, so insubstantial was it – then he had been shocked to realise that she had a world more slavish and demanding than he could have endured. It was this, too, which had led him to the act – rare among those he worked with – of taking the children off her; his principal satisfaction was always, as now, to look back and see Emily alone – for then, he thought, she must be relieved and happy.

Afraid of drowning, May did no more than paddle – Harry was soon sitting scraping out the sand and making a castle. John walked backwards and forwards, offering Alice to the waves it seemed. He offered little else. Perhaps the knowledge that this sea pressed down on him when he was working beneath it made him restless: whatever it was, he was soon bored and he felt a darkness, seeping in like the sea, coming from nowhere this fine day, but irresistibly settling on him as it had done in the cottage.

'We'll go and see if we can ratch out some bird nests,' he said, abruptly.

'Come on. Here. Dry your feet on my jacket.'

He went away from St Bees' Head to the lower cliffs at the southern edge of the small bay, waving to Emily and, with the return of the wave, getting an injection of enthusiasm which led him to organise a race – sending Harry and May well out in front before he himself began to run. Alice screaming with pleasure in his arms so that he laughed aloud and kissed her as he ran, the large boots thudding such footprints into the sand as looked indelible.

Emily had hoped they would come back to her – but when she saw May and Harry run away in front of their father, she let them alone, deciding against going after them. She knew that John wanted to have them for himself sometimes.

A wind came up with the tide and it was too fresh just to sit. Sarah had not yet come back from the village but Emily had no hesitation at leaving the bags and coats unguarded. The red sandstone cliff of the head drew her towards it and she walked towards boys playing among the rock-pools, past women like herself planted in the middle of their family's stores, the sea's edge dared by a few paddlers, only one man swimming, a game of football starting up.

Mr Stephens was returning to his bicycle to get some drawing paper from the bag. This bag sat most impressively on the back mudguard. He had fitted it out himself and it was so built that two dozen eggs could be carried in it without any fear of their being broken. When the breeding season passed, he took out the frame and inserted a minute system of drawers for his paper, his chalk, pencils, rulers and the new geometry set. His 'book of the moment' would fit in there too, still leaving room for the french chalk and glue, the scissors and the patches. His sandwiches and flask of lemonade were in a small pack which he carried on his back. Dressed in stout tweed suit, with his mackintosh strapped on to his handlebars, he was then ready to meet any day.

Emily recognised him but was too shy to approach him. So much so that she was tempted to turn around and be off to prevent any possible embarrassment that might come to him as a result of having to engage himself in the act of remembering – and perhaps pursuing – that encounter they had had when he had given her shelter at Cockermouth Hiring. Though he did not at first recognise her, Mr Stephens was very conscious that a woman was about to pass near him. Still unmarried, that last ten years had encrusted him with bachelor habits which his hobby had greatly encouraged. He was too old now for that willing flirtation into which he had been prepared to enter with any girl – and too young to regard himself as irrevocably single; too aware of his feelings to regard himself as a misogynist, too

cautious before their implications to permit himself to trust in
them. Marriage was his dream and as yet he was still able to
regard it as a happy perfection – no less would do – which one
day would slip on to him as neatly as his coat.

The path at the cliff-foot was narrow and he stood aside to
let her pass. She looked away from him – but the definite
impression of that action caused him to look at her more closely.
Then he turned away, afraid to be caught staring. Emily was
within a yard of him and had to glance up in order that she might
indicate to him that he must step to one side for her to pass –
and she was glad to see the evidence of remembering in the
concentration on his half-averted face. Aware of the necessity
for his small retreat, Mr Stephens turned to her, thus using the
excuse of courtesy as a stalking-horse for his gathering curiosity.
The nod which she returned to him for his well-mannered
stepping back contained a confidence to which the formal and
inconsequential nature of this small passage lent no intimacy:
his returned inclination was thus the more vigorous – acknow-
ledging, too, that there was more cause than common politeness
for them to greet each other. Yet the very vigour of his bobbing
head was an unsuccessful joggling of his mind to unloosen the
cause. Passing by him, Emily was amused and she smiled; but
she was relieved, now, that she would avoid an embarrassing
exchange and this forbade her eyes to light at the signal from
her mouth. Stephens sighed, too slight a sigh for anything but
the incident just concluded, reaching Emily's ears like a plea for
more time – as it was meant to – and causing her to hesitate for
a moment, wishing that she could throw off the wrappings of
this prohibitive sensibility and straightforwardly address him.

'Tallentire!' he said. 'Mrs Tallentire!'

Beaming with pleasure, Emily turned and bowed, slightly but
so easily inclining from her waist as made her appear much
younger than she was. Mr Stephens clutched off his hat and
held out his hand.

'Robert Stephens. You – we met at Cockermouth – oh, ten,
twelve years ago.'

Slowly her hand went out to his, she watched it rise before
her, saw it coarse in his slim white fingers.

'My sketching paper got wet,' he said. 'Silly of me. I dropped it in a puddle. But I always bring a spare block. How's your husband?'

'Very well, thank you.' Her hand slid out of his, no pressure having been applied by him or her. 'He's over there with the children.'

'Children! O yes – you were – children, eh? Deary me.'

'It was May I was carrying then,' she said.

'And how many more?'

She paused. 'Two more, Harry and Alice.'

'Goodness,' he replied. 'Well. I've often thought about you.'

'You were very kind to us.'

'Oh – no, no. No, no, not at all. Often – thought about you. You were such a – how can I say it? – you were such a – a handsome young couple: so lively,' he said, rather forlornly. Then, 'Of course, you still are – as you were – I should have recognised you immediately. But I get so absorbed – there were some shovellers I was trying to get down, and then I saw a redshank – even more unusual around here, you know, must be the weather. And I couldn't decide which to do. That was when I dropped my pad. Still on farm-work, your husband – Joseph, that's it! I've been trying to remember his name – Joseph.'

'John. No, he's in the pits now.'

'John. Yes. In the pits eh? Well,' Mr Stephens looked out to sea, 'the conditions are improving I'm told.'

'They won't be improved until they shut down the mines altogether,' Emily returned, calmly.

'I see – Yes – Well, we must burn wood. Except there are so few trees now. I'm sure that's one of the reasons the fowl-mart has disappeared.'

'Has it?'

'H'm? Yes – it has. And the short-eared owl's becoming rarer now. They think birds can sit on stones, you know. Well so they can – you'll find thousands of herring-gulls nestling on these rocks in season you know: but it would be a dull world with only herring-gulls to look at, wouldn't it?'

'Yes,' Emily replied with great gravity, hoping that she would thus conceal the giggle, which ran up her stomach as rapidly as a lizard. 'Yes, it would.'

'It would. It would. They never think about what they've got – always wanting more. And they frighten away all the delicate things of the moment. True, Mrs Tallentire, true. Have you seen the golden plover?'

'No.'

'There you are. You should have done. They're frightening him away. Sometimes I think the world's going mad, Mrs Tallentire. It breaks irreplaceable things so carelessly.' He smiled. 'You can tell I'm still a schoolmaster, can't you?'

'Oh . . . where do you teach now?'

'Maryport – ugly place – full of miners – not, of course, I mean – the cottages they have to live in – they *are* ugly, aren't they?' The wistful end of the sentence truly craved an apology.

'They're better than some places,' Emily replied, briskly.

'O yes. Everywhere's better than *some* place – isn't it? I mean – the world's a circle. Never ending.'

'That's something to be *thank*ful for, isn't it?' asked Emily, not at all confident before this method of talking but happy to keep going, having observed that the man had ducked so determinedly into his hobby out of shyness and been more than willing to caricature himself through fear of becoming over-intrusive. She liked him.

'Yes, yes I suppose it is. Maybe this is another period when things become extinct – and somewhere others are growing or changing to take their place.' He smiled. 'Maybe *we'll* become extinct, eh, Mrs Tallentire?'

'Good gracious, Mr Stephens. Why should we?'

'True. True.' He paused. 'But if things keep changing at this rate – we'll soon have nothing left to invent.'

'We can sit back then,' she laughed.

'Yes. Sit back. Yes.' He paused. 'I'm going that way,' he continued, nodding in the direction behind her. 'Would you – I suppose you want to be alone.'

'No. I'll be pleased to walk with you, Mr Stephens.'

'Will you? That's very kind. I'll just get my pad – this one's ruined I'm afraid.' He laughed at her, 'Though I could always use it for *water-colours*, I suppose.' His smile stopped on his face, waiting for the response to his little joke. When it politely came, on went the smile, thankfully.

When she thought back on those next two or three hours it would amuse her to imagine them as a flight. For, once on the trail, with gulls and waders and peregrines to point out, Mr Stephens' confidence was restored, and from being restored, it leapt to action. He was gallant and considerate helping her across the rock-pools, taking her by the easiest routes – and soon he began to abandon his dependence on birds and chat to her in a way which freshened her thoughts. Yes, she wondered what it would be like to be married to such a steady, gentle man: not that John was other than steady in his ways, not that he could not be gentle – the defences went up like a drawbridge – but John's steadiness was all in his turning over the weekly money – that done he would allow himself any extremity of mood before her, or merely subdue her by that awful indifference to what was around him. While Mr Stephens, she thought, would be steadily curious in the world around him, not forcibly questioning it as did Seth but ceaselessly prodding this fact, that object, something in him that would spin out a lifetime. And then, because he talked to her so, she relaxed and lost that strain she so often had before John – before most of the men who had ever come to the house with him – when the silences would be stretched by contradictory interpretations until it was rent by temper. Talk made Mr Stephens more open, he was not afraid to remark on his attitude towards anything – and even in that short time, she found herself able to redefine her own feelings because of his statements about his own, whereas with John, things were defined in disruption or left unspoken, so potently unopened that they sank below the soil of the mind to fester and fructify there, hidden.

This flight, then, so unexpectedly come upon, forgot her worries – and when John – trailing the children, discovered her she was sitting on a rock, her bare feet splashing in a pool looking over Mr Stephens' shoulder as he sat beside her, sketching.

'What the hell are you doin' here?'

'This is Mr Stephens, John,' Emily replied, immediately.

'I don't care if . . .' then John saw the disturbance on the mild face which turned to his and stoppered his outburst abruptly. 'Alice was mopin',' he said.

'Oh – poor thing. Here. Let me take her.' She came across, her feet lifting wincingly at each step.

'They're so tickly these rocks.'

'Thou should keep shoes on.'

'Yes. There we are. Poor lovely. Did she think mammy had run away?'

'She did!'

'Mr *Stephens*, John,' Emily whispered, 'Cockermouth.'

'Oh!' John looked at the figure scrambling upright, with legitimate intentness, relief coming with the recognition. 'I didn't recognise you – Mr Stephens! How are you then?' – the words were shouted across the short space; perhaps the sea encouraged such volume.

'Oh – very well, Mr Tallentire. Very well indeed.' The hand came tumbling over. 'Thank you. It's so very easy to slip on those rocks. Yes. Deary me. Cockermouth. I hope you haven't been anxious about your wife, Mr Tallentire – I should have thought to tell her the time but you see when I'm sketching . . . you must have been very anxious.'

'Not a bit, Mr Stephens! Glad to see you – keeping well are you?'

'Yes. Thank you. Very. I was telling Mrs Tallentire that the black-headed gulls are more numerous this year than I've ever seen them.'

John looked up – and in doing so caught the wink in Emily's eyes – she alone had observed his slipping from forced to spontaneous speech, as the break on a wave, which could not be wholly successfully withheld – and she knew that if she could catch him in this way it would flick him back to her as neatly as could be. It worked, he returned her wink. If only she could have told him how that simple reaction penetrated her more deeply than any thousand hours with Mr Stephens.

'More gulls, eh?' said John. 'Well they must be finding this territory good for breeding, eh, Mr Stephens?'

'Quite so,' replied the schoolmaster realising that, whatever the danger he had so clearly felt, it was now past. 'It's the salmon boats, you see. Well, all the boats. D'you know, there are about three hundred along this coast now. All from Cumbrian ports. Of course, the bye-laws are very good – but even so, it's too many boats, I think. I have a friend who tells me that they've cleaned the herring out entirely.'

'Have they now?'

'O yes. Scuppered him – if I may use the word. But of course, the boats are useful for the gulls.'

'It's like that song – Ilkley Moor baat 'at, Mr Stephens. You know – t'worms eats t'man and t'birds eats t'worms and we eat t'birds so we eat t'man.'

'I know the song, yes. *Ducks* eat the worms. *Ducks*. Yes. It's very popular in Yorkshire.'

And again Emily wondered at Mr Stephens – that he could be so nervous in front of people as to shy away into part of himself that had been almost entirely absent while they had talked together, him drawing, she dabbling her feet in the water, on the rock.

'Mr Stephens – would you like to come and have your tea with us?' she asked. 'We have plenty.'

'Well – I do bring my – it's very kind of you – but, well . . .'

'Come away, Mr Stephens!' said John, encouragingly. 'Thou's most welcome.'

'Thank you, I *will* come.'

He let May wheel his bicycle and Harry held his hand.

Sarah had got to the provisions first and shook hands with Mr Stephens after a most energetic gobbling of the sandwich and dusting of her palms on her skirt. Soon, she was comfortably settled.

'Don't you find it funny – living on your own?' she asked him.

'It is a little,' he admitted, again relaxing now that he had cleared the introductory hurdle – and innocently finding in Sarah's directness the possibility of airing questions about his bachelor state in a much more serious and satisfactory way than usual. 'Yes. I suppose you would call it unnatural.'

'*I* would,' said Sarah, stretching out her legs, the skirt hem flapping prettily over the small boots, propping herself up on her elbows. *'Most* unnatural,' she added – and laughed.

'Yes. And laughable, too. You know, sometimes I think that I was made to be a bachelor.'

'No man is,' she retorted.

'Exactly. That's always my conclusion. Still,' he went on, 'there's nothing much I can do about it at the moment.'

'Isn't there now?' asked Sarah, thoughtfully.

'Have another sandwich,' said Emily.

'Don't you have even a housekeeper?' Sarah asked. 'Surely you could afford one.'

'Yes. I suppose I could. Well – I certainly could. But – well, I like to think that the first woman in my house will be my wife.'

'That's nice,' said Emily.

'It's *right,*' Sarah countered, as if the distinction were a correction. 'I've known men who never got past housekeepers and ended up by marryin' them – or just pretending you know. There should be wives in there.'

'Thou's wise to tek time,' said John. 'Tek all the time there is.'

'John Tallentire?'

'Yes,' smiled Mr Stephens. 'You're a bad disciple of your own teaching.'

'Well – mebbe for me it was different.'

'Yes.'

'It's the same for everybody,' said Sarah. 'They should do it just as soon as they can. Get on with it.'

'I agree,' said the schoolmaster.

'Do you ever come to Whitehaven of a market day?' Sarah enquired, lazily.

'No. I'm teaching.'

'They have a small market on Saturdays as well.'

'Do they? Of course they do. I know they do.'

'It's very interesting,' said Sarah.

'It's exactly like any other market,' said Emily, 'and possibly no better than Maryport's.'

'Maryport's!' Sarah exclaimed. 'If he's been no further than

*Mary*port market then he *must* come to Whitehaven of a Saturday afternoon. Maryport's nothing!'

'Well. I might try it.'

'You do.'

John had the greatest difficulty in keeping a straight face before Sarah's relentless incitements and when she added, 'There's ducks and pigeons and geese and aa' that sort of thing there – dead, mind, but there again, it'll give you a better chance to draw them. All that at Whitehaven market!' then he rolled over and picked up Harry to chuck him in the air and have an excuse for laughing.

When Mr Stephens left pushing his bicycle over the grass to the track, waving to them and quite moved that May came to escort him – he gave her threepence – then John was even more entertained at Sarah's defence before Emily.

'What you mean "poor man"?' she demanded. 'He's better off than our John for a start. And he's old enough, isn't he? I thought he was *very* pleasant, anyway – and anybody could see he just needs a bit of encouragement to open him out. I bet he's a different man altogether when he's opened out. Anyway – you could tell he liked me to talk to him – anybody could – and it's a good job I was here or he would have felt out of it. He liked Veronica as well.'

'He never *said* anything to Veronica.'

'But a mother can tell, Emily, a mother can tell these things.'

(When Sarah did leave them it was not with Mr Stephens – never seen at Whitehaven market – nor anyone prepared for or considered but one who, like the first, came and took her, accepting the baby as casually as he expected Sarah to follow him back to the town he came from. Which she did, leaving as suddenly as she had arrived. Emily was convinced that, had she been accidentally out when Sarah had danced in to collect her clothes and her child, then she would never have discovered what had happened to her.)

That afternoon, however, Sarah brooded on Mr Stephens. Because she recognised that her resentment was caused by just a little jealousy, Emily was more openly affectionate with John than usual. And as they left the beach and walked slowly over to the coach stop, the freshness of the day's sea air seemed to mature on them, and the slowness of the children's steps spoke of a richness of running and seeing which nourished the parents with the knowledge that the day had been well spent. Emily heard her skirt trail on the grass behind her and she wished it could always be so, it was like the sound of the waves. A wind blew in from the sea and she snuggled more closely up to John.

Three children. John steady now in the pits, all silly hopes and uncertainties irrelevant now to the life that was set plain before her.

John was thankful that he had not lost his temper too often or too badly with the children. The thought of being home soon, the children abed, Emily with some work of her own to do, himself away, maybe for a drink, maybe to the allotment – would make it easy to be pleasant enough on the way back. It was impossible to live without Emily and his family: yet to live with them was almost unendurable.

But were these the only thoughts he was to have? This, his life, now settled on this plot, pit-cottage, an outing to some predictable place; was this all? So it was. So, in the beginning; no, it was the same then. But despair came over him when he contemplated such a life. It should have been enough – but it was so much less than enough, he thought. Day by day all he saw was what he threw in his own face, and it blinded him to what could be seen. And before vision went altogether, he wanted to see, he wanted to reach out, and perhaps to touch it with his hands.

SIXTEEN

He read the notice for the third time.

THE WHITEHAVEN CAB & GENERAL POSTING CO. LTD.
COACH BUILDERS, CARRIAGE PROPRIETORS & CARTERS
REGISTERED OFFICE, TANGIER STREET

These stables are occupied by a large stud of well-seasoned,
thoroughly reliable horses which places them in a
position for supplying on hire at the shortest notice –
Landaus, Broughams, Phaetons, Dogcarts and Wagonettes
of every description. Hearses and Funeral coaches:
Funerals furnished in the most modern style.

'No sudden bereavement, I trust,' loaded with anticipation
and coated with self-congratulatory politeness – the cleanness
of accent being a matter of great pride – the words came from
a small, well-dressed old man who had approached John from
the other side of the market and stood behind him biding his
time.

'Mr Errington!' John took the offered hand. 'Well. What's thou
doin' here?'

'The market,' said Errington succinctly, and coughed. 'No
. . . bereavement – then?' he repeated.

'Oh – no. Nothin' o' that.'

'Ah well,' said the old man. 'At least you'll know where to
come.'

'Yes. Still as cheerful, eh?'

'Now. Don't mock, John. As a man grows older his mind
begins to dwell on his funeral. I saw one in Wigton last week –
and, do you know, they couldn't even manage matching horses!
It looked badly.'

'I don't expect t' corpse complained.'

'It was Mr J. T. Ritson. A very respectable fella. I felt embarrassed for him.'

'Well, thou's'll hev to coom here to be buried then.'

'Who said anything about being buried? I'm still fit enough for a man ten years younger than me.'

'Yes. Thou's taken good care, Mr Errington.'

'I have. And I intend to continue in that direction.'

'What's'te think of our market then?'

'Fair to middlin'. I'm glad I came – but I think I'll skip it next time. Your wife's mother's only poorly, you know.'

'Yes. I do know.'

'And George Johnston died last week – did you know that?'

'No.'

'Robert Fell the week before.'

'Yes?'

'Mary Jane Wallace just before him.'

'Ay?'

'Freeman Robinson isn't lookin' good.'

'He nivver did.'

'Well he's worse since his brother died. That was George.'

'It was.'

'And old Frank Hewer fell down a ladder – broke his back: very bad.'

'Sounds like an epidemic round Wigton way, Mr Errington. Thou'd better clear out.'

'All me fields is let,' said the old man, testily.

'I see.'

'Well – you can catch a cold if you stand about. That sea's all very well but it shouldn't be allowed to play on the chest.'

'No.'

'Good day then.'

'Look after yourself, Mr Errington.'

A needless warning. The old man wrapped his coat collar around his throat and battled through the warm spring air. No jokes now; John remembered that the old man had once delivered 'witticisms' and riddles as readily as some men give away sweets: he regretted his flippancy, but not enough to pursue his former neighbour through the market. Still, he thought, as long as Errington was getting around the markets there could not be a great deal wrong with him.

He himself had come this holiday morning to buy some brass studs for a small stool he had almost finished. They had been quickly got, but he had made no immediate rush to be away, preferring to dawdle around the stalls, masking his aimlessness and the femininity of the action by a small furrow on his brow which was to serve as evidence of an instantly justifiable search.

There was only enough money in his pocket to buy a couple of drinks. This was no cause of concern. Indeed, John and Emily had considered themselves decidedly well off since his work in the pit. They took no holidays beyond the very occasional day-trip to the sea. The house, once furnished, stayed as it was with Emily quite capable of replenishing knick-knacks, repapering the walls, replacing whatever was broken out of her savings from the housekeeping. John had one good suit. He was not much of a betting man just as she was not concerned to be flatteringly represented by her children's appearance: shoes were a problem but with care on her part and a few extra shifts on his, most of the children could be satisfactorily fitted out at Easter. Though to many their income would have seemed incredibly small, it might be said that they had few financial troubles. All that came in went out and there was sufficient for John to have his few drinks on a Saturday night, for Emily to feel the pleasure of being able to hunt down a small bargain on some Saturday afternoons at the market.

Propping up this attitude was the memory of what things had been like when John had worked as a labourer; though his youth had dissolved any incipient bitterness at the meagreness of the wage yet, looking back, John saw that for Emily those must have been hard times. And for Emily, whose attitude to money had been formed in a labourer's cottage early in life, the terms 'poverty' or 'subsistence-level life' would have seemed insulting as well as inaccurate. Insulting to those before her who had managed on so much less. Occasionally she had to scrape – and when the big strike had been on a year ago in 1912, she had been forced to cuts and stratagems, to skimping on her own food and regulating the number of slices of bread for the children, selling small treasures and taking the utterly distasteful step of asking for credit – but in normal times she had no complaints. She would have been ashamed to give sentence to them, there, where she daily saw real poverty. Where there were families whose numbers had grown so large that the least break in the man's work would crash them all to Homes and workhouses or near starvation. Where there were men drawing the mean sickness pay, made the more ill by the sight of their deprived families. Old people huddled in the corner of a kitchen on the five weekly shillings of pension. People not quite competent enough to hold on to proper jobs reduced to the scraps of labour which took every hour they had for miser's returns. Though a small town, it was large enough to breed that number, almost caste, of the very poor who swirled sadly and dispiritedly about it like sediment in a bottle. On 'The Tops' where they still lived was many a woman who could not give shoes to her children, and each wife, like Emily, with a man bringing in steady wages, was accustomed to the consistent behests of two or three neighbours; thus, daily, as she lent a sixpence or some bread or a pat of lard or gave away something too small now to fit any of her own children – she knew what the grind of poverty was – and through John's job, she escaped it.

Her escape was his confinement. Sometimes he would be overawed by the obligations which made his work so necessary. On a good day, when he was cheerful, working in the backyard making a rabbit-hutch for Harry – then he would feel as if an oppressive weight had been lifted from him: his cheerfulness now not, as before, coming out of the conditions of his life, but at such times as he could forget them. So far he had been lucky: there had been four bad accidents since he had come on to the coalfield and he had been involved only marginally in one of them: that time a piece of timber had torn across his calf – but he had been off work only two weeks. Otherwise, a ceaseless routine into which, at thirty-three, he felt himself settled for life. Without appeal. Now rummaging around the market to appease indistinct murmurs.

As soon as he noticed Emily, he drew back behind a stall to

watch her unobserved. All the children were with her, including little Sarah, now just old enough to refuse to be carried, but still too small to walk very far. John smiled at the listless and dutiful expression on Harry's face: if there was anything the boy loathed, it was going shopping, preceded as it was by all the brushing and washing which superimposed a plaster-cast cleaner self on him, so tightly fitted that it took even him a good hour to break it all. Now, as the stiff chunks of wet hair broke away from the head at the back and one stocking hung slackly over his boot, he was beginning to win through – but John could appreciate the struggle.

The occasion for their appearance in force was May's return. For two years now she had been the hired lass on a farm – she had not wanted to work in a factory or a shop and Emily had discouraged her from going into service. Her wage was four and six a week, and four shillings of this was sent home; thus, as throughout England, the younger children were fattened by their older brothers and sisters. It did not occur to Emily not to take this money, nor did May think herself in poor circumstances: she knew, moreover, that things had been harder since Sarah's birth and, as she loved the baby as if it had been her own child, the thought of her money going towards her made her positively glad. She walked the four miles home each Sunday afternoon to deliver her wage but had never more than an hour to spend with her family on that day. All the more, then, did she want them to move as a group, herself to be constantly among them when, as now, she had her week's holiday.

It was at this time that Emily would buy her a dress, or a pair of shoes, or whatever necessity was required by the girl. May was uncomfortable that so much money should be spent on her; at the same time, knowing that she herself had earned the money, she was determined to miss no opportunity of having it spent on her: yet that secondary feeling made her miserable. She was foolishly generous, giving effort, time, consideration and such possessions as she had to anyone who asked. Mrs Fenwick, her employer, had merely to nod to a pile of darning in the evening and May would take it up – though she had been up since four-thirty doing hard and heavy work all day. 'May this, May that' – yes she would help lift the potatoes if Mister needed an extra hand, yes she would thin the turnips, as she did nothing with her two free hours on Saturday afternoon – it was too short a time to go home in – and so yes, she would help with the ironing. Even out of those sixpences she kept for herself each week, she would hoard enough to bring back sweets for Harry and Alice, a ribbon for Sarah, a piece of chocolate for her mother.

John watched her, feeling tender towards his first-born. She had never recovered physically from the effect of those few months of his despair: she was a lumpy girl – her hair lustreless, her hands fat-fingered like a man's, she wore spectacles, she slouched as she stood – and yet John's eyes were drawn to hers with a wonder which his other children could not inspire in him. For there was such innocence there as reminded him of Emily when he had first met her: though what in Emily had been open was masked in May; what had flicked the hazel of his wife's eyes with excitement was calm on his daughter's face, the one expression seemingly careless amid abundance, the other often forlorn, set in a sadness; but this could not conceal the similarity. Through a gap in the canvas of the stall's side, he looked long at his daughter.

Emily had put on a little weight after the birth of Sarah, but it suited her, drawing the slim frame more firmly upright, giving a confidence to her walk which made it slightly slower, rid of that hustling scurry which had previously threatened to turn it into a run. She wore a hat and the hair could never be so strictly managed that it failed to loosen a little and sink some way to her shoulders, with the luscious thickness of a swathe.

She bought some thread and a thimble from the stall and turned away. John stepped out and came up to them, swept up Sarah and walked along to the shop.

'We thought we'd get May's dress at Studholme's, this time,' said Emily. 'The one we bought last year at the market wasn't much good, was it, May?'

'It was aa' reet, Mam. Honest it was.'

'You said it split after a week.'

'I mended it.'

'I should think so – but it shouldn't have split after a week.'

'Let's get her a hat, as well,' said John. 'She couldn't have one at Easter. Have one now, May.'

'I divvn't like them.' May blushed with the effort of denying her father's wish. Impassioned to further defence by a complete understanding of the love and favour which the suggestion contained, she was impelled to excuse herself fully. 'I look like a silly calf in hats.'

'Thou's look pretty,' said John.

'Nivver that,' May murmured. Then, 'Mam – I can easily do widdout a dress.'

'So we can go home,' said Harry. Adding, 'See, Mam. We needn't 'ave come.'

'You need a frock for summer and that's that.'

John pulled at face at May to excuse her mother's authority and went into Studholme's with them.

'Please go away, Dad,' May implored him.

'No, lass. Aa'd like to see the fit-up. Aa can't bide to be wid' yer mother when she's shoppin' – but Aa'd like to see thee set.'

'If Dad stops, I'm not goanna hev one,' May said, miserably.

'See, Mam,' repeated Harry. 'We needn't 'ave come.'

'Now don't be silly, May. He wants to make sure you'll look nice.'

'I can't git one wid' *him* there, Mam. I just can't!'

'Thou's a simple maid,' said John, affectionately moving over to hold her shoulders.

'I am.' May was but a touch from tears. 'I'm very simple, Dad – so please go. Oh – let's all go, Mam. Please.'

'See, Mam,' said Harry. 'We needn't be here.'

As they stood just inside the door with the deep bay of the shop running into twilight, long counters meeting in eternity, a host of assistants hovering, pale in front of the darkly papered walls, they made up an obstructive gaggle, now teasing, now pleading with May, until the shop-manager set off from his control seat deep beyond the children's wear, and bore down upon them, boring his way through the damp air by the propeller action of rapidly dry-washing hands.

Sarah cried and Emily sent John off with the baby – allowing

Harry to slip out and join them while she stayed with the two girls to meet the last push of the manager.

'We want a summer frock for this – young woman here,' said Emily, pleased to have turned it so well that the Manager himself was thus obliged to conduct them to the frock counter.

John went home and deposited Sarah with a neighbour before going over to his allotment. Harry had raced ahead of him, changed back into his patched playing clothes, and been out of the house long enough to score a goal in the back alley before his father's arrival.

The allotment had long been as John wanted it and now he had not much interest in it. On principle he kept it neat, for economy's sake he kept it productive, but it gave him little satisfaction. He would do what he had to do and then walk over to the edge of the cliff, sitting down there to look, as now, at the ships, the collieries, the town in which he had spent more than eight years of his life, feeling in its streets as much underground as he did in the pits which ran from it.

If he could not lift himself from the shadows in which his blankness had left him by dwelling on his memories of the glorious light which had once lit his life, then perhaps more action or even movement would provide a first foothold.

When the children were all in bed that night, he told Emily about the sign he had seen advertising the Whitehaven Cab & General Posting Company.

'I was thinkin' of askin' them if they wanted a driver,' he said.

'Whatever for?' The reaction unnerved him: she ought to have known without words.

'What d'you mean, woman? Because I want a change – that's "whatever for"!'

'Well – you change if you want to. We shall have to get out of this place.'

'That'll be no heartbreak.'

'It's been a good house.'

'We can find one just as good.'

'Just as you please.' She paused. 'When'll you be changing?'

'I haven't said it was certain.'

'No. No you haven't.'

She got up and adjusted his boots inside the fender. They needed no such adjusting.

'You would like to work with horses again, would you?' she asked, softly, though not timidly, as she returned to her chair – purpose achieved in breaking the rise of his temper.

'Mebbe.'

'Well, I'll be glad. Anyway – I never like to think of you way down those pits, under the sea. It's a fearful job.'

'It pays well.'

'I know it does, dear.'

'This would certainly pay less.'

'I expect we'd manage.'

'I expect we would,' he returned glumly. Then, catching the sound of his dismal response, he laughed.

'What would'te think of us then – Eh? Up on a coach – gee up there! Horses peltin' on – ridin' through t' town – or mebbe I'd get a country run – eh? Git along there! O hell – it's be a *change* Emily.'

'Are you sick of the pits?' she asked, laying aside her work to look directly at him for the first time.

'Who isn't?' he answered. 'No more than anybody else, thou knows. But some mornings, when that cage clangs and that bluddy bell rings, and down we go, cramped together like cattle – and I get out to see t' same tunnels goin' on for miles, ready to smother me up, and thousands like me, that pick-axe the only thing that I've got to fight wid – well it makes me feel I might as well drop dead there and then and be finished wid it. Hackin' and squirmin' about – like a mad thing, Emily – pickin' away at that coal – there's nothing gives, nothing. Thou rips it out – and then there's more. There's nothing grows, nothing answers. Emily; a man could *be* his pick – he's worth no more.'

'Well, go and see them in the mornin',' she said.

'I will.' There was some satisfaction in this final agreement. He felt the reins in his hands, the horses breaking into a trot.

The following morning, on his way to the company, he met Seth and was alarmed the way his brother bundled him into a shop-front and stood there, frightened, his large eyes scanning the street ceaselessly.

'Ted Blacklock's got a gang out for me.'

'Where are they?'

'They were standin' outside t' committee rooms but I came out back way.'

'Did they see thee?'

'No. But they won't wait all day. I heard him say he would settle me first and then beat ivverybody else wid his whippet this afternoon. I think they're still drunk from yesterday, John.'

'How come?'

'They were in Larry Allen's 'til five. Blacklock got in a card game wid' this sailor-fella and they wouldn't stop.'

'Let's go to t' docks,' said John. 'Come on – we can move around down there.'

John was upset at his own initial reaction. For he resented his brother's unspoken plea for help and could not stop thinking of the job he had set out to try for. He overcame this by taking his brother into his entire protection: willing him to put himself in his hands.

It was equally useless to go to Seth's lodgings or back to his own house. Later in the morning, John saw Harry and told him to tell Emily that he was with Seth and would be out for most of the day. If anyone came – she could say he had gone off to see the whippets.

The two men dodged about most of the morning. John went into the town at midday to see if the gang were still around – and just escaped observation. Blacklock, taller than most of the miners, was there in the streets with four others, hunting along the pavement like a pack of boys in their gestures, wolves more like in the ferocity of their obvious intention. People stepped into the gutters as they approached and the confidence grew on them as they saw the startling effect they could have without so much as a spoken threat. John stood in an alley on the other side of the street and felt their purpose smack into his face. He let them pass, bought a couple of pies and went back to Seth.

Seth's behaviour had often threatened to get him into trouble. It was a pity that it had to come from such a dangerous man as Blacklock. Soon after the committee meeting which John had attended, Seth had caused a nasty scene by standing at the entrance to the pit urging the miners not to work with Blacklock, who not only refused to join the Union but was totally against it. As a hewer and shift-leader he was doing well out of the present system.

He had not joined the Union then, but soon afterwards, when the opinion of the majority hardened, he did join – and Seth, utterly without vindictiveness, ceased to bother him and was annoyed if anyone reminded him of how he had once publicly denounced the man. He gave it little significance. But Blacklock never forgot it; he boasted of that. Then the Union had moved forward through more strikes towards the big one – and Seth, though he never rose above the level of an ordinary committee man, had more and more work to do, was sought out, even listened to. And in the strike, Blacklock dare not touch him.

Now sufficient time had passed and the span of the grudge had given it the quality of an epic revenge in Blacklock's mind. He was after him.

Though he knew that Blacklock would be out with his whippets in the afternoon, John thought it wiser for them to stay away from the town centre – and he took his brother to the side of a slag heap where they sat and looked down on the rocks.

'They're nothing but drunken savages,' said Seth. 'I should really just walk up to them and tell them what I think.' The tone robbed the words of all confidence.

'Thou couldn't,' John answered. 'They'd kill you.' He paused. 'I wouldn't go up to them on me own neither,' he added.

'Blacklock thinks that if he can intimidate me – then he can intimidate all the committee. He wants to smash the Union – I'm just a start.'

'It's nowt to do wid' t'Union. Better if it was. Blacklock wouldn't dare move against t'Union now. No. It's thee he's after, Seth. And he won't settle 'til he has thee. Now he's started, he won't rest.'

'Well, I can't keep away from him all the time. He'll have forgotten by tomorrow.'

'If he has, there'll always be somebody to remind him.'

'I'm spendin' no more afternoons on a slag heap,' he smiled. 'Let's work it out a bit.'

'There's nothing to work out. He's a stupid, drunken fool, that's that.'

John was silent and sadly he thought of Seth. The violence was all in the words. Even strike action had to be orderly. In his charge for knowledge he ran into the cannon's mouth but he treated his body as if it were of no account. Now, faced with a direct attack on it, he was not so much afraid as helpless. Fighting was not at all uncommon, yet the prospect had caught Seth unaware. As they sat there, John felt for his brother's loneliness. Wished he had provided more of a family for him. The efforts Seth had made had been for them all: all of them now should help him. At least his own family should. This idea of the brothers uniting for Seth appealed to him romantically; a candle to the flame of his own first vision with Emily. Besides, something had to be done; by avoiding them in this way, Seth had done no more than thicken the scent.

'What we do is this,' said John. 'We send to Maryport for our Tom' (another brother, who worked on the docks there), 'we get hold of Isaac. Fred Stainton'll come in wid' us and mebbe that fella sometimes knocks about wid' thee – Harry Barnes. That'll mek about half a dozen. And we meet up wid them and tek them on. There'll be no rest 'til it's out.' He paused. 'And *that's* certain,' he concluded.

Though such a fight seemed futile to Seth, such a cooperative effort appealed to him. And gradually John managed to get it into his head that the alternative was to run away or be badly beaten. Seth was slow to take the full impact of this – blood could not run through the bandages of his ideas. *He* would not have assaulted anyone. John's persuasion was tempered by the melancholy realisation that he was urging his brother to a necessary action which with finer instincts Seth wished to avoid.

In the end, however, it was done, and Seth set off for Maryport to get Tom while John went home to send May for Isaac.

They met the next morning. The four brothers, Fred Stainton and Harry Barnes. John was full of himself. Isaac insisted on sending Harry down to Blacklock's to tell him they were coming. For without due warning they might have caught Blacklock alone and that would be 'poor does', said Isaac. 'We would be stuck then, lads. We couldn't be six to one. Poor does a'together.' The arrangement was that they would meet that afternoon, the last day of this holiday – and fight it out on some waste, the south side of the Docks, hidden from the town by coal heaps, sparkling with minerals streaked under the bright sun.

Blacklock sauntered up with seven men and after an awkward almost shy preliminary few minutes when the damp sea air threatened to fizzle the whole thing out, Isaac demanded whether they were for business or not and this peremptory question from a stranger was sufficient spark to set if off.

As they fought the children who had gathered around them grew in number and men who had vaguely heard of the fight came up to watch. The fighting spread out over the waste down to the rocks beside the calm sea. All the men were strong from the work they did and the number of those involved meant that even if a man was badly knocked down, he could still recover in time to pitch in again. The only sounds were the grunts from the men, the boots on the black rocks, screeching black-headed gulls. It lasted for over an hour and because of Isaac, Seth's side were winning when the crowd suddenly slid away and the men stumbled and scattered along the waste and rocky shore as two policemen pushing their bicycles came from behind one of the heaps to survey the small groups of men walking off. They stayed until the place was cleared.

The fight lost John the opportunity of changing his job, for as he explained to Emily, he could not now leave the pits. It was impossible to think of working anywhere in that town but with those he had fought. That she did not understand his explanation was no cause of wonder to John, who did not understand it himself. But it was much the same as that impulse which forced him to meet up with his brothers soon afterwards and volunteer for the war.

SEVENTEEN

Joseph was born soon after the start of the war. He was the most difficult of the children – worse even than Harry had been, and Emily found that she had not the reserves to cope with him. She was then doubly glad that she had moved from the town to a cottage near John's parents, for her mother-in-law was a good help and would take Sarah off her hands for a whole day. Alice and Harry were at school, May had shifted to be close to her family, near enough to come over on midweek evenings as well as on Sunday afternoons. When May was there she could just about manage Joseph. At other times he was too much for her and she would sit back exhausted on the chair after he had had a feed, with neither the strength to button up her dress nor the energy to whisper protests against his crying. She never forgot those afternoons. As she lay there, she heard her own breath, whimpering in the silent kitchen; and she wondered that it might stop. Then once more Joseph would begin to cry and her face crumpled before this simple assault. Outside was the quiet garden which Harry kept so well for her – already, at twelve, a hard worker. Across a field, for the cottage stood alone, was the house of John's father and mother. Below, on the plain, Wigton, Wiggonby and the places she had grown up in. She should have got protection from all this – yes, May *was* coming that evening, *was* coming, *was* coming – but the baby would not cease its cries and she could not move from the chair to the cradle, there was no strength in her. A particular dab of distemper on the wall would fascinate her and the shape would rivet her eyes so that all in the kitchen led to it, that senseless shape, that meaningless shape, and tears came down her cheeks as she weakly tried to pull her gaze from the shape which was the only hard thing about her, the rest insubstantial as the air which threatened to withhold its benefit from her: she closed her eyes and once more saw the shape printed on the screen of the black lids.

She remembered the long enchainment to her son, Ephraim, and the lock which Jackson's assault on her had put on her emotions; like a magnet this shape of despair drew to it all the filings of unhappiness. May's cold, stunned face when they had settled as squatters in the abandoned cottage. John's impenetrable misery at that time, his face, dead. Images of horror came to her and sucked at her bare breasts, scraped the stretched belly, clawed the slack, lifeless thighs and she could only wait for them to pass for she had no power to make them go. No John to help her, and as Joseph grew and that terrible first year passed, it was on John's absence that she laid the cause of her terror. She heard of other women pining for their husbands and by the line of comparison slowly pulled herself once more above that shiftless fear.

In this situation, May thrived. Her bulk seemed ablaze with premature mothering energy. She could not think of her father at war without tears – yet his absence relieved her of the strain of appearing well before him, which, undertaken as an impossible burden, had oppressed her to a stunted representation of what she might have been. Emily longed to hear her singing as she walked across the fields, marching along, her clogs like army boots – and she loved to see that broad, innocent face beaming in at the window before coming in; immediately to pick up little Joseph. Soon he was called Little Joseph to distinguish him from John's father, who was very pleased at this first repeating of his name among his grandchildren. Emily had done it to please – grateful for the way in which the old man had found her a cottage and helped her to move there.

Joseph was not only pleased at the christening of the last boy, he was delighted that John's family were near him. He had seen his own children scatter away – more often than not blessed by a well-delivered 'good riddance' – and none save Sarah, who, as he told her, he could have done without, had brought their children to him on more than the most perfunctory and fleeting visit. The outbreak of war had changed him. After a drunken evening to celebrate it, he had gone off to Carlisle to volunteer and though he had lied emphatically, his true age – fifty-eight – had been winkled from him. The laughter which had then met him, as he was pushed back by the dozens of younger men impatient to be in, and the solitary afternoon he had spent adrift in the city – seeing everywhere men who would be accepted where he was refused admittance, feeling the thunder of war over the calm sunny skies of the medieval market city and himself no more than able to shake his fist at it, shrinking away as he thought he heard someone or saw someone who might recognise him and so bring him to relate his stupidity – a desultory, shambling figure, his very stockiness and strength making the cringe in his eyes the more pitiful – all ending with the dark of night slinking home, this had taught him more than his age. For though his life had been cut off from many things – all turnstiles opening to wealth, privilege or breeding being closed for a start – he had never been excluded from that in which he had seen a part for himself; until now. He saw that he would be left in the countryside with the children and the unfit – and the old men, he thus marked as one of them.

This self-pity had been strong in him when he heard that Emily was finding it difficult to manage in the town: another child was due, May was too far off, the money was scanty; and the self-pity had watered the roots of generosity. He had restored an abandoned cottage, settled for it at a month's rent and even gone himself to bring her over. Until then, the war had been a permanent Sunday; and the spirit quite lacking from his conventional Christian obeisances had found a faith in that observance; for *this* could not be done now because of the war, cock-fighting was out because of the war, you did not drink to drunkenness on the side-lines of a war, you watched every word and gesture in Wartime.

But Harry had mocked that glum observance on the first day of his arrival when he had sworn back at his grandfather and catapulted the old man to a chase which had lasted for half an hour ending with Harry near the tip of a long beech branch and Joseph holding on to the trunk, cursing and threatening him, afraid for them both if he tried his own weight on the slender arm. Emily had seen the beginning of the pursuit, the small boy scurrying away before the stout old man, diving through a foxhole in a hedge-bottom, wriggling through the bars of a gate, the two of them galloping along the skyline like comic opposites held together by an invisible rope which would never let them apart – she had seen this and laughed at it, but worried that the earlier reputation of Joseph might rise again through his newly assumed responsibility and regretted the panic which had spurred her to move to where she would be so dependent on him. She need not have done. That invisible rope became visible as the boy and his grandfather became inseparable: through Harry, she and the others were permanently accepted under Joseph's protection.

May would not go up to see her grandfather no matter what the order or the temptation. Even Alice, whose childishness made her less liable to persecution, and Sarah whose prettiness gave her a certain immunity, were far more pleased to come home than was polite. For May saw in Joseph that domination of children which often ran to real persecution – and it reminded her of her father in his severe moods. She expected not to speak at meals, unless spoken to, she expected to stand in the line while Joseph finished his dressing and hold out the collar, to serve on him at table, to clean his boots, to fetch and carry for him, to be controlled by him in all matters of dress, manners and fact – this she had learned to do for John: but she could not accept to be hit, to be sent out of the room, to have her supper taken from her, to be blamed for nothing just because he was in an accusing mood; she never forgot being tied to the table leg with a length of rope, her father leaving her there all evening, and while she had not the power of answering back which is given to many rebels, she was sufficiently independent to fight as she could by avoiding what she did not approve of. She stayed with Emily.

The older woman was glad of her company. As Sarah had done when they had lived in Crossbridge, May brought gossip to the isolated cottage, and the premature oldness of the daughter matched the mother's last lingering with youthful looks and ways, making them sisterly in their interests.

When letters came, that was a day of talk and re-reading, remembering and prayers. For not only did she receive John's letters, but Seth wrote to his mother, and Isaac's wife would send over letters received from him and from Tom. When a letter was received from John, Emily would have Harry go over to where May worked so that she could slip down in the evening. The girl always read most carefully, and then skipped through it again, still not permitting herself to utter a word, and then she would return it to her mother, blushing as she remembered the 'Dearest Emily' which had begun it, and wait for it to be read aloud to her. As her mother read, the most marvellous parcels would float before the young girl's eyes, parcels stuffed with sweets and socks, black puddings which he particularly liked, magazines, chocolates, tobacco, parcels which she would the next morning begin to save for until Emily would check their size and off they would go, the nights of posting being the sweetest in May's life, as she thought of the brown paper being torn open by her father and all those good things there to cheer him up. After once more looking through the letter, she would play waltzes on the old gramophone and dance around the kitchen floor with her mother, happy in the proof of their father being alive and determined to let that happiness be enjoyed by Emily before the inevitable withdrawal to fear and sadness.

The first rush across the Channel, created by the widely recorded zeal of the volunteers, broke on the rocks of the German artillery, and telegrams of death washed back to England like flotsam from the wreckage.

'I'm with Jackson Pennington,' Isaac wrote. 'John knows him. Ask Emily about him – John and him had a fight! Last night I piled up some in tin drums and slept seated on top of them. Mud's worse than Wedham Flow. Our Sergeant-Major was killed last night by a bullet that bounced off Alan Pape's helmet. I tell you, I get sick of sitting in these holes. You would think that Cumberland would disappear when you're so far away but it doesn't. There is never enough news. A man must be the easiest thing to shoot at in the animal kingdom, my love. But don't worry – they say it'll be over soon. And tell Emily not to worry about our John. It was nothing but a flesh wound and I saw him before they took him off. He was happy enough. He might even get sent back! Lucky him!'

John had been slightly injured in the leg. He was taken to a base hospital and just as he finished his convalescence, sent back across the Channel, but only to the Isle of Wight to be a blacksmith there.

'It's my own fault,' he wrote. 'I couldn't bide doing nothing at the hospital so I used to get down to one of the forges and help the fella there. Norman Allen he was called, from Staffordshire. Then some Captain seen me and asks a lot of questions and the next thing I know I'm in the Isle of Wight. It won't be for long though, I hope. They promised me I could go over with the next big lot. It's nice working with horses again.'

Sarah arrived on the day of Seth's long letter. She had another child with her, a boy, Reginald: apart from that indisputable evidence she appeared not a day older nor a jot different from Emily's last memory of her.

'Where's your man this time?' Joseph's first question.

'He's fighting, like everybody else!' She shouted at her father, hitting him unwittingly at that point most vulnerable in his temper's frail armour. As before, the choice was to have her roam the district as a vagabond – a travelling advertisement of his hard-heartedness – or take her in. Which he most begrudgingly did, knowing that the two children would be left with his wife while Sarah pranced off. He managed to slip a bridle on her this time, however, for he would only agree that his wife look after her children if she would enlist as a land-girl. After spying out all other possibilities, Sarah declared herself willing and was posted to a neighbouring farm.

The war settled to those two armies separated from each other by a few waste yards, the trenches, two long cracks across the face of Europe.

'And sometimes,' Seth wrote, 'when we're back from the
lines, me and two other fellas go up on this little hill – mont,
it's called in French, no higher than a slag heap. They're both
from London. We lie on our backs and just look at the sky
and talk all night. They can talk about anything – they talk
about why we're here and where we're going. It's an education
just to listen to them. And you can see the battle going on in
the distance, the flares like shooting stars. The ground shakes
when the heavy artillery let fly and you know what it's like
before an earthquake. I've never heard talk to match these
two. They can go on for hours and never repeat themselves.
One of them said that "War is the way men revenge the
sacrifice of their cheated instincts". I copied it down then and
there.'

'Come on!' Sarah urged.
'But I'm tired, my love. May'll go with you,' Emily replied.
'May's staying to look after the children, aren't you, dear?'
returned Sarah firmly. '*You* come. You never get out and you've
still a good figure, Emily. You should walk it or it'll turn fat on
you. Nothing looks worse, especially when you're married. They
think they can pick you up like an old cushion. Look at how I've
improved since I started on that bluddy farm. *You* must come.'
Once Sarah had set her mind on something it was impossible
to deny it her unless you were prepared to be violent. For no
protestations could be offered which were stronger than straw
before her mowing will, no excuses could be invented that could
not be challenged, no rebuffs that would not be returned with
no hard feelings: she would stand and insist and, unless picked
up and thrown out, have her way. Emily was certainly no match
for her.
The two women walked across to the road and went some
way south along it. To their right about three miles away was
that first drift of fell which marked the perimeter of the Lake
District in the north-west as the fells around Crossbridge did to
the south-west. To their left, Wigton, the plain, the Solway, the
Scottish hills, as clear as the fells this soft summer's evening.
Sarah had not even bothered to put on a cardigan and her brown

arms were bare. Emily had taken her shawl and this, with the hat she wore, strands of grey hair filtering around her neck, flashing white as the low sun caught them, made her appear rather stern beside the gallopy walk of the younger woman.

At first she had been irritated at being dragged from her book but as she walked she sensed the air, the view, the memories of country roads, nourishing those buds in herself which had been without sustenance for so long. She breathed easily and the nightmare of those moments when she had sat and seemed to see the air hovering before her mouth unwilling, unwilled to enter, could be thought of without fright. With Sarah on this summer evening all was well.

She wondered at that. The country was turning into a Machine for War, so the papers said – and the lists of killed and wounded spread over a page every week in the *Cumberland News*. She saw the photographs of men leading wounded away from the battle, of broken weapons and soldiers ready to kill and, most movingly to her, a group of men cheerfully posing for a photograph, waving and smiling to the camera as if they were at the sea-side. Yet here, in a country at war, she could feel calm and cheerful – even though her own husband was away from her. As once she had learned that she could contain many loves, for parents, husband, children, friends, so now she saw that she must contain many contradictions within a struggle: for the clouds would not roll over in fallacious thunder, the roofs would not split in agony at the desolation of the empty beds beneath, the people did not wring their hands and shut out all but grief: though only a total surrender to sorrow would have portrayed what they felt, yet they could still smile and talk of other things. And here she was herself, on a little outing with Sarah, enjoying it.

'They came yesterday night,' said Sarah.

'I heard tell of it.'

'Mary Franks saw them. She said they looked like murderers. She got the creeps and ran home.'

'We must go past as if we were out for a normal walk,' said Emily, firmly. 'Nobody likes to be stared at.'

'But they're *Germans*,' said Sarah.

The prisoner-of-war camp was no more than a mile away, and as they approached the gate of the huts which were set in a small pine copse, Emily was embarrassed to discover that they were not the only ones inquisitive. There was a small crowd, some of them had biked up from Wigton, pressed around the wire; retreating no more than a temporary yard when barked at by one of the guards.

'Let's go back,' said Emily. 'We won't see anything.'

'But we must look,' Sarah returned. 'There's no harm in looking – and we've come all this way now. What would we say to folks if they knew we'd come all this way and seen nothing?'

'We could say we had seen them.'

'That would be a fib, Emily,' said Sarah, unctuously.

They were rewarded by the appearance of the prisoners as they came out for their evening air. All were silent as the strange men moved around most normally and even laughed once or twice. They looked at the sky and commented, perhaps, it was later hazarded, on the weather; they moved with a listlessness proper to that institutional dogma called Exercise; one of them spat – but in the opposite direction – and another made a mild face at a little boy who was clinging to the wire top and fell down to the grass in immediate terror. All these actions were carefully noted down and when, on their return to the huts, the men began to sing, amazement and satisfaction competed for attention in the response of those outside the wire.

'They look all right,' said Sarah. 'Nothing special. But did you see that big one, Emily? The one who winked at me. Didn't you see him wink? The one who had the cap on the back of his head. He was *nice*.' She paused – and then made her declaration. 'I don't expect they're much worse than anybody else. Hm. What d'you say? Emily? Emily, you're crying. Emily! Don't. You know I always start up as well. Don't cry, Emily. Please.'

'I was thinking – John could be shut up like that in another country. He could be shut up just like that.'

'Oh, Emily,' Sarah moaned. 'That's started me off. Don't say things like that. It's not fair.'

'They said I could go over with the big batch,' John wrote, 'and I got out of the smithy to get ready for it. Then the day before embarkation some blacksmith breaks his arm and I've got to stay. Why can't I get back there? Sometimes I think I'm selfish to complain. I mean, a lot of men would be pleased with my job, and I should be glad I'm needed. But it isn't any good, especially since our Tom was killed. I wanted to get a gun and murder the lot of them.

His railing against the fate which had landed him in a safe spot appeared touchingly comical to Emily; but that was the easier interpretation of it. She knew that his frustration at being away from the battle would be once more savaging the contact between his actions and his feelings and feared that this time the line would be irreparably cut. And she, too, felt his anxiety as a cruel privation and found herself wishing that he could be back on the front, despite the danger. When she caught herself wishing for that, she wondered that her feeling for John could be called love – for it was without doubt wishing him nearer death. Yet she was not ashamed of her sympathy for his situation.

'Some of the men here are sick of it all,' Seth wrote from a hospital in Surrey, 'and I agree with them. We just sit there and kill each other. Nobody moves. We could be in those holes the rest of our lives. It isn't the ordinary man that wants war on either side. Generals and Politicians and Big Business make wars to please themselves. I saw some German prisoners before I came here – they were just like us. We gave them some biscuits. If they'd been three hundred yards away, we'd have given them bullets. It makes no sense. One night me and Fred Stainton was out on patrol. We crept about through no man's land: when we put our ears to the ground we could hear the tunnelling: there was gunfire everywhere. We found a man hanging over some barbed wire. He was a German. *He'd* been out on a patrol, I suppose, and caught it. I wanted to see him and waited for a flare. His face was all shot off.'

He recovered and spent his leave in London before going back.

'I suppose you've heard about our Seth and his carryings on,' Isaac wrote. 'He thinks that if we all stop – that's an end to it. And so it is. They would just walk all over us then. Do you remember me telling you about Jackson Pennington? He got killed last night – the bravest man I ever saw. He was our Sergeant that got Seth recommended for a rest – battle-fatigue – and he deserves it, really, he's been out here since it started. Jackson caught it out on a night patrol: he always liked to be in among it. He'd been an army man most of his life, you know.

'Here's a coincidence – soon after our Tom got it I saw that another Tom Tallentire had caught it. He was an Australian and I found out that his father was the brother of our father – Robert that went to Australia with Jim. The same man told me that there was two other Tallentires about – Tom's cousins – I would like to meet them because they must be my cousins as well – but doubt if I will. Things are much the same here.

'It looks as if I'll never get away from here,' John wrote. 'I might as well be at home for all the fighting I see. But never mind, I must make the best of it. I might go back to a smithy when I come out – or I would if I could afford to set up myself. Some of the men say that horses are finished. I can't see that. They'll always be needed on the farms. Ted Blacklock's here. He isn't so bad when you get to know him. He says he's never been happier – no wife and kids to bother him. He drinks like ten.'

Harry was now past his fifteenth birthday and his life with Joseph had helped to make him look older. He had taken work on the same farm as his grandfather and the bond between them, which had now lasted for three years, prospered. Joseph took the boy into pubs with him, he introduced him to all the men they met; on his fifteenth birthday he had given him a gun that he had acquired second-hand, an old weapon, but still a gun. He called on him on Saturday afternoons to go out somewhere just as a young man might call on a friend. He delighted in Harry's aptness on the farm and took more care in teaching him how to do things than ever he had done with his own children. Harry repaid these favours by accepting them – for he thought it was important to be with his grandfather and relished the old man's talk of times past, of the tricks they used to get up to and the way they had to do things. They were inseparable.

Emily wished sometimes that the boy would take some friends nearer his own age, but when she saw the flush on his face at night as he set off for some poaching or smiled at the swagger in his walk as he came back with a few rabbits after an evening's shooting, then she saw that he was content and did not interfere.

Indeed she could scarcely wish him differently, so husbandly did he care for her. Since their first arrival he had made himself responsible for the garden – laying it all to vegetables, not a flower-seed sown – gone out to collect wood for the fire, taken upon himself to regulate the conduct – even the dressing – of Alice who was only three years younger than he was, but 'so that she's off thy hands, mother,' he explained. He would run a mile to the shop at the slightest request and dauntlessly play truant from school on market days so that he could go down into Wigton and make himself useful for sixpence or a shilling brought back to her untouched. Emily had never been able to chat to him as she had done to May and Alice and as she was beginning to do with Joseph, but she saw he was straining to make himself her protector, and she loved the authoritative scan of his eyes each time he entered the cottage. 'You're my man, now your father's away,' she wanted to say – but she shrank away from it, knowing that he would find such affectionate sayings distressing.

In all matters proper to his love for his mother he was scrupulous and undeviating – but he lacked that playfulness which can make affection nourish itself on its own regard. She knew that he did not lean on her as John did: Harry's support had an independent foundation – and though she was relieved by that and admired it, she found that she would catch herself saying: 'I wish him no different. He's right as he is,' with as much regret as pride – for she wanted to be closer to this son whose constancy and daring offered her so much love. Though she hated him to go out with the gun, she would often choose that afternoon to take the air herself, hoping to see him walking with his grandfather in the fields, the gun so casually hung in his hand – and the action so quick and definitive when he pulled it to his shoulder and fired. Or when she went to the farm to collect the washing that she took in, she would deliberately dawdle back with the big basket, selfishly pretending that it was too heavy so that he would notice her and tie up the horses to drop his sickle and race across to her – and that eager, considerate expression on his face was one she would have made any pretence to see.

She still smiled at the memory of the night Joseph had got him drunk, how he had stayed out in the washhouse, ashamed to come to his bed and she, worried into going out to look for him, had found him there, asleep on the wet flags, shamedly groaning that he had let her down and so must leave her. He was so far gone that he had been obliged to put his arm around her neck as they walked to the cottage, and she hugged this rare physical intimacy to herself, his lean body now just a shade taller than her own, pressed against her, dependent. But mostly she had to be content to observe at a distance, and when John came back on leave Harry quite disappeared – so overawed was he by the sight of his father in uniform and so shy before the open affection between the man and woman who were his parents. Then she wanted to call him, to have John call him, to let him share with them what his guardianship made so easy – for he had left school before fourteen and every penny from his work went to his mother which, with May's wage and the bit that John could send and she herself could earn took them away from the scanty scrapings of the opening two years of the war – but he would not be called.

When Harry spoke to her other than on domestic or local matters, it was about the war. Lloyd George was calling on the chapels to give up their congregations, the entire country was becoming a factory, the Germans were caricatured as beasts and monsters who must be destroyed at any cost and the bitterness and doggedness of those at war infected the boy with an ambition to be fighting; and no poultice of Emily's could draw it out.

Later, she realised that she had known what would happen and been unable to do other than ignore it. That week, two letters had come – both of which upset him. One was from Seth who told them that he was being discharged 'on medical grounds' – and Joseph's sneer at that brought Harry the shame of having an uncle who was perhaps running away. The other from Isaac whom he idolised: in it, Isaac wrote that he had had a leg blown off and his back was peppered with shrapnel, 'they come in and hack a few more bits out every day,' he said, 'just like as if I was a pit and the doctor was a miner. Still, it means the fighting's all over for me, I'm afraid.'

When Harry failed to come home for his supper that night she was annoyed – but it was not unusual for him to eat with his grandfather – though it *was* his habit to let her know whenever he intended to do so. She covered the plate and put it back in the oven and sat down to read. Alice, Sarah and Joseph were in bed, May would not be down that night – she had looked forward to spending the evening in Harry's company. He was very deft and would sit with his feet inside the fender, carving a piece of wood into a toy for Joseph or Sarah, the yellow shavings blown on to the fire, one by one. His knife moved so silently through the wood that her pages rustling was the only sound.

She could not settle without him.

Word would have been sent her immediately if he had been hurt.

She started a letter to John but had no heart for it. She took up the darning basket, put it down again, checked the plate in the oven, lowered the pulley to feel the washing, and wound the cord around the two hooks with meticulous attention to the task.

All this was losing time. But she did not want to believe that he had gone and she willed herself to maintain her illusion. She went out to the washroom and discovered there sufficient kindling chopped for a whole month. That was conclusive.

Joseph borrowed a pony and trap from the farmer and they set off along the night road, the lantern bobbing on the trap, an indistinct beacon. She had put on her coat but the finest drizzle soon made it sodden and the cold clothes soaked her frigid flesh.

'He'll have med for Carlisle,' said Joseph. 'We should catch him before he reaches it.'

She nodded and concentrated on fighting against the shivering fit which came on her. There was no moon and Joseph was forced to drive carefully. Through Thursby they came upon two soldiers walking back to their camp: Joseph gave them a lift and Emily looked at their uniforms, her silence chilling their friendly chatter. The slow steps of the pony were like the ticking of a clock, relentless.

They did not pass him on the road.

'He'll be sleepin' out somewhere to be at the Recruiting Office first thing,' Joseph guessed.

'We must drive around and look for him.'

When the pony became too tired to go further and Joseph weary of moving through the empty streets of the city – the pony and trap bumping over the cobbled stones lit only by smudges of palest yellow from the few gas lamps – even then Emily would not stop. She left Joseph with the trap under an archway near the town-hall and walked about the streets until the morning, the drizzle turning to steady rain, the cold set white her face until it was strained numb. She had little chance of meeting him but there was nothing would stop her looking.

They had some tea in a café near the recruiting-centre. The hot liquid scalded Emily's tongue and that first sip was all she could manage.

Joseph kept his eyes to the window and he saw Harry arrive, well before the office was due to open, walking almost shamefully down the street as the morning workers hurried along the pavements. His grandfather brought him in and produced him before Emily with pride.

'He slept in a barn at Cardewlees,' he said. 'We went right by him.'

'You look tired,' said Emily to her son, 'have some tea to freshen you up.'

She waited until the tea had been brought and Harry had drunk from the cup before further speech. In truth, she knew that she had to store her strength, for the night had penetrated her and she ached with the wet cold.

'If thou teks us back home, Aa'll just run away again,' he said, quietly – and Emily wanted him to look at her so that she could win or lose him with full face, but the boy's head was bent down over his cup.

'You're too young,' she replied, very low. Then her voice rose. 'You're not yet sixteen, Harry. They won't let you in.'

'There's younger than me in,' he said. 'Arnie Barwise told me that they're desperate for anybody now. I can pass for seventeen and a half.'

'I could go and tell them your real age.'

He shook his head, still refusing to look up.

'Thou wouldn't do that, mother. Thou couldn't do that.'

'I could.' What was meant to be firm was frail.

'No,' he smiled confidently to himself – and had that smile been given her directly, had he looked at her when the knowledge of his mother's love brought that smile to his face – then she could have said no more. Even the few words spoken had wrenched more from her than she thought she could bear.

'Oh, you shouldn't go,' she said, 'it's wrong even for you to think of it.'

'Why's that?'

'Live while you can,' she replied. 'Please. Wait the two years.'

'It'll be over then.'

'So it's just the killing you want!' This, her one flaring. 'You want nothing but that. You just want to be there to fight. It's nothing else!'

'But what else is there to do?' he asked, eventually, his face drawn up, made anxious by the vehemence in her words. He saw the tears in her eyes and looked away once more. Her crying was his only fear. Knowing it, Emily drew a breath which racked the aching of her body and forced herself not to cry.

'I shall miss you,' she said.

'Aa'll send all me wages,' he returned, eagerly – and that she could not bear. Her feeling broke and she wept.

The two men regarded her uncomfortably. Other voices in the café were lowered and Emily's sobbing alone was heard.

Harry put out his hand and touched the clasped fingers of his mother. She quietened at that and stopped as his hand gripped hers more tightly.

'I'm sorry I was so silly,' she said, abruptly stopping, reaching in her bag for a handkerchief.

'That's all right,' he replied.

'There. I'm better.'

'So thou'll not mind?' he concluded.

It was Joseph again who brought her down to Carlisle some weeks later to see Harry off at the station. This time she did not weep.

On their way back, Joseph said:

'He's better there, Emily. Aa said nothin' – remember – nowt that mornin' thou talked to him. It wasn't for me to come between you two. But he's a lad won't settle 'til he's doin' what he thinks has to be done. Once it was in his head, Emily – that was that. There's nobody on earth could have shifted it out. And if somehow thou'd forced him to stop on – if thou'd pleaded and tormented him – thou would nivver have been forgiven. And his spirit would have been broken. Thou must just hold up, now. Hold on, lass. Thou can do no more.'

The pain in Emily's side, which had begun after that night of searching for her son, grew and developed into pleurisy. When Seth came back, ravaged and stunned in his expression, she could speak to him for no more than ten minutes and then she was exhausted: yet there was so much she wanted to ask – about what it was *really* like there, what chance Harry had. Isaac's 'performance' on his wooden leg raised only the pretence of a smile in her. As Joseph mooned his lonely way about the farm, Emily scarcely left the cottage, for even when the illness passed she had no will to stray from the sanctuary that Harry had made for her.

He was killed three days before the end of the war. When John returned he found her set on leaving the cottage. The land around it reminded her only of her son and John took her back to the town, himself returning to the pits.

EIGHTEEN

The year after the war ended, the Crossbridge Friendly Society had one of its greatest days. Founded in 1808, the Society had served the village as an unmilitant co-operative, labourers paying in a few pence a week as a guard against sickness and accident. It had never been sufficiently militant to attempt to raise the standard of wages or improve the conditions of work of its members, its inclination was rather to provide a safety net below the wires of paternalism. The fifteen-piece band was its real pride – among those instrumentalists, committee men flourished serenely; an oligarchy of sounding brass – while its joy and to many its purpose was this day, the last Friday of June, the day of the Club Walk, that Walk being a formal affair from the pub to the church and back: the rest was sport, food, entertainment, drink, gambling, racing, competing and fullest debauch.

John decided to go up to it. He was now in the privileged position of being able (with sufficient notice given) to manipulate his work to such an extent that he could get a specific day off. May was not able to come but he kept the other children from school so that they could enjoy the outing. And it was a good occasion for tempting Emily out of the house, getting her into the fresh air, reviving that body which had begun to retreat from all life.

They went from the town on one of the omnibuses belonging to the Whitehaven Cab and General Posting Co. Ltd. A favourable morning, money in the pocket, nothing to do but enjoy themselves. John took Joseph on his knee and they counted the number of horses they could see.

Indeed this day was a wake for many dead. The foam of welcome at the war's end had soon been licked off and it was only now that the deep spring of relief could cascade in the dry fountains of peace. In some parts of the country this led to whirlpools of near-revolution – soldiers refused to obey their orders, strikes were mounted. In others, as here, there were times of calm: the pool already being re-filled. Throughout the land memorials were being erected in the churches forever to display the long list of English dead. Tattered banners leaned bedraggled in the corners of the altar; in France the acres of white crosses stretched across the flat fields, a harvest barren of seed; and as yet the folly of the peace settlement, which was such as could insult even the stupidity of that war, was unperceived, its retribution uncomprehended. Nor would there be many more of those Walks, for the Government had taken upon itself to insure and protect all citizens, offering better terms than the Friendly Society which, pierced at the root, was to lose its members.

In 1919, however, its funds and functions could still claim to be firm. If the days when men came up and stayed the week, sleeping out in Lund lonnin, spread over the village like a sacking army, if those days were gone – then *the* day itself had still the power to attract crowds and legends. John breathed more happily as the coach went through Frizington and saw the fells very near. He bounced his son on his knee and was rewarded by a flush and a smile from Emily as she told him not to be so noisy in front of everybody. But he took this as his cue to increase his exuberance. All on the omnibus were going to Crossbridge and the air was a curtain of rough tobacco, cleat leaves or aniseed which some of the men still smoked for economy's sake.

John, looking at the hills, imagined that he could see the shepherds coming down for the day's events, the cowmen leaving the fields, the labourers hurrying through the milking, and once again, it seemed, the character and form of the country he had grown up in could meet in celebration as if the war had been not a severe operation on the people – one that would change its face and form – but a wound only, deep, to the bare bone, but capable of healing with new skin grown from the old.

In his fortieth year, John was at his prime: whatever despair and frustration he had, it could not be seen on such a day. If it had given him little else, his work had brought him indisputable strength, the rhythm of it beating now as the very pulse of his life and his days cast in iron through that ceaseless, intense throb. While any release from such toil could not but be furbished with all the ornaments of delight – no baubles scattered through the evenings of many leisured days – but the spirit of festival, bottled up through the most of the year. And he knew there would be the sports he had enjoyed before the war, the men with the stories, the dialect and tricks and feats: he joggled his child impatiently, longing to be quit of this slow conveyance so that he could push himself among it.

Emily was very pale, as always now, and she wore the black dress she had worn at Joseph's funeral. For the old man had survived the news of his grandson's death by a mere six months: he had been knocked down by his own horses while ploughing but there was little doubt in anyone's mind that he would never have let himself in for such an accident or, even so, would have been well able to recover from it, had not Harry's death so affected him. To please John she had stitched some white lace around the neck and on the cuffs but these added more to the frailty of her appearance than to its gaiety, and in her bag was a pair of large scissors, secretly packed, with which she would trim Ephraim's grave. She made an effort to be cheerful, for John's sake, and also because she could not but think herself self-indulgent: others had greater troubles . . .

Mrs Sharpe had just that year come into The Cross and this was to be her first big Club day. She was a pretty-faced young woman, a farmer's daughter, used to catering for large gangs of men after harvest or hay-timing and after her marriage she had rushed at the chance of taking over The Cross which she managed through the day as well as looking after the small farm attached to it while her husband continued to earn his regular wage in the iron-ore mines. This day, however, he too was one of her many helpers.

The night before all the furniture was taken out and Jo Howe the carpenter came to board up the stairs. Sawdust was put on the floors. Forms and barrels were set out at the back for people to sit on. The Cross was in the corner of the field where the day's entertainment took place and all the back windows on the ground floor were opened and used as bars. Mrs Sharpe and her helpers not only did for the pub but for the marquees which rose overnight in the field. As a sole peg to those insubstantial tents, The Cross took the weight of the day.

She expected to feed at least 250 people for dinner at midday and well over 500 for high tea. The food arrived at this small country pub much as the wagon-loads of feed must have come to a castle at the time of a great feast. Ninety pounds of beef, ready cut, came up hot that morning from Cleator-Moor Co-op. Six hams were boiled and carried off the waggonettes to be stacked in the small kitchen. Over a hundredweight of potatoes had been peeled the night before. Mrs Sharpe herself, with Miss Graham and Mary Edmonson, had roasted two legs of ham, two of pork, and prepared more than a stone of green peas, two dozen cauliflowers, two dozen cabbage and a stone of split peas. Eight hundred teacakes had been baked around the village and more were to come from the ovens throughout the day, as well as bread and cakes and biscuits. Dozens of jars of home-made jam were got out, pints of cream and preserves. For the puddings, she had the help of the older women – Mrs France from Crossgates, Mrs Jackson from Bird Dyke, Mrs Parker from Hoodge Cottage, and Miss Graham: twelve plum puddings were made, twelve rice puddings, rum sauce for the plum puddings, ale got ready for the Crossbridge Pudding (buns steeped until soft in hot ale and served with seasoning and spirits to taste) and twelve herb puddings. The children had collected for a week the ingredients for the herb puddings: rhubarb, nettles, blackcurrant leaves, cabbage, cauliflower, leeks, sour dockings, barley, Easterman giants – twenty-one different ingredients topped by whisked eggs. Before the dinner, the eight carvers came, each bringing their own knives and steel, Tam Wrangham, Harry Edmonson, Joe Wood, Jo Stoner, Joe Jackson, John Dalzell, Tom Cowman, John Eliot, and the rasp of steel on steel cleared the throats of all who heard it.

At nine-thirty the band assembled outside The Cross, among the horses and wagons, men moving in with food, women rushing about with pans. Jo Branthwaite stacking up the crates of bottled beer which would fortress-fill the small back-room for the length of the day. The coachload of Licensees arrived from Workington with the Brewery's compliments and at the Brewery's expense from the coach straight into the field – the church service would be full enough with local people. Children panicked with pleasure running around people's legs like chickens avoiding capture – and the President of the Friendly Society, Harry Wilkinson, brought out the silk banner from the pub – gold and blue it was – unfurled it, presented a pole apiece to the Secretary and the Treasurer, nodded to the bandmaster – and led off for the ten o'clock service.

They were standing in the aisles as the vicar went through the short office. The band accompanied the long hymns and the packed congregation settled back as comfortably as they could to attend to the sermon for which the vicar received a guinea from the man at the Hall. A new family there. The old one which had been there since it was built, now died out, the last son killed in the war, the last act of the father being the erection of a cottage, called Le Plantin, to be lived in rent-free by a poor widow of the parish.

The sermon done, the band lined up once more and the vicar marched with the President back to the field for the day's entertainment. As she heard the band leaving the church, Mrs Sharpe put the potatoes on to boil and five women in nearby cottages did the same. They would be boiled, mashed and put into earthenware pots with a blanket tied around them to keep them warm.

In the field the President gave his address – embracing the membership list, the funds, thanks to the creator for the weather, and to Mr Tyson for the hurdles, a throwaway reference to a new cure for sheep-scab, a remark on the founders and the official opening of the Club Walk.

John and Emily arrived just as the President began his address and after it, with the rest of the crowd, they walked over to watch the sports. In the late morning there would be the terrier racing, whippets after dinner and the sheep-dog trials, fell-racing and field sports in the late afternoon, hound dogs in the evening, the band playing continuously except at meal times, and hawkers, gipsies, bookmakers, side-shows, displays and old friends, monkeys on barrel organs, a blind man with a fiddle – all the day long. Now, however, was the start of the wrestling – Cumberland and Westmorland style, supposed to have been left in the two counties by the Romans. The men stripped out in woollen vests and long-johns, black trunks, soft black plimsolls, crouching crab-like against each other, each chin on the other's shoulder, one arm above one below that of the opponent, swinging up for a grip against his back which, once held, signified the start of the contest which ended when one man broke the other's grip.

Emily took the children away to see inside the big marquee and John settled down to enjoy the sport. He had already nodded and talked to many of the men from the village, the conversation always the same mixture – beginning with references to those dead in the war, continuing on the present condition of the bereaved, from there to the improvement of life in the village since the doubling of labourers' wages in the war years and concluding with tips for the races – and stayed for a long chat with Mr Pennington who had given over his farm to his two remaining sons, living with them in his old age. John told him what Isaac had written about Jackson and Pennington was so grateful for this praise of his son that he treated John to a complete appraisal of the prospects on the farm, no meagre or easy confidence from one to whom nothing but that land had held real substance even during the war itself.

Now John sat and watched the wrestling – more than glad to be joined by Isaac. Their first remark was to express mutual amazement at Seth's sudden marriage – an arrangement which had prevented him from being here this day: both knew the woman, both had heard gossip of her, both disliked what they had heard, both thought Seth a sad fool – neither said so.

Isaac was working 'like old Nick, John boy. Nickerdemus himself!' – setting up in a butching business, 'for it's the best Aa'm suited for now, me boy' – but still he would not miss such an outing. Indeed, the false leg and the back even now embedded with bits of metal, had stopped him from doing very little that he wanted to do. He had made up his mind to ignore his injury. His years in the trenches had lost him some of his weight –

which helped – and the broad face was cut by lines like faults on its grainy surface. 'If Aa sit down and mope – Aa's finished!' he said. So, as soon as he had felt well enough, he had gone off on a hunt. All day he had stuck at it though the other men, seeing the blood come through his breeches, had tried to send him off. He had spent the night 'wid' me stump in a basin, lad, like a bit of raw meat hanging in a dish' – but the statement had been made, the tempo set – and three days later, 'bandaged up to me belly, lad' – he was off again with the hounds. Since when he had hunted regularly, sometimes prevented by the considerations of his business but never by those of his stump.

'Aa fancy Alan Stott,' said Isaac, looking at the two heavy-weights now slinging up their arms for a grip, 'Aa fancy him to win it.'

'What price is he?' John asked.

'They'll give thee four to one now. They'll shorten when he wins this round.'

John went across and put on a shilling.

The two men were still wrestling when he returned, which was unusual as the contests generally lasted for no more than two minutes, often less.

'Stott can't git his buttock in,' said Isaac grimly. 'That other fella must have a double-jointed backbone.' He looked intently at the wrestlers but continued to address John. 'Aa've tried to git back into wrestlin' myself,' he went on. 'But fust time Aa did it Aa vanyer brok t'other lad's toes – wid' me stump. T' umpire sed Aa'd a "unfair advantage". Ay. Aa hed to drop owt on it aatogither. There! He's got him. My Christmas – Aa thowt they were ganna cuddle up agen each other aa day. Well, if he can beat yon rubber-bones, he can lace anybody else.'

They all had dinner together in the marquee, where Isaac's wife revealed herself with her children and agreed to look after Sarah and Alice while Emily took Joseph down to the church. The men were beginning to lay into the drink and devoted all time apart from that to talk and inspection of the dogs.

John walked Emily and their son to the gate.

'I could nip down and hev a look ower it,' he said.

'No. You stay. I won't be long.'

'Don't go, Emily,' he said, abruptly. 'Thou'll just be upset.'

'I'll be fine.'

'Thou looks for trouble,' John continued.

'You just go back and enjoy yourself.'

'How can any man enjoy hissel when thou's mopin' and crying down yonder?'

'I won't mope.'

'Sorry. But thou looks so lost, Emily.'

'No I don't. I'm enjoying it.'

'The way that's said goes against the words. You look so miserable these days, Emily.'

'I don't! But I will if you keep on at me.'

'Dis thou remember when we first came to this spot?'

'Yes. I do.'

'We used to walk up to Cogra Moss.' He hesitated. The dogs were barking for the beginning of the races. 'If thou wants, I'll tek thee up there now.'

'No. You want your sport.'

'We could be there an' back in an hour.'

'No. Go back.' She smiled at him and touched his arm. 'Thank you, John. I'll get better – just – let me do it my way. Please.'

'Well don't be long down there then. I'll expect you back for tea-time.'

She nodded and watched him go back into the field, soon hailing someone, laughing with them. She wished that she could throw off this burdened, gloomy atmosphere which had settled on her. It made John restless and she thought it unfair of her to impose that on him. Sometimes she caught sight of herself in a shop-window and almost laughed at the enclosed dreary reflection which returned to her; many, many were in worse position than she was – this she kept telling herself so often it became her only weapon to alleviate her despair, yet the weapon more often worked against than for her, hammering her down into her unhappiness. She thought of Mrs Kemp, a widow, a husband and two sons lost in the pits, a brother killed in the war, a daughter who was backward – but this piling up of comfort by contrast was no good; Mrs Kemp would appear to her as someone to be pitied, yes, but also someone whose list of disasters over-weighted the pity until it broke into helpless detachment. Seth she was more sorry for, who ailed nothing but had come back from the war frightened out of all his former certainty: and still she shuddered at the way in which he had once 'claimed' old Ephraim, allowing none of the other relatives to take any charge of him, drawing on to himself by main force the one member of that large spread family who had been so fated, planting him in those bare lodgings like a living note to himself. Emily had never been able to take much to Seth.

If only, she thought, as she left the field behind her and walked down to the church, if only she could get rid of this pain in her side. For things were easier for them now – and she ought not to drag them down. She was afraid to admit the pain – afraid that she would be sent off for a long operation and the family split up. It was this greatest fear which made her move and act in such a self-constricted way: for she was sure that once her illness was declared, then she would be taken up with it entirely – and there would be no alternative for the children but to send them out to relatives. She would never have that.

In the churchyard now, she called Joseph away from the graves and took him along the narrow path which led to that of her first son. The small hummock had been shorn by the caretaker at respectable intervals but she wanted it, this once, to be perfect. The noise from the Walk came down the fields to her on the wind and she worked quickly, afraid that bodies might follow the voices and she be found clipping the grass with scissors in the empty cemetery. Afraid, afraid, afraid of her own shadow.

Yet the more she worked at the grave, the calmer she felt: and saw clearly through her confusion a glimpse of order and simplicity, or a rule behind the disturbances which drift on the surface of life. That same impulse which sends anthropologists to lost tribes to discover the mould for all subsequent castings, and thinkers to myths and legends to find codes and correspondences, that which makes the Golden Age of all times so persistent a legend, however vulnerable – an understanding, come to some through intellect, to herself through her senses;

that clarity and beauty were there beneath all that men piled upon it; – and yet the feeling which this insight gave her was one of sadness only. Those hills around seemed mournful.

She insisted that John and herself stay on in the evening for the dance in the assembly rooms. Many women took their children into the dance and so she had no qualms about that. And Alice, awed by the occasion, guarded the sleeping smaller children while Emily danced with John.

John had been well set for a drunken day when she had returned to tell him that she would stay – but so pleased was he with this evidence of her willingness to try to 'come out of herself', as he said, that he steered himself away from that port. They danced until she was exhausted but John, inflamed by drawing her to him once more, mistook the colour in her face for excitement and easily persuaded her to dance some more. The room was packed with those from the Walk and the thick air made all the children tired so that soon the three of them lay across chairs in a corner, warmed by their coats, oblivious to the noise of the band, the shouts from the men as they whopped at the tunes, rocked by the shaking of the wooden floor.

'I can dance no more, John,' she said, finally. 'I couldn't go another step.'

'Thou mun come outside for some air,' he replied. 'Don't worry about Alice and them. Charlie'll keep an eye on them. Won't you Charlie? There, see. Come on. Thou's startin' to look pale again. Let's have some air.'

They went from the assembly rooms, manoeuvred their way through the coaches and bicycles and walked a little way up the road. The crescent moon could have been papered on the clear sky and beneath it the tops of the fells were clear. The air was chilly but John held his wife around the shoulders, her head slightly against his shoulder, their steps matching.

'Would you like to come back to farm-work, John?'

'I was just thinkin' that myself. Just that minute! That very thought.'

'Well?' And in her, too, was a tremor of pleasure that they were once more close: like copper through rust, the vision flashed.

'It's a better feelin' here, isn't it? Better for the children an' that.'

'You must – what about yourself? John?'

'Me? Oh – I'm easy, Emily.' He laughed. 'More true to say I'm finished, really.' He wanted her contradiction.

'That's not true at all.'

'O, it is.' He paused; why could he not go on, catch the vision? 'It is,' he repeated, lamely.

'But – you've got all the time you want. You could do whatever you wanted.'

'Don't be daft,' he grinned, further to disarm the gently delivered rebuke. 'My alternative is work or work. Well, that's all right. There's many got no choice.'

'What other people do doesn't matter,' she protested, vaguely recognising a direct echo of her own encircled reasoning. 'You shouldn't be bothered about that.'

'No,' he answered. 'Mebbe so.' He hesitated. 'Let's stay where we are,' he said, 'mebbe – mebbe later, we'll change.'

'But what d'you *want*?'

'Want. Yes. I've thought on that as well. But my Wants come up so fast that they throttle me, and the next minute they're gone, as if they'd never been. I've wanted many things – but I've seen that they could be done widdout, just the same. When I was in that army – I wanted to fight, and got over it when I couldn't. I want thee to be well, lass, but if thou's not so strong – that's how it is. There's Wants that's never seen the light of my day – and how glad I am they've stayed out of sight. I want nothing, Emily.'

She bit her lip to hold in her reply. It could not be that he, too, felt himself hollowing, emptying. He looked so well, so strong, surely that was not the shell only.

'Oh, John,' she said. 'John.'

He paused. 'Yes, Emily?'

But she did not know what to say: why did he not know? 'Take me back.'

As they walked back to the dance, she leaned heavily against him. She needed him to be the same: they had grown apart, and neither would speak of the chasm at their feet; they had the power to touch only, not to heal. She began to cry.

'Thou's taken ower much out of thissel,' he said, reproachfully. 'Come on. We'll go home. We must be careful now, eh, Emily? Cut our coats.'

NINETEEN

John felt that he had failed. Emily's illness worsened and a tide of persistent consideration swept quickly over every other feeling in the house, making it impossible for him to reach out sharply to her for fear of jarring the fragile hold.

In that quiet terraced cottage, with Emily lying upstairs, refusing to leave the house, May back with them having thrown up her job at the farm to come into the town and work in a factory so that she could manage the home, himself taking Joseph down to the allotment when he finished his supper so that the place would be quiet, removing his boots in the backyard, the carrier of news of his wife to all who met him so that he walked the streets like a muted cryer, his information known to all but all who knew him concerned to indicate their own concern at his changed circumstances – there he thought he would go mad. Never to talk directly to her again, never to be able to show her how he felt except by the lap of small attentions.

'Blind, blind, blind amid the blaze of noon.' This he was. Feelings uncomprehended, undirected, feelings alone, it seemed, had been given him – and blinded him from understanding. It was as if, shorn of the training of reason, deprived of the leisure for speculation, and no believer in the strictures and aids of a dogma – all that he was had been forever churned into those impulses and sensations which rushed through him and left him unaccountably. Now he wanted to claim Emily back to himself – but though he talked to her and reached out for her, it would not work: and he knew as he sat there beside her bed that he had lost. Between the blindness of his own volition and the necessity of his daily life had been formed the inevitability which he had finally acknowledged.

On his return from the war, sprung with the resolutions and

energy which his frustration had generated – he had been ready for anything as never before in his life. The bloom that was then on him had survived Harry's death, held to the year following, been there still that day of the Club Walk, now a year past. But the fruit had not followed. For Emily had bowed herself over her grief – and he had let her alone: alone he had tried to mend the hopes, fragments of a vision. In a few months only it seemed of no more substance than the declarations of a schoolboy. He got into his pit clothes and latched the front door behind him, walked down the middle of the street to be joined by all the others, nearer the pits indistinguishable from them and like them taken into the earth and along the dark roads under the sea. It seemed a fool's fancy to have ever thought that it could be otherwise.

There was no one for him to turn to for he needed not an intermediary but a past self. So he sat there, reassuring her, and sometimes she would be strong to come downstairs and he would find her there on his return, and once, even so ill, she had set out to meet him, getting only a few yards down the street before Joseph had to run and fetch a neighbour to help her back, and she looked at him with such a look as filled him with helplessness and wrung him, for though he could return it, he could not secure it.

May came home to prepare the midday meal for the three younger children. Afterwards, she took a tray up to the bedroom for her mother. May, unmarried, plain and heavy, had assumed maternal command over all material matters with a determination which slowly revealed that she intended to keep it so when the worst happened. Always the one most concerned with family, she worked against the dread of having them split up. To prevent this, she did everything that her mother had done – and then more – feeding the three younger children, seeing to their clothes, their cleanliness, their manners, keeping the house spotless, employing all her energies in stratagems to ensure that there would be a cooked meal waiting for her father when he came back from the pits, all in the shadow of her mother's approaching death and in fear of the disintegration which she was sure would follow. The girls who worked with her in the factory – most of them younger than she was – thought her devotion passing praise, formidable in its single-mindedness and for that reason difficult to bear. May was aware that she was becoming increasingly isolated, excluded from the gossip and practical jokes, spoken to with special consideration as if she herself had been the invalid. It was she who wrote letters to other members of the family – a practice which had never been more than desultory among them but in her attempt to underpin the household, May contacted aunts, uncles, cousins and grandparents all over the country – merely to give them news. Wanting the letters to be evidence of her capability and intent. She even managed to overcome the dread she had before her father – though this victory was never more than a mask – and would sit to be attendant on him while he ate and after he came down the stairs from seeing his wife: knowing that he had always liked to have Emily available for talk, making herself so available, though she would not sit in her mother's chair.

None of this was easy for her. For she had always discounted herself – Sarah was prettier, Alice more clever, Joseph the boy. Harry had been admired for qualities she could never have: she had always had to fight for a place, first between her mother and father and then among her sisters and brother – and she alone had carried the weight of knowledge of her father's retreats which had been expressed towards her in unendurable sullenness, and her mother's words which had cut even more deeply into the daughter. Indeed, May was compounded of memories which bruised her whenever she thought of them: she was as sensitive as the princess to the pea of people's feelings towards her, towards each other, towards their circumstances – and this made her life a continual stumbling for she imagined herself to be intruding continually, leaving on the wrong note, forever breaking across the current of emotion which conducted life between those she loved, and those from whom she would always be somewhat excluded by the fact – the principal fact in her life – that she was taken for granted, by herself, by others, and, she thought, rightly.

What made it possible for her to come through was a temper,

an anger which had rarely much play but in private rendings of herself when she would cry or shudder into her body: physically taking as blows the words that barbed her mind. This anger now was that her mother should be ill. She idolised Emily: she loved to watch her move, even now, when the wasting disease had rolled away that first slight thickening of early middle age and Emily was as thin as she had been slim as a girl – she loved to watch the delicacy of her mother's gestures – delicacy of all characteristics being the most desired by May and the most adamantly denied to her. A thousand panics swept the young woman each day, in her stomach, in her throat, before her closed eyes until she thought that from anywhere, rooftops, streets, the sea, a thunderbolt would come and destroy her, destroy them all – and to combat those terrors she found that her teeth clenched, her hands tightened as if in a fight and she fell upon the forces which dared threaten her so. Her mother was not to die, and that resolution released positive forces in May long repressed or channelled to the swamp of work – and the anger that such an event might occur gave her all the strength she needed to work, to look after the family, to nurse Emily and attend John, and to contain her own fear which woke her in the dark, bottling up her mouth.

Emily vowed each night that she would get up in the morning, but when the dawn came she had no will – only the wish that John would not slide out of the bed beside her, would stay – lie with her all the day so that she could lean against his strength. She said nothing, but when he heard the first ring of the alarm and banged his hand on to it so that it would not disturb her, then she prayed that he would put his arms around her, not go, not go as he gently did, easing out carefully, holding down the sheets and blankets so that a draught did not come on to her – taking away what hope of life she had. He brought her a cup of tea and a slice of bread and jam which he placed on the bedside table before bending to kiss her brow – and she, eyes closed to bless this kindness, would counterfeit a calm awakening.

Downstairs he sat before the fire to fry his own bacon and toast his bread. He liked the kitchen to be his own at this time, the only moments when he was alone, and the senses opened

in sleep would fill his mind with sweet thoughts – even, occasionally, now, despite his wife so ill above him – while the kettle
boiled on the fire and the frazzled bacon crunched saltily on his
palate. His toes played against the edge of the fender through
his stockinged feet and the shirt and trousers, warmed by the
night's fire, sat comfortably on him. He remembered the frozen
wet trousers he had climbed into at his first job on that farm and
the memory always made him feel a lucky man.

Now, as ever since Emily's condition had worsened, his
fingers were reluctant as they pulled at the laces on his boots.
He had heard May get up and dress all the children upstairs with
many a shush! and stricture to silence: she would not bring them
down until he was gone. But whether to go, whether this would
be the day – he pushed his legs out stiffly in front of him and
pulled on the long laces as if they had been reins. He closed the
back door quietly and turned, at the bottom of the yard, to wave
up at the children whose faces were pressed against the back
bedroom window. Then into the back-alley, immediately walking
over to the middle of it, his head looking down at the scoured
stony ground. When he came out of The Tops on to the streets,
his pace quickened and he hurried as if to encourage the day to
go faster.

Often, as he pushed back a tub of coal along the seam, he
would want to abandon it and continue that walk back to his
house. It seemed madness to be working so when he could be
spending time with her – and yet he accepted that he would and
should work each day, saw nothing remediable about the day's
absence.

May brought Emily a second cup of tea before she went off
to work. Then the children came in to kiss her good-bye before
school – and the house was her own until mid-morning when
one or another neighbour came in to take a shopping list from
her, build up the fire, make yet more tea – almost all the
nourishment Emily had, for she ate sparsely – and chat about
her health. 'How's your chest, Mrs Tallentire?' 'How's your
breath, Mrs Tallentire?' 'How's the pain today, Mrs Tallentire?'
until Emily thought that she was no more than a combination of
ailments, each demanding a child's consideration. In this time,

though, after the children had gone – before the neighbour came, she tried to get up. She would relax for a little while, culling back what sleep there had been in the night, trying to make tranquil the tensions in her body, and then get out of bed and begin to dress. She made herself do this at her former speed, not allowing the illness to grip and drag at her, thinking to cheat her body back to its former self by observing all that she had been. And every morning she had to sit down on the half-descended stairs, sit in that gloomy staircase feeling her cold sweating break against the cool air, her lungs fill and almost choke her with coughing, fingers wrapped in on themselves, her only thought to get back to bed so as not to be found so weak. She had to crawl back up the stairs, her knees catching against the long skirt, pulling it from her waist until her blouse came out.

After dinner there was no chance: the children began to arrive home from school and sometimes the doctor came. Emily would not have allowed there to be any chance of the children seeing her distressed. John had shifted the bed so that she could prop herself up with pillows and look out, through a gap in the opposite terrace, to the allotments, the sea and across it, these fine summer days, the Scottish hills. Then she would read a little or knit, or, occasionally – as a treat with which she rationed herself most carefully – look at photographs and re-read the letters John had sent her from the war. There was a photograph of Harry with the Londsdales, the men in shirt-sleeves, one of them holding up a shaving brush, his face lathered, and Harry, arms folded, a cap squarely on his head, a slim pipe self-consciously clasped between his teeth. He, too, had sent her a few letters from the war.

As she looked out, at the red-bricked terraced houses – so neatly laid out when seen from this height – under the clear light the bricks and lines, the white window frames and occasional black-coated women moving in the confined spaces – she experienced a feeling of gratitude which she would neither explain nor reveal. For the noises – the few cars on the streets, the sirens at the pit, the more daring talk of the young women as they came back from the factory – came up to her window like tremors from a new world. Her own world had been one which, with few enough digressions, went back for centuries on the land in villages so that whatever changes occurred they had not shifted the central hub of a woman's life – the cramped conditions, large family, carefulness in all things material, the rhythm and obligations the same. As she lay and looked out, she was grateful to be protected from what was coming. Yet she had never been afraid before now of what might be unknown before her: had as much led as followed John to that village unknown to them, to the mining-town foreign to her. But this gratitude soaked her body as the balm to the illness; and as the tuberculosis sapped her so, to slow surprise, she let go, let go without fear – and even the pain of not being able to tell John, and the sudden clutching in her throat when she knew that soon she would part from her children, these passed: she lay, palms down on the blanket, hazel hair well mixed with grey, long over her shoulders, falling on the black shawl, and looked past the chimney pots to the grey sea.

It was towards the end of the summer. John had now lived for so long in that narrow vein of subtly changing hope and despair, each week shortening the distance between them but still the extremes oscillating like a compass needle that will tremble between the very closest points, that he was not more than usually troubled by the doubt as to whether or not he should go out to work that morning. He took her the tea and kissed her forehead: it was once more damp though he had wiped it clean and dry only a few minutes before as he had got up. He parted the curtain a little and closed the door quietly behind him.

And in the pit, that afternoon, when there was a small rush a few yards up the seam from where they were working, he remembered later that he was calm enough. Even more calm, perhaps, than the five others as they sat down and extinguished their lights. It was too dangerous to try to dig out through the slack fall but Alec Benn, who had been nearest to it, said that it was nothing but a small rush. They knew that a rescue party would be there in a matter of minutes and themselves released, they thought, not much later than their normal time.

When Joseph came from school, he would come into his own

house and go upstairs to change from his shoes into his clogs. It had become a small conspiracy between Emily and her son that he go into her bedroom to do the simple change. She was often asleep and this time, as others, he sat on the edge of the bed, changed, and then waited for her to stir at the interruption which his pressure on the bed gave to her breathing. This time she did not stir, and he sat, waiting, slowly numbed by the cold and fear of his own stillness. Found there shivering with the full sun on his face, holding the dead hand.

As the men went into the seam they discovered that the fault ran right back. To dig there, however carefully, would bring the roof down on all of them. They had to go down another shaft and cut in from a parallel seam. The miners cycled quickly across to the next pit where the seam was cleared of work and from there they pushed towards the trapped men.

At midnight, frozen in the dark, with the water running down the walls as if the sea above them was beginning to seep through, its immeasurable weight taking this chance – as it had done before – of crushing those ceaseless workers beneath its bed, John could scarcely keep still. He knew that all of them had equal troubles, all were in the same danger – and this communality alone restrained him. But, in the dark, his mouth opened wide in soundless cries for help – to get out and back to Emily – to see her once more.

With the women at the pit-head was May. She had helped to lay out her mother and dumbly allowed the children to be divided out among the neighbours. Now she waited for her father.

The trapped men had soon guessed that they would have to go out through the other seam and the realisation had silenced them completely. As the morning came, however, they began to talk to each other, all speaking with very deliberate casualness about football, their friends, the town – the gossip of the day. Alec Fisher, the oldest man there, had been trapped three times before and that was a distant comfort to all the others: his 'luck' became the centre of their talk, the one thing always referred back to, chafed about, encouraged as they drew out of him other instances of this 'luck'; at cards, in growing leeks, in every smallest matter that would yield. John was the second oldest man, the other four were young, two in their early twenties, two in their teens.

When they heard the picks in the other seam they cheered and knocked back at the wall. That simple knock brought a small rush down on them and they were prevented from digging to meet their rescuers. John was furthest away from the sound. As the men came nearer the falls in the trap grew more frequent. Alec Fisher felt for an area that could be propped up, so that they might make a small shelter for themselves within their hole. For by now it was obvious to all that the nearer the rescue party came, the harder their blows – the more certain it was that the crumbling roof would crash down on them. But there was no timber for the propping – nothing to do but wait as they were.

Joseph had run down to the pit-head directly after his breakfast and he wriggled through the crowd to join May who took his hand, made no reproach.

Warned by the silence of those within – for Alec had ordered that they stop hammering back at the oncoming party – the rescue party slowed down and stood back to allow one man alone to work and he most carefully, making a path less than two feet high and propping it all the way. Almost all the men in the rescue party were related to those within: Seth was there for John.

Patiently, almost delicately, his nerves more wracked than his bruised bare body, the miner picked at the last few feet. With no more than inches to go he stopped and listened. He could hear Alec, who told him what the trouble was. But the only other way in was by another seam entirely, would take another day and meet the same problem. He passed the message back and was dragged out by his feet to let in someone fresh to make the last cuts.

A small hole was made. Within, the falls had become so steady that it seemed to pour slack and small pieces of rock. Those nearest went out first. John would be the last. Each one had to crawl over the hole, and the movement of each caused another, heavier fall. John gripped the wet coal about him, bracing himself so that he could lift himself from his position with as little disturbance as possible. Alec Fisher went. It was his turn.

He pushed his hands on to the floor and so levered his body clear. Then he placed his feet out and used both hands and feet to crab himself forward. As he left what had been his seat, a fall descended on it. Slowly, patiently, he moved forward. His feet went into a pile of slack. He would have to stand. The hole was about five yards before him. He eased himself upright and dived for it. His head caught a low sagging piece of roof and it came down on him. The fall was heard and Seth, who had come to the front waiting for John, slithered through the narrow shaft and right into the hole – another man behind to grab his feet. He saw John's hands and the top of his head and shouted to be held as he leaned in and pulled, heaved his brother out of the rubble, pulled him clear.

John was still unconscious when they buried Emily. Unconscious as Seth over-rode May's cries and sent out the children to various relatives. His head injuries were severe, his back lacerated.

No one told him of the death of his wife, even when he did come round. It was thought better not to. But as John felt some strength come back to him, he thought only of her. The mumbled reassurances to his questions about her did not satisfy him. He was allowed no visitors but Seth those first two weeks. May accepted that she could not go as she would not have been able to conceal her mother's death.

After two weeks John was out of danger but still extremely ill, often delirious. That night, however, he did something he had tried to do each night since he had collected his senses. He got out of the bed.

He was in an isolated room and luck came to him – for he found the place where his clothes were and slowly put them on. His forehead was bandaged, more bandages wrapped around his body – and every noise he heard came through thick walls of cloth, each movement he made went slowly through a dense curtain. Standing, holding the door ajar, his boots held in his hand, he waited until the sister went past his room into the general ward. Then he went out. The night air cut at his face and he could remember nothing of what followed. Nor, afterwards, would he have it spoken of in his presence.

He had to see Emily and thought that she was at Crossbridge, in the first cottage they had had, waiting for him. They had put him in Whitehaven cottage hospital and he came down the drive on to the dark streets where he took his only bearings – for then, turning his back on the pits and the sea, he began to walk towards the fells. There was a moon, a dry night.

It was more than eight miles to the cottage and he did not stop. When his balance left him and he staggered across the road or into a dyke, then he would right himself immediately, calling on himself to go on, to see her, the only woman he had known, the woman he had to see before she died.

He collapsed a few yards from the old cottage and there he was found at dawn, as if dead.

He left his mother's house in mid-morning. Taking the back road to Wigton, he passed Old Carlisle and saw the boys playing among the grass-covered mounds of the old Roman Camp. He stopped and looked for Joseph who had sat alone by Emily when she lay dead; but the boy was too absorbed in his play to notice his father.

He turned away when he heard the clock of St Mary's church strike ten. The Hiring would have started now.

As he walked down the hill, he felt his jaws clench at the reply that would have to come through them when, soon, he would stand in the Ring looking for work. But the jaws would have to unclench – work had to be found.

'Is thou for hire, lad?'

Yes; he was for hire.